"Do you belie

Jake had issued ———————————— ore. "Let's put it this wa———————————, oppor- tunity *and* expertise. You're a prime suspect, whether you like it or not."

"Answer me one question, Kate," he said, his words hot with feeling. "Why'd you come back to Silver City, to a town you claimed you hated?"

"I came back to make a home, to settle down."

"The truth is, you came back to settle an old score. A long time ago what you felt for me was a lot more than suspicion. But things didn't go right and now you're trying to burn me."

"The past is over and done, Jake." Kate wouldn't let herself remember how much she'd once loved this man. "I've put it behind me. I suggest you do the same." With that, she walked away.

Jake took a step to follow her but stopped and watched her instead. The promise of beauty she'd had as a teen was now full-blown. She'd grown up but she was still dangerous and willful. When she'd first returned to Silver City, he'd hoped they could rekindle what was once between them. But now he knew Kate had a different agenda. She'd come back not because she'd learned to accept the past. She'd come to bury it. And him with it.

Dear Reader,

With his nine lives and wicked sense of adventure, Familiar is everyone's favorite crime-solving cat. And we're delighted to bring you another of his fast-paced, fun-filled mysteries in the FEAR FAMILIAR series.

Caroline Burnes was thrilled to read your letters asking for another Familiar adventure. She has the pleasure of living with the prototype for Familiar—her own black cat, E. A. Poe. In this book, Caroline introduces another sidekick, Ouzo, a dog who bears more than a passing resemblance to a black rascal that holds a place in her heart. In one of her many adventures with Ouzo, Caroline took him to obedience classes. After a brief session the trainer took her aside and said, "I've diagnosed the problem. The dog is smarter than you."

We're thrilled by your response to the FEAR FAMILIAR mysteries, and we urge you to look for more feline adventures in the months to come!

Regards,

Debra Matteucci

Debra Matteucci
Senior Editor & Editorial Coordinator
Harlequin Books
300 East 42nd Street
New York, NY 10017

Familiar
Fire
Caroline Burnes

Harlequin Books

TORONTO • NEW YORK • LONDON
AMSTERDAM • PARIS • SYDNEY • HAMBURG
STOCKHOLM • ATHENS • TOKYO • MILAN
MADRID • WARSAW • BUDAPEST • AUCKLAND

For Julianne Moore,
who comes at editing
with the deft touch of an editor
and the sensitivity of a writer

ISBN 0-373-22452-4

FAMILIAR FIRE

Copyright © 1998 by Carolyn Haines

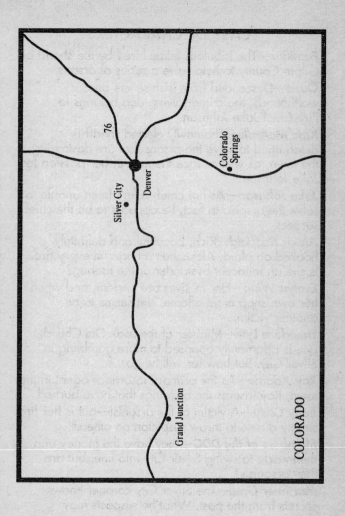

76

Colorado
Springs

Denver

Silver City

Grand Junction

COLORADO

CAST OF CHARACTERS

Familiar—The fabulous feline hired by the sheriff of Gilpin County to help solve a series of arsons.

Ouzo—Descended from Irish setters and wolfhounds, the crime-solving dog belongs to Fire Chief Jake Johnson.

Kate McArdle—The newly elected sheriff is determined to solve the arsons that are destroying the town, as well as face the fires of her passion for Jake Johnson.

Jake Johnson—As fire chief, Jake's been unable to solve the arsons. In fact, he appears to be the chief suspect.

Alexis Redfield—Rich, beautiful and definitely hooked on plaid, Alexis has a finger in every fire. Is she an innocent bystander or the firebug?

Evelyn Winn—Her motives are unclear, and when her own shop is set aflame, she seems to be another victim.

Theodore Lyte—Minister of the Look Out Church, Lyte is adamantly opposed to more gambling in Silver City. But how far will he go…?

Roy Adams—As the primary insurance agent in the town, Roy insures the buildings that have burned.

Betty Cody—A victim of the arsonist—but is her fire simply a ruse to throw suspicion on others?

Members of the DDC—They have the money and the muscle to swing Silver City into line, but are they arsonists?

Mortimer Grell—The Silver City coroner knows secrets from the past. What he suspects may destroy Kate.

Chapter One

So this is the land where Buffalo Bill and Calamity Jane roamed. Where men came to find their fortunes and live the American dream. Makes me want to don a pair of chaps—Naugahyde, naturally—and some of those spurs that jingle, jangle, jingle. I could even work up a rendition of "Happy Trails" if Pistol-Packin' Mama here would quit giving me the evil eye.

My, oh, my. I can see by the glint in her beautiful green eyes that I'm going to have to prove my sleuthing abilities once again. Oh, the tedium of a doubting woman. Now I ask you, gentle reader, why would a woman answer an advertisement about a mystery-solving cat and then not give the feline in question half a chance? I mean, I just flew into town and she brings me straight up here to this smoldering mass of timber and stone.

Speaking of smoldering masses, my new employer, Miss Kate McArdle, is one hot number. That mane of red hair bespeaks a temper out of the Fahrenheit range, and those green eyes could certainly ignite sparks. But those long, gorgeous legs don't match the cruel pistol she's carrying—or the tin badge. Nope, I wouldn't hesitate to say that Sheriff Kate McArdle would look a lot better in a Las Vegas dancer's costume than her drab tan uniform. Of course, I get the impression that if I tried to make her see it my way, she'd pop the cuffs on me and put me under arrest. EE-yow! An image for later study!

I'm here to work, and I absolutely detect that this place went up like a fireball from Mt. Vesuvius. Even Mr. Magoo on a bad day could figure that out. But the reason a lot of criminals turn to fire and explosives is because, by the nature of the crime, it doesn't tend to leave a lot of evidence behind. It's going to take some poking around, and the idea of getting my elegant black suit all sooty and smoky-smelling doesn't hold a lot of appeal at the moment.

But it is troubling that someone would deliberately burn a church. What's the motive? That's what's put a twist in my knickers, figuratively speaking.

The problem is that the altitude here at what remains of Lookout Church is rather high. I feel the need for fluids, as in cream or a delicate bouillabaisse with perhaps a few succulent morsels of crab floating on top. Yes, that sounds perfect.

Hey, we've got company. Looks like an official red fire vehicle. Uh-oh, I can tell by the way Kate's tensing up that this isn't the cavalry coming to our assistance. Jeez! The man has brought a large, black hairy beast with him. Criminy, here it comes bounding over at me like something from one of Sir Arthur Conan Doyle's moorish nightmares! The damn beast is wagging his tail in puppyish fashion and almost grinning. Grrrrrrr!

HANDS ON HER HIPS, Kate McArdle watched as the man and the black dog picked their way over the charred timbers. Although the dog viewed her eagerly, tail wagging, the man ignored her and kept to the other side of the scene. Kate knew who he was—and knew she didn't have the authority to make him leave the scene of the burned church, though that was exactly what she wanted to do. Jake Johnson was a skunk.

As he bent to carefully examine a pile of stones that had once formed the back wall of the sanctuary, the morning sun glinted in his dark hair, catching the chestnut highlights. Kate turned back to her own investigation, only then noticing that the black dog was down on his forepaws, tail wagging in the air with roguish playfulness as he teased the black cat she'd just flown in from Washington, D.C., a cat who had helped solve seven other mysteries all around the world.

"Hey!" she yelled at the dog. "Shoo!"

Instead of running, the dog turned to her and gave what almost resembled a grin. "You are as dumb as a mud fence," she said under her breath. "Beat it."

Tail still wagging, the dog waited.

"Ouzo! Ouzo!" Jake called.

The dog took off—in exactly the opposite direction. Kate had a moment of satisfaction. So, Jake still had his way with things. She couldn't stop her grin.

She bent to the blackened timbers where Familiar had turned his attention. The cat was more—and less—than she'd expected. He'd arrived, first class, without a hair ruffled from the journey. He'd been completely composed, his golden-green gaze studying her for the entire trip out to the remains of the church. She'd thought it best to let the highly touted detective cat start at Lookout Church, the latest fire in Gilpin County—and the one that had put the heat on her to solve as the newly elected sheriff. Even as she watched the cat delicately paw at a piece of charred wood, she knew that if the fact ever got out that she'd *hired* a cat to help her solve the arsons, she'd be one long-gone law woman. The folks of Gilpin County would shame her out of town—for the second time.

And solve the series of arsons that almost paralyzed Gilpin County she would, if only Jake Johnson would stay out of her way! She cast a glance across the rubble at him. He was collecting more evidence. She couldn't help wondering what had prompted the area merchants to instruct her to keep an eye on his investigation. An active eye. After all, she wasn't the fire chief, Jake was.

As if he had read her mind, he suddenly stood and came toward her. The black dog was at his side. Watching him walk across the ruins of the church, Kate was intensely aware of her surroundings. The sky was so blue it touched her heart. The gentle breeze brought the scent of fir and the last chill kiss of winter. Jake lifted his hand to shade his eyes, and Kate felt such a strong sense of *déjà vu* that she felt almost light-headed. Beside her leg, the cat's back went up at the approach of the dog.

"Easy, Familiar," Kate said softly. "We can handle both of them." Her words were calm, but her heart rate had increased. Jake Johnson was capable of anything— from a casual greeting to a tongue-lashing. Along with being a skunk, he was known to be extremely territorial. She remained perfectly still, waiting as he walked directly toward her.

When he was three feet away, Jake stopped. His expression said that he'd tolerated all he could. "What exactly do you think you're doing? This is clearly marked as a crime scene. You're tampering with an ongoing investigation." His words and stance were a challenge.

Kate's hand strayed to the shiny new badge on her

left shoulder. "As sheriff of Gilpin County, I'm investigating."

"Arson falls in the domain of the fire chief." Jake edged closer. "Which is me."

"Yes, I'd say you know a lot about fires," Kate answered slowly. The yellow flare of anger lit Jake's eyes and she knew she'd hit her target. "I'm willing to concede that point. But the fact remains that someone is setting fires in Gilpin County and you haven't been able to catch them."

One corner of Jake's mouth lifted in a smile. "And I suppose you're just the *woman* to do the job?"

Kate felt his gaze on her hair, her face, her neck, moving slowly down her body. He wasn't going to play by the rules. It was up to her to be the professional. She nodded. "The folks of Gilpin County elected me, and that's what I intend to do."

"I see." He studied her face a moment longer. "I was shocked when you came home and ran for sheriff, Kate. Maybe I shouldn't have been, but I was. I guess I expected you to do what you said. When you left Gilpin County fifteen years ago, you vowed you'd never come back. But here you are, just a living, breathing contradiction of your word." There was anger in his voice. "It might have been better all around if you'd stayed away."

"I changed my mind." She didn't owe Jake an explanation. He was the last person on earth she had to justify her behavior to.

"Yes, you do seem to have a way of doing that, don't you?"

"Back off, Jake." The words came out quiet and deadly. "I've got as much right to be in Silver City as you do. Maybe more."

"More?" His left eyebrow came up in that familiar arch.

"My *family* helped found this town. Remember?"

For a long moment they stared at each other, green eyes daring amber ones to take it an inch further. Jake nodded. "I'm glad you've been able to accept your heritage, Kate. To a person with less to do, the idea that you've returned as sheriff might make an interesting study in psychology. But I don't have time for this. I'm going to have to ask you to leave. I've got a long day here trying to find some evidence of how this fire started. I don't need you stomping around."

A bark crackled through the air, causing them both to turn and stare at the black feline, fuzzed like a Halloween cat. Butt poking in the air, Ouzo wagged his tail and barked again in an effort to goad the cat into running.

I can see the canine has the training of a Snopes with a single-digit IQ. And I question the sanity of a man who travels with such a creature unrestrained. It's obvious to me that Kate has her own negative feelings about this dynamic duo. But if this black demon inches one tiny little bit closer to me, I'll have to resort to a claw in the tip of his nose. Ah, he's backing away. Look at him. What a slobbering fool. Good grief, and humans love them because they're loyal! Have you ever heard such a crock? They're too stupid to be anything but loyal!

"Damn! Can't you even control your dog?" Kate asked, striding toward the cat and dog. "If he harms one hair on that cat's head…"

"Ouzo, come." Jake slapped his thigh in an effort to get his dog's attention. "Ouzo!" He gave Kate a withering look as he stepped in front of her. "Ouzo, get back over here and get to work. I didn't bring you here to chase a cat.''

Just as Jake drew near, Ouzo bounded away, leaping the rubble as if it didn't exist. "Dammit, Ouzo.'' Jake stopped beside the cat. He looked at Kate and then back at the cat. "What in the world did you bring a *cat* out here for?'' His eyes narrowed.

"Familiar is my companion.'' Kate said it with as much disdain as she could muster. If Jake found out the truth… "He's a far better companion than that black nuisance you brought with you.''

"Ouzo is—''

"A pain in the butt. Obviously he learned at his master's knee.'' Kate's chin lifted a fraction of an inch. "Go investigate, and leave me alone. I'm doing my job. If you don't like it, take it up with the Silver City Merchants' Association. I didn't ask for this extra duty.'' She turned away, pleased with her frontal assault.

Jake paused for a split second, ready to fire back a reply, but the cat's claws hooked into his cuff, holding him in place. "Come on, boy, I've got to get to work.'' As he bent to unhook the paw, he looked closer.

"I'll be,'' he said. Beside Familiar's paw was a charred and twisted piece of metal with a stub of a red wire attached. Instead of touching it, he stood and retrieved a pair of long metal tweezers and a plastic bag from his pocket.

"What is it?'' Kate stepped cautiously over to the cat.

Jake retrieved the device and held it up in the air for her to see. "It's a detonator. Whoever set this fire used a timing device. If there was any doubt, we can definitely prove arson now.''

"Meow!''

Kate knelt down beside the cat. She lifted his chin

with one finger as she gently scratched. "I'll be damned. The cat found the timer."

Jake put the plastic bag in his jacket pocket before he answered. "It was Ouzo who discovered the timer. The cat just happened to be standing here."

"Ouzo? That dog?" Kate looked up in disbelief. It was exactly like Jake to have the plain facts under his nose and then to twist them to suit himself. It was just like him! A flood of anger washed over her. "You're saying, after that cat almost rubbed your nose in the timing device, that your *dog* discovered it?"

"Ouzo is trained to sniff out evidence of arson, bombs, even drugs." Jake wasn't going to give an inch.

"That black ragamuffin?" Kate shielded her eyes from the sun as she gazed in the direction she'd last seen the dog take. "The only thing that dog can find is trouble. Besides, it was Familiar who found the timer, Jake. Surely you aren't too pigheaded to see that."

"A fire cat? Are you telling me that's a fire-detecting cat?" Jake pointed at the black cat with disbelief. "There's no such thing as a fire cat, Kate. Now if you'll just clear out of here, I'd like to gather some more evidence. I am the fire chief, this is a fire. Ergo, you don't need to be here."

Kate hooked a boot heel on what remained of a cedar beam and met Jake's amber gaze. "Now that you have some hard evidence, the area merchants are going to expect an arrest." The rash of fires that had plagued Silver City had begun to look suspicious even to the people who supported Jake as fire chief. No one had pointed a finger, yet, but Jake was drawing a lot of ugly attention to himself.

Jake's fists clenched. "Are you honestly saying you think I'm somehow involved in these fires?"

Kate could feel the raw emotion in Jake. It came from him in waves—a tightly controlled fury. A split second of intense memory knifed through her. She knew what it was like to stand beside Jake when his emotions were running strong. What it felt like when his passions were directed at her.

The memory was so unexpected, so deadly, that she felt her knees weaken. "I don't know what I think," she said. She looked past Jake at the vista of burned rubble and charred wood. She had to concentrate on the factual, on the present. She hadn't come back to Silver City to wallow in the past, she'd come to prove that the present was what mattered.

She focused on the blackened remains of one of Gilpin County's largest churches. Lookout Church had perched on the highest point of Sentinel Mountain. There wasn't another building around for miles. Below the church was the land of the Double J Ranch—or what was left of it. Jake's ranch had been the first in a long string of properties to burn. Some folks were saying he'd collected a hefty insurance claim. That thought brought a jolt of adrenaline that steadied her. "You'd better arrest someone, Jake, and put an end to these fires."

"Kate, there's a lot of water under our bridge, but I can't believe you think I was involved in any way in the destruction of property. Especially a church."

The rush of satisfaction she'd expected wasn't there. She looked into his eyes and was caught for a moment by the amber light. She'd seen her future in those eyes once upon a time. "I can tell you that members of the city council called my office. One or two of them are positive you're involved, at least in covering up some of the evidence." There was no point in soft-pedaling the truth.

Jake looked away, then returned her gaze. "You didn't answer my question. I asked you what *you* believed."

Kate glanced down to make sure the black cat was still near. This was not going the way she'd hoped. Instead of the rush of victory, she felt only tired and disheartened. "You've got the timer, now maybe you can begin to make some headway on this case." She didn't meet his look.

"I asked you if you thought I was guilty?" Jake's words were brittle with emotion.

It was a challenge Kate couldn't ignore. She lifted her face and stared into his eyes. "If I had the evidence that proved you to be the arsonist or in any way involved, you'd be locked up." She forced her chin up and steady and didn't back down, though she had no heart for this any longer.

Jake shook his head slowly. "Is that it? You don't have the proof. So in your eyes, I'm guilty?"

She saw the hurt in the set of his jaw, the way he compressed his lips as he nodded. Kate had expected to hurt him, but she surely hadn't thought to feel the stab of regret that made her own voice roughen with emotion. "Look, Jake. You've got a motive for every fire that's been set. You've got opportunity, and the good Lord knows you've got the expertise. You're a prime suspect. Whether I like it or not."

"Answer me one question, Kate. Why did you come back to Silver City? You were long gone, nothing but a memory. Why come back to a town you claimed you hated?" His words grew hot with feeling.

Kate's own temper answered the challenge. "I've got as much right to be here as you do. What do you mean, why did I come back? I came back here to make a home, to settle down."

"The truth is, you came back to settle an old score. You're letting your emotions control you." Jake shoved his hands in his pockets. "A long time ago, what you felt for me was a helluva lot more than suspicion. Things didn't go right, and ever since you came back to town, you've been trying to burn me. I'm not completely responsible for what happened in the past, and I'm not at all responsible for these fires. Now as the fire chief, I'm ordering you off the premises."

Kate swallowed the angry words that welled in her throat. "That past is over and done, Jake. I've set it aside. You need to do the same. What's happening here has nothing to do with a couple of kids fifteen years ago. Five buildings have burned in Gilpin County. Five. Prominent businesses and homes. That's the issue. Not the past. Keep that in mind. I'm going now, but I have every right to examine this property, or any evidence you might find. If you try to block me in any way, I'll take it to the city council. I hope you won't make me do that."

"You're hoping with every fiber of your being that I will. That way you can get me fired and then frame me any way you like." Anger made his eyes glow with a wolfish glint. "Now leave before I do something I regret."

Kate felt the pure wind of reason wash over her. She looked at Jake and saw an angry man, one she didn't know at all—had never known. "That hot temper of yours has gotten you in trouble before, Jake. I'd hoped you'd learned to control it. I guess not." She scooped up Familiar and walked away without another word.

Jake took a step to follow her, but stopped. Kate

McArdle was a woman with an agenda. When she'd first returned to Silver City, hope had sprung up that maybe they could rekindle what had once been between them. It had been a stupid thought, and one that had reopened a painful wound. Kate was still Kate, with all the raw edges and anger. The promise of beauty that she'd had as a child was now full-blown. She'd grown up physically, but she was still the same teenager emotionally. The same dangerous, willful person.

He sighed. With each step she put more distance between them, and Jake knew it was unbridgeable. Kate had returned to Silver City, but not because she'd learned to accept the past. She'd come to bury it. And him, too. He watched her drive away in the old pickup that now bore the insignia of the Gilpin County Sheriff's Office.

"Ouzo!" He whistled at the black dog, who came rushing toward him. "Damn it all to hell, Ouzo. How is it that every time I turn my back, you're into something else?" He knelt and began to pull the stickers from the dog's thick coat. "You've lived out here for at least five years. Other dogs avoid these things. I think you roll in them."

Ouzo gave only a low whine and licked Jake's hand. His big, brown eyes begged forgiveness.

"Right. I know you're playing me like a fiddle." Jake tugged the last sticker free. "Now earn your keep. Sniff around here and find something." He grabbed Ouzo's fur. "Who did find that timer? You or the cat?"

"Arf!" Ouzo wagged his tail. "Arf."

"It had better be you. We're not being beat out by a team of a hard-hearted woman and a cool cat."

"Arf! Arf." Ouzo put his nose to the ground and began to work.

AH, SWEET MALARKEY, my territory has been invaded by a creature of the feline persuasion. A cat and a woman, a team of feline and female! 'Tis a thought that would send a lesser dog into a frenzy of wally-globbering. But this flame-haired sheriff, a lass with the hair of a wild Irish princess, is the kind of woman who would set a poet's tongue to wagging and a dog's tail to thumping. It is a troubling sight—to see one of the dear creatures of the feminine persuasion with a pistol strapped to her hip. The cushion of her soft bosom is no place to pin a star!

As a dog with a history, I know that all creatures have a place, but this is the West, where men are men and dogs are their partners. Ranching, mining, gambling, chasing Mrs. Tanner's cats and Mrs. Williamson's horses, jumping in Mrs. Carter's swimming pool—this is not the work of women. And certainly not a place for a cat.

I can see that the sheriff and her new sidekick are going to have to take a fall. A gentle fall, let me hasten to add. A wee, gentle fall. You see, the problem is that Jake suffers from some deplorable code of honor. Though the lass and the black devil cat are plainly trespassing on our case, Jake will do nothing to stop them.

I'm under no obligation to follow the rules or to even acknowledge that there are rules. I live by the code of the West—Don't get caught.

It's a long and glorious family history from whence I've sprung, one of skullduggery and the art of the quick escape. It was many years ago when the first of my line, Rustling Red, came over from the Old Country. He was a handsome rogue with a roving eye and a talent for herding other people's cattle and moving them. Red developed a reputation—and a bounty—back in County

*Cork, so he headed out west where his talents were in
high demand.*

 *He was running with a band of rustlers when they
stopped over in Silver City for a night of whoring, gambling and cheating at cards. 'Twas there, on a moonlit
night, that he lost his heart to a handsome border collie
who had come into town with her mistress. Though Red
was a rascal and a rogue, he was also a romantic. One
look into the eyes of Sassy and he was a goner.*

 *The Irish setter blood mixed with the collie, and a new
breed of dog was born. Handsome, smart, and with a
bent toward a criminal nature that has passed from generation to generation, until finally it culminated in the
ultimate criminal mastermind, me. Lucky for Jake I'm
here to look out for him.*

KATE EXAMINED the reports that had become an inch-
thick stack on her desk. She recognized Jake's hand-
writing, the neat letters, the professional black ink. She
could find no fault with Jake's investigation. He'd gone
by the book—completely. There simply wasn't enough
solid evidence to provide a lead. With a sigh, she put
the reports on the desk and looked at the cat. Familiar
was perched in her office window watching the hundreds
of pedestrians roam through the main street.

 Silver City had started life as a mining town with a
rich vein of silver that had drawn prospectors from the
safety of the settled East. It had been a wild western
settlement with an abundance of saloons and the
boom-or-bust men who drank hard and fought harder.

 In some ways, Silver City had been no different from
the other mining towns that dotted the Colorado landscape. In other ways, it was very different. Silver City
had boasted a doctor *and* an opera house. And one of

the finest whorehouses in the entire West. One with a legendary madam who was known for her solid business sense, her beauty, and her generous heart. Silver City had been born at a time when the West was a wild and woolly place, and the men and women who populated it were larger than life.

It was a time when a man could stake a claim and become rich overnight. Or else work his entire life away without anything to show for it but an empty hole in the ground and failing health. The landscape was dotted with those empty mines, and the hastily buried remains of poor prospectors who hadn't made it through the winter.

It had been even harder on the women.

Now Silver City was one of the hot casino spots. A different kind of vein had been hit—one that brought in the nickels, dimes, quarters and silver dollars as the one-armed bandits spun and whirred and the roulette wheel jumped from fortune to bankruptcy. The old town had been carefully preserved—every inch of it—and turned into a gambling mecca.

Kate got up and went to the window and began stroking Familiar's sleek black hide. The cat had been a surprise. She'd read about Familiar and his ability to solve mysteries. But she hadn't really believed in him. Not until he'd discovered the timing device.

And he *had* found the device. No matter how much Jake claimed it was the dog, it had been Familiar.

"You've been awfully quiet," she said, scratching the cat's ears until she was rewarded with a loud purr. "Are you thinking about the arsons?"

"Meow." Familiar arched under her hand. He hopped to the floor and went to the small refrigerator she kept in her office for the cream she liked in her coffee.

"I do swear I've never seen a cat who could eat his

weight in food. Your owner, Dr. Curry, warned me that you had distinctive tastes.'' She went to the desk drawer and pulled out a can of smoked oysters. ''So I got these for emergency food.''

''Meow!'' Familiar stood on his back legs and pawed at the can.

''You also have a way of getting your point across.'' She opened the tin and put it down for the cat. He dove into the oysters with gusto.

Kate went back to her desk and picked up the reports again. The clearly established facts were that all five fires were set. At first Kate had not wanted to believe that the Double J fire should be counted in the more recent arsons. The ranch had burned some ten months before, but it was clearly a fire that someone had deliberately set. Jake had found clear evidence of arson in each case. The problem was that he hadn't been able to find clues as to the arsonist. Five fires and no solid clues. It was troubling.

Even as she pondered the possibilities, Kate's gut knotted. Jake Johnson was a skunk. He'd broken the unspoken code of the West and treated her in a manner that no woman deserved. But men weren't what they used to be all over the country. His lack of chivalry didn't mean he was capable of being involved in the destruction of a total of 2.3 million dollars worth of real estate.

Jake was a heel, but that didn't make him a firebug.

But in all five fires, he hadn't been able to come up with a single suspect. Even brilliant criminals made an occasional mistake. And in the past, Jake had been pretty good at solving arsons. Why had he suddenly lost his abilities?

The logical answer was that the arsonist was either

Jake or someone he was protecting. And Kate found herself chafing at either answer.

So what was her problem? Why was she pacing her office, tying her own gut into knots on a Saturday evening when out on the streets the gamblers were coming in by the busload?

Not a damn bit of it made sense.

The sound of footsteps outside her office made her stop pacing. Her private office door burst open, and she took in the large man dressed in black. He strode into her office as if he owned the place, his silver hair a cloud of indignation around his head.

"'Vengeance is mine, saith the Lord,' but if you don't find out who burned down my church, I'm going to take matters into my own hands."

Chapter Two

Kate's eyes narrowed and she pointed to the chair beside her desk. "Have a seat, Reverend Lyte."

"I have no time for sitting while the devil who set fire to my church runs free in this community. Five times he's struck! Five buildings have burned. Why, Betty Cody is homeless. Homeless, do you hear? And my flock is homeless. Tomorrow is the Sabbath and where shall we gather to sing God's praises?"

"It's not going to rain. Maybe an outdoor service would be a novelty." Kate closed her eyes as soon as the words left her mouth. She didn't like Reverend Theodore Lyte, but getting smart with a man who'd lost a church wasn't going to make life any easier.

"Sarcasm is lost on the Lord," Lyte informed her in a pious voice. "Now who burned my church?"

"I don't know. Have a seat. Maybe you can give me some clues?"

"Me? Clues?" Lyte grew indignant. "What are you implying?"

Kate patted the back of the chair and walked around to her own. "Sit down, Reverend. Tell me a little about your church members."

Lyte took the chair but he sat on the edge. "I've been

over this with Jake. I told him everything. I didn't come here to repeat myself, I came to get some action."

"Bear with me," Kate said in a patient tone. "Roy Adams asked me to get involved in this investigation only this morning. I went up to the church. It's a fact that the fire was deliberately set."

"It was?" Lyte put a hand over his heart. "That's what Jake said, but I didn't believe it. I swear, no one would deliberately burn down a house of the Lord."

"In case you've forgotten, Reverend, there's been a string of fires in Gilpin County. Homes, businesses, even Jake's ranch. So far, we've been lucky in the sense that no one has been injured or killed. But we may not continue to be so lucky."

"Who would do such a terrible thing?" Lyte asked.

"I don't know yet, but I can assure you we're going to find out." Kate pushed aside Jake's reports and picked up a clean pad and pencil. "Let's start with obvious suspects. Is there anyone who would want to see Lookout Church burned? Someone who might benefit in any way?"

Lyte gave her a blank stare. "We haven't been a perfect church, but we've tried as hard as humanly possible. We've done everything to make this a better community. God doesn't approve of all this gambling, all of this human folly, this waste. We've preached against it, but gambling is legal here. We've taken our stand up on the mountain where we're above the errors of human nature. We always take a higher stand."

Kate nodded. "Is there a member of the congregation who has been unhappy? Someone who may have felt…left out?"

Lyte started to answer, then paused. "I don't think someone burned down a church because they felt left out." He eyed her. "Do you? And what about the other fires?"

Kate mentally gave Lyte a point for possessing more intelligence than she'd first thought. "No, I don't. But I have to remind you that there's been a rash of church burnings across the nation. None in Colorado so far, but the burning of your church could be unrelated to the other fires in this community. At this point, we can't assume anything."

Lyte nodded. "I like that. I like the fact that you're looking at this from all angles."

"So, there's no one who might have a grudge against the church?"

"I didn't say that." Lyte looked down at his fingers, which he shaped into a steeple.

"Is there someone who made threats against the church?"

Lyte continued to contemplate his fingers. "Not against the church."

"Against you?" Kate leaned forward. Now this was getting somewhere. There had been nothing in Jake's report regarding a personal vendetta.

"The angry words were directed at me *and* the church. You see, for some time now Lookout Church has needed to expand. Our congregation has grown. We have children we want to pull above this den of iniquity here in Silver City. Our young people can't walk the street without the sound of slot machines or the laughter of women calling them inside casinos..." Lyte looked at Kate and hesitated a half beat. "I mean, we needed a bigger church, better facilities for our young, more parking. But we're bounded on all sides by the same property owner, and he refused to sell us any more land, though it's undeveloped."

"And the owner would be?" A bad feeling crept into her gut. At one point in time, the Double J land had covered most of that area. But times had been hard for Jake. She'd assumed he'd sold some land, since he wasn't ranching.

"Jake Johnson."

Kate's pen began to slip in her fingers and she clutched it tighter. "The Johnson ranch?" she said, though she needed no clarification.

"Yes, the Double J property extends up Sentinel Mountain and surrounds the church. The land is virtually useless to a rancher, but Jake refused to consider selling us even fifty acres, not even that bare section which is nothing but a rock slide waiting to happen."

Kate digested this new tidbit. "What exactly did Jake say?"

"He said he'd never sell. He said that ranch was his heritage and if his father hadn't lost his mind and donated the original deed to the church, we wouldn't be sitting out there today. Then he told me to get off Double J property and never come back."

"Sounds like Jake didn't want to sell." Jake had always been crazy about the Double J property. It was mostly scrub grass and rock, but he'd loved it like it was Kentucky bluegrass. Loved it more than…anything.

"We needed that extra land and I told him it was a sin against God to withhold it."

Kate couldn't help the smile that briefly touched her face and gave her striking features a soft glow. "I'll bet that really sizzled him."

"I thought he was going to strike me."

"Listen, Reverend, you see that land as a place to build more church. That's Jake's heritage. That land has been in his family, and believe me, family members have died protecting it from claim jumpers and squatters. Jake is a little touchy about his property, but it doesn't sound as if he actually threatened you."

"Not then, but later. He came up to check out what we were doing at the church. He found that we'd been using a tiny piece of his land to load supplies. He was livid. He made us haul off the supplies on the spot."

Kate had no trouble imagining that scene, either. It wasn't wise for a man to let another use his land. Use meant possession, and possession was nine-tenths of the law. If the Reverend Lyte doubted that, all he had to do was ask the Native American tribes who had once owned the entire West. "Okay," she said. "So Jake valued his land and he maintained his perimeters. That's a rancher's right."

"Are you defending him? I thought you were supposed to find the man responsible for starting these fires and punish him, not protect him."

Kate held out her hand. "I'd calm down, Reverend, before I went off making half-baked accusations like that one. Are you claiming that Jake burned down your church?" She leveled a cold green stare in his direction. "Think about it before you answer. This is a serious charge. If you make it, you'd better be able to back it up by signing a statement."

"I have no proof." Lyte rose from his chair. "That's what you're here for, to get the proof."

"And I will, but let me give you a little warning. A friendly warning free of charge. Don't go accusing Jake or anyone else of a crime unless you have proof. A lot has changed in the West, but a man still has the right to defend his honor. Even against a preacher."

Lyte nodded. His mouth lifted into a smile. "You don't like me very much, do you?"

Kate was slightly taken aback. She didn't like him, but she'd tried not to show it. "I'm not paid to like you."

"That's right. I can understand why you don't, though. Family aversion to the good Lord and his commandments. Have a good day, *Miss* McArdle."

He left the office as abruptly as he'd come. Kate leaned both hands on her desk, stunned by his parting shot. Since she'd returned to Silver City not a single soul had mentioned her family. Not even during the election, when she'd thought it would surely be used in a smear campaign.

The fact that she was Kitty McArdle's granddaughter could have made headline copy—Descendant of West's Most Prominent Madam Now Seeks a Badge. But her opponent hadn't used it, and no one else had either. She'd begun to think that she'd finally separated herself from her grandmother and her infamous house of "playful kittens."

She'd been wrong.

She watched the minister walk toward his car, determined not to let him get under her skin. He was a pompous ass, and it was no wonder Jake wouldn't sell him a foot of land.

She returned to her reports, determined to find the common link between the fires. She knew they were related. It was a gut feeling, and she'd learned to trust her gut.

JAKE COLLECTED the bags of evidence and stowed them in the car. Ouzo had gone to work and uncovered a footprint left in a puddle of melted wax. Jake could only hope that it was a print left by the arsonist. But it was almost too good to be true. The fire starter had never been so careless before. But then he'd never burned a church before, either.

One of the things that was so frustrating about this case was that there seemed to be no clear connection between the fires.

The fire that destroyed the Double J ranch house had been set ten months before. It didn't take a lot of imagination for Jake to recall the roar of the flames as they shot into the night sky. Most folks around town had felt that the fire had freed Jake of the burden of the ranch, which was nothing but a financial drain. It was true that the insurance money had given him a sense of freedom that he never thought he'd have. The ranch house and barns had been properly constructed and insured appropriately. Of course the land was another matter. It had never been worth much. Jake's grandfather had bought it for next to nothing from a couple of prospectors who went belly-up. Then in an effort to establish a working ranch and a fine home for his family, Jake's father, Jacob, had heavily mortgaged the property. But with the insurance claim Jake had been able to pay off the bank and own the land free and clear.

What no one had considered was that Jake's entire personal history was gone with the house. Every photo. Every personal item that connected him to his family and the land that his father had loved so dearly. Insurance money couldn't buy those things back.

He carefully nudged a clump of blackened stone. As he bent to examine a paper beneath it, he found it was a page from a hymnal. A memory surfaced, and he recalled a twelve-year-old Kate standing in front of the Gilpin County School assembly singing "Amazing Grace." Her voice had been true and pure and lovely to listen to—until someone in the audience had begun a catcall about Kate's grandmother. Kate had halted the song and stood stricken like a wild animal, then she had fled. Not another single time had he ever heard her sing. And he'd never thought of that moment again until now.

A glimmer of understanding came to him. As usual, his epiphanies were a day late and a dollar short. Jake had identified strongly with his father, and therefore with the land his father loved. Kate, on the other hand, was trying desperately to escape the heritage that had been handed to her. She'd burned to get out of Gilpin County and leave behind the dancehall image of a grandmother who acquired her money in the sporting life—and the mother who'd walked out with a high-stakes gambler and left her sixteen-year-old daughter to fend for herself.

While he'd been hanging onto his range-land inheritance as hard as he could, Kate had been kicking free. Neither one had ever really stopped long enough to consider the other's needs. They'd only recognized their attraction to each other, and like a lot of teenagers, they'd acted on it.

He felt the heat rise up into his face at the memory of the nights they'd shared. Kate was a woman who gave herself body and soul, when she decided to give. There was no doubt that he'd loved her. But he hadn't been willing to sacrifice to have her. She'd given him a choice, and he'd chosen the Double J.

Now his ranch was gone and his father was dead.

And Kate McArdle was back in town as the sheriff.

He groaned out loud and looked around for Ouzo. "Here, boy," he called. "Let's load up and get this stuff ready to send to the lab." The black dog bounded into the car.

"You know, Ouzo, women are a treacherous breed. My advice to you is to stay away from them completely.

I've figured something out today. Something about Kate. But I can promise you, if I try to explain it to her, it'll only lead to a fight.''

"Arf."

"You're one smart dog."

Jake was backing around when he caught sight of the white compact headed up the road. The church had been the end-of-the-line destination, so there was no doubt the car was headed toward it. Foot on the brake, Jake waited. When he saw the florid face of Roy Adams, mayor of Silver City, Jake rolled his eyes.

"Roy," he said as the window slid down. "Something I can do for you?"

"You can catch the maniac who's setting these fires. That *is* what you get paid to do, isn't it?"

"Not exactly," Jake answered, knowing he would only make matters worse but unable to resist the impulse. "Technically, my job description has more to do with keeping the fire department manned and ready for emergencies. Arson investigation is a secondary area of my work."

"Don't cite your job description to me! I wrote the damn thing!"

"Okay," Jake answered calmly. Roy's face had turned another five degrees redder. It was time to back off or risk a mayoral stroke.

"The CEOs of the Dandy Diamond Casino will be in town tomorrow. They're scouting for a site for a new casino, but they're worried about the arsons we're having. I want you on hand to give them a report that will reassure them that you're hot on the heels of the arsonist. We can't afford to spook these people. Silver City needs what they can do."

"I think the last thing Silver City needs is another

casino. That's all we have. Even the opera house where Kitty and her girls danced and entertained is now a gambling den. Isn't it about time we tried to preserve some of the original town? Hell, the next thing I know, you'll be selling the fire station to a gambling interest.''

"You're not a historian, you're the fire marshal. I want you at that meeting, giving that report."

"But I'm not hot on the trail. In fact, I don't have any evidence that leads me in any direction. Whoever is setting these fires is pretty damn smart.''

"Well, find some clues. And do it before tomorrow. I want you at that meeting, and I want you to have some progress to report. Is that clear?''

"I get the idea you'd like me to fabricate something."

"I don't care if you have to dream up a suspect. Just have one, and have him nearly caught. Is that clear enough?''

"You're the boss," Jake said.

"And don't bring that hound dog to the meeting. This isn't the Wild West anymore. Folks don't take their livestock with them to meetings.''

"Technically, Ouzo is a dog. That's not really livestock.''

Adams's eyes bugged with fury. "You know what I mean. You show up and leave that hound at home. You're on thin ice, Johnson. Half the folks in town think you're the arsonist. Don't push me. I'm one of the few people holding the line in your defense. Don't take that for granted.''

Jake felt the truth of Roy's words like a slap. This was the second time in less than four hours he'd been told he was the prime suspect.

"I don't think I have to say this, Roy, but I didn't start those fires.''

"Quit making it so hard for me to defend you, Jake."
Roy rolled up his window and headed back down the
mountain.

Jake eased the car into gear and followed at a much
slower pace. As he descended Sentinel Mountain, he
came to a point where he could look over the valley
below. The remains of the Double J looked like a giant
bruise on the land. Jake reached across and stroked
Ouzo's thick black fur. "I remember the day you strayed
up to the ranch, Ouzo. Johnny Marino named you for
that Greek liquor he was always drinking. He said you
had a sneaky kick like ouzo." He patted the dog again
then pressed the gas. "We'd better get this stuff to the
lab."

THE FIRE STATION was right across the street from the
sheriff's office, and Kate was watching when Jake pulled
in. She continued watching as he unloaded a cardboard
box and went into the station house.

His reports were spread across her desk, and she had
come to one conclusion. The only thing that linked the
fires in any pattern was that at some time in the past,
Jake Johnson had had words with the property owners.
Every single one of them. And then their homes or businesses had gone up in flames.

She went back to her desk and looked at the chart
she'd drawn. Counting Lookout Church, three fires had
been started with a timer. In another, gasoline had been
used as an accelerant. The fifth fire, which had been Roy
Adams's insurance company, had been electric. All of
the fires had required some degree of skill to start.

Kate pulled at her bottom lip as she reexamined the
reports. It didn't make sense that Jake would have de-

liberately included every shred of evidence that pointed at him.

The Double J had been the first fire. Then Betty Cody, a member of the city council who'd tried to get Jake fired, had lost her home. Not two weeks later, Roy Adams's insurance company had burned—after he'd told Jake that he wouldn't reinsure the Double J if Jake rebuilt. The fourth fire had been Lester Ray's saloon, right after Lester had publicly accused Jake of starting the other fires. And now Lookout Church. It turned out, in addition to what Lyte had said, that Jake and the preacher had also gotten into an argument right in the middle of town. Jake had made some unflattering remarks about a preacher who felt that a church needed movie theaters and bowling alleys. And Lyte had retaliated from the pulpit in recent sermons.

Kate went back to the window where she was joined by Familiar. Together they watched Jake bring out a cardboard box and put it in the trunk of his car. One thing about Jake—he didn't mind a public argument, and he didn't back down.

"Stay here, I'm going to talk to Jake." Kate slipped into the leather jacket that she'd owned since her college days at the University of Colorado. When she'd gotten her master's in criminal justice, she sure hadn't thought she'd use it to run for sheriff in Gilpin County. In fact, she'd been so eager to get out of Silver City that she'd run over anybody who got in her way. Even Jake Johnson.

As she stepped out into the fading afternoon sun, she remembered the day she left town. She'd packed up everything she owned in her beat-up old pickup. High-school graduation was only hours behind her. She and Jake had planned to elope. They had spent the last six months of high school planning the way they'd hightail it out of town and over the county line to the closest judge. It had seemed like a perfect plan.

Except that Kate had assumed they'd both leave for college together, and Jake had assumed they'd move out to the Double J.

The upshot had been that Kate had packed alone. Holding back her tears, she'd climbed behind the wheel of her truck and started out of town—forever.

Jake had been standing right outside the old saloon that still bore Kate's grandmother's name and the nude painting of her in the bar. She remembered it clear as a bell. Jake had stepped into the middle of the street when he saw her truck coming.

He wasn't moving, and she wasn't slowing.

She could still remember the feel of the truck's steering wheel in her hands, the tears that almost blinded her as she pressed down on the gas. He'd chosen not to go with her, and he certainly wasn't going to slow her down. That was exactly what she was thinking as she drove straight at him.

Jake's father had dived from the sidewalk and knocked Jake out of the way just as she'd careered past him, hell for leather, headed for the interstate and freedom.

And that was the last time she'd seen Jake Johnson—until she'd come home to run her election campaign. Except for in her dreams. Yeah, old Jake had certainly torn up her subconscious over the years. That was one reason she'd come back to Silver City. She was going to exorcise Jake Johnson and the whole problem she had with her grandmother's past and her mother's abandonment if it was the last thing she ever did.

"Jake!" She jogged across the street toward him, the fringe on her jacket swinging in the breeze.

Jake turned and felt his heart thud. "Why, if it isn't Calamity Jane. You look mighty western," he said.

Kate felt the flush begin at her toes and work all the way up. "Well, uh, thanks." For a split second she forgot what she'd come to ask him. "Did you find anything else up at the church?"

He motioned her toward the car and reopened the trunk. "A footprint. It was mixed in the wax and mud. It had rained just before the fire."

"That's good." Footprints could be very useful forensic evidence.

"Maybe. You know as well as I do that it could be a print from the fire team. That isn't likely, though. It looks like the sole of a casual shoe. The fire boots have a distinctive pattern."

Kate nodded. "The road up to the church has been sealed, but that doesn't mean we successfully kept everybody out."

"The arsonist hasn't been careless in the past. A footprint just doesn't seem to be his...style."

Kate filed that information away. "Listen, I've been thinking about putting a couple of deputies on night patrol. I thought if you had a couple of firemen and we could get some cooperation from the other branches of law enforcement, maybe we could discourage this guy."

"I don't think a few uniformed folks walking around town will discourage him, but it couldn't hurt."

"How about you and I pull the first shift this evening?" Kate was as surprised by the suggestion as Jake. Based on the degree of heat they'd generated up on the mountain, they were highly combustible. There was no point in putting themselves in a situation where they would fight and argue. At last she gathered her scattered thoughts. "I mean it would be a show of good faith if we did some of the grunt work. I'm new as sheriff, and you've got your own PR problems. This couldn't hurt. And I owe you an apology. Reverend Lyte just paid me a visit and I had to jump on him about accusing people without evidence. I did the same thing earlier today."

Jake looked down at the box of evidence. "If that's an apology, Kate, then it's a first, coming from you. I accept, but I can't pull a shift with you tonight. Since it's Saturday, I thought I'd drive this evidence into Denver. I didn't want to wait for one of the delivery services and the crime lab is waiting for it." Jake didn't look at her.

Kate felt her embarrassment as keenly as a wound. "Right. It was presumptuous of me." She shrugged one shoulder to show him and herself that it didn't matter. "Later, Jake."

Chapter Three

Kissable Kate, formerly known as Pistol-Packing Mama, is cruising the town and I'm left here with a bunch of dry reports. But this window gives me a good view of Silver City, and I must say the inhabitants of this place look like a cross between blue-light shoppers at K Mart and high rollers from Monte Carlo. Throw in a few buffalo hunters, old hippies, generation X-ers and it's a mass market that no television show has come close to touching. Not even Vanna could clap for big money and get the attention of these people. Look, there goes a granny in sneakers, eyes glazed like she's been eating lotus plants. There's something about gambling that turns folks into zombies.

Night has fallen, and in the glimmer of the neon lights and the raucous shouts coming from some of the casinos, I can imagine what life must have been like during the late 1800s. Kate's been gone a couple of hours, so I've had plenty of time to poke. What I've discovered is a family history that would make a bestseller. It would seem our hot-tempered sheriff is the descendant of Katherine West McArdle, the first infamous Miss Kitty. Just down the street is the old opera house, which Miss Kitty built with her personal savings and where traveling stars stopped to perform and lend an air of culture to the otherwise wide open, Wild-West settlement.

When the opera stars weren't in town, Miss Kitty sang and danced to an audience far more appreciative of her charms than those of some Italian soprano. Keeping up with the latest fashions, Miss Kitty held literary readings in the afternoons and cancan dances at night. A hardworking miner and his golden nuggets were soon parted, once he fell into the cunning ways of Kitty and her Kittens.

The talents of Kitty's girls drew men from all over the West. And Kitty's shrewd business sense made her a wealthy woman, one of great independence and outspokenness. So I can see a real family resemblance here. Except that my Kissing Kate upholds the law. The modern-day Kate bears an uncanny physical resemblance to the original Kitty, except that the old Kitty broke laws hither and yon, always leaving a man with a smile on his face.

And Kissing Kate is the first of her line to walk completely on the right side of the law. It appears her mother took a long hike with a fast-talking man. No wonder Katie girl is so sore about the past. You know, I once heard a famous author point out that we love our horse-thieving, pirateering relatives as long as they are at least four generations removed. Any closer and they are an embarrassment instead of fodder for a good story. This is Kate's problem. She can't bury the past because it's local legend and because it's not so past. Too bad humans can't learn a more feline approach to life. I have my scars and my old wounds, but I live for today. We cats have nine lives, and I intend to wring every drop of living out of every single one. Mayhap I can teach Kate a few valuable life lessons before I solve this arson mess and head home.

What is that I spy? Why, it's that moth-eaten dog. He's sneaking out of the fire station as if he were up to no good, which of course he is. God didn't make him a dog for nothing. I'd better follow. Besides, I think I smell grilled swordfish with a light dill sauce. I'm not complaining about the grub—yet. But I will say Kate doesn't have the palate of a great chef. She needs just a little refinement. Something else I can help her with.

Ah, it feels good to be moving, and with just the exact pressure of my shoulder against the door—voila! Super Sleuth is on the prowl!

JAKE GLANCED at his watch. It was not even ten, and he'd be back in Silver City in plenty of time to walk a shift with Kate. So why had he avoided it like the plague? Because he was a coward. Kate had walked over and apologized for her hot words. But Jake had made a discovery about himself that no amount of apology could fix. And he surely owed Kate one. He'd let her down, and the least he could do was tell her that he finally realized he should have left Silver City with her. He shouldn't have made her choose between him and a new future with a clean slate.

"Damn!" He thumped the heel of his hand on the steering wheel. Tonight would have been the golden opportunity. He'd felt something between them when she'd walked across the street, her buckskin leather jacket swinging in the breeze. Whatever magic they'd shared as teenagers had, for a split second, been rekindled. And like before, he'd let it slip through his fingers. He was as bad as one of the old-time prospectors who used to pan for gold, never seeing the precious silver that slipped beyond his grasp.

"Damn and double damn!" Jake hit the steering wheel again. When he got back to town, he'd use the crime lab report as an excuse to track her down. He maneuvered a sharp curve and the city limits of Silver City burst upon the night. As always, he was struck by the garish glare. He didn't like the idea of another casino in town. The entire county was being taken over by gambling interests, and there was little left of the small community that he'd grown up loving. But perhaps that would make it easier, in the long run, for Kate. He pushed his thoughts aside as he planned his next moves. He'd hurry to the fire station, shower and change clothes. He didn't expect Kate to hug him, but he'd been up since dawn and his body was tired and his clothes worn.

As he passed one of the casinos, the Ruby Slipper, he caught the black flag of a tail that almost made him brake. But he'd left Ouzo securely locked in the station. Ouzo was a regular Houdini, but not even he could have gotten out of doors that were padlocked and secured. Especially when he'd been left in the living quarters on the second story. With access to the stairs blocked, the only way to ground level was the fireman's pole. Not even Ouzo... Nah! He kept going, parking at the curb of the Royal Flush Rosery to rush in and buy a bouquet of flowers—just for the hell of it.

In less than three minutes he was pulling into his space behind the fire station.

He used his key to open the heavy metal back door. He had six daytime firefighters who worked for him, but at night he was on his own, unless there was a blaze. The city council had been talking a lot lately about building a new fire station, and Silver City desperately needed one. The town had grown by leaps and bounds in the last two years, and the city services hadn't kept pace. Truth was, Jake wasn't too inspired by all the changes. He'd enjoyed small-town life—before the casinos. Now, maybe it was time to think about giving up his job and rebuilding the Double J. Or else moving on.

The irony struck him hard, and he handled it with a grunt and a wry grin. Just as Kate was coming back to Silver City, he was thinking about leaving.

He took the stairs to the back door of his private living quarters two at a time. The stairway gate, which had originally been plastic, then wood, and now cast iron, was still in place. Ouzo had eaten the plastic and wooden gates. Wrought iron had been the ultimate solution.

"Ouzo!" He whistled, listening for the dog's response even as he unlocked the gate. "Ouzo."

An ominous silence greeted him.

"Ouzo!" He didn't bother relocking the gate but hurried into the kitchen area. The garbage was knocked over, but there was no sign of the dog. He went to the den, where the sofa still held the imprint of the dog's body and a Spaghetti-O can was wedged in the cushions, licked clean. Ouzo had definitely been there. But where was he now?

"Dammit all to hell," Jake said, able to clearly visualize the trouble that was sure to come. It had been Ouzo he'd seen slipping around the corner of the Ruby Slipper. And right down the street from the casino that had once been a hotel were Mrs. Tanner's cats. Ouzo had been caught at least a dozen times chasing the felines. Susan Tanner had promised if the dog came one more time that she'd call animal control and have him captured and destroyed as a public menace.

"Ouzo," Jake said, angry and worried. Well, the

shower and change of clothes were out. He'd have to find the dog and then worry about finding Kate.

He turned back to the stairs. He never saw the black-jack that came out of the shadows and caught him a glancing blow on the side of the head.

Jake crumpled to the floor, oblivious to everything around him.

KATE'S STEPS SLOWED as she neared the old opera house, now called the Golden Nugget. The ping, whir and clatter of the one-armed bandits floated out on the night air, along with the tinkle of a player piano and the sounds of laughter. Kate didn't have to step inside to see the painting of her grandmother that still hung over the bar. Even though she wore her hair in a modest French twist and her figure was disguised by her uniform and gun, she was a walking replica of the woman in the painting. Her namesake and nemesis, Katherine McArdle. Miss Kitty.

Standing in the cool night air, Kate felt the past come alive. Kitty had died when Kate was a child, but the memories were as vivid and fresh as if they'd happened only yesterday. Even as an old woman, Kitty had retained her flamboyant ways, and her total lack of remorse at her career as a madam. She'd built a comfortable house on the outskirts of town and managed the dance hall and saloon from there, dressed in bright red loungewear and turbans. In the middle of the front parlor of her home was a grand piano, which Kitty played with bawdy abandon, entertaining her friends, and Kate. Kate had loved her dearly. Until she'd gotten old enough to realize how Kitty had made her money.

At the age of twelve, Kate had refused to have anything to do with her grandmother. A year later, Kitty had died, unexpectedly, of a stroke.

The saloon style door swung open and a laughing man came out, a dazzling blonde on his arm. Arms linked together, they continued down the street, stopping at the next casino and looking in. Still laughing, they went inside.

The sight of them gave Kate a cold and unexpected ache. She moved away from the Golden Nugget and went down the street, stopping at each alley and walking behind the casinos. She'd chosen to walk the casino beat without a backup. She had deputies who would have been glad to partner with her, but she'd wanted the solitude. Seeing Jake earlier in the day had left her in a pensive mood. And Reverend Lyte had opened the door on a line of speculation that wasn't headed in a good direction. Was Jake guilty? All Kate knew for sure was that he'd loved his ranch more than he'd loved her.

Jake was firmly in her mind when she saw the black dog ambling along the street. Silver City had a leash law. One Jake obviously didn't feel compelled to obey. Kate shrugged. She was the sheriff, not the dogcatcher.

There was the sound of barking and an aggravated yowl. She hurried down the alley toward Mrs. Susan Tanner's house. Sure enough, Jake's black dog had treed a big yellow cat. Tail wagging, the dog was leaping in the air and snapping at the cat's tail.

"Ouzo!" Kate spat out the word and was amazed at the way the dog turned to confront her. He instantly dropped onto his belly and began to whine and grovel. "Easy, boy," she said, amazed that the mere tone of her voice had sent the dog into a spasm of abject fear. It was almost as if…no, Jake would never mistreat a dog. Never. Jake's soft spot for animals had been one of the problems at the Double J. Jake had found it hard to sell the cattle he did manage to raise on the hardscrabble land.

"Ouzo?"

The dog came to her, crawling on his belly. At her feet he began to lick her boots.

"Hey, fella," she said, kneeling down to pet him. "It's okay, but you can't chase the cats."

Susan Tanner's porch light blinked on, and the petite woman came out, a bathrobe wrapped around her.

"Is that black devil after my babies again? I swear, I've warned Jake enough. Now keep a grip on that dog while I call the dogcatcher. That animal's going to the pound, and Jake can pay the fine to get him out."

Kate eyed the dog and then Susan Tanner. She was a lovely old woman, but a little overprotective of her cats. "Scram," Kate whispered, and released her hold on the dog.

Ouzo took off without the need for any prodding. His black tail disappeared around the white picket fence and he was gone.

"Sorry, Mrs. Tanner, he got away."

"Was it Jake's dog?"

Kate considered. The one thing she didn't want to get involved in was a dispute over Jake's dog. "I can't be certain, but my deputies and I will be walking a beat every night until the arsonist is caught. We'll keep an eye on your cats for you, and if we see that dog again, we'll nab him."

"Thanks, sheriff," Susan said. "I voted for you. It's about time we had a woman who knew how to get things done." She stepped back in the house and flipped off the light.

Alone in the dark, Kate smiled. She'd have a word

with Jake about the dog. A friendly word. In the morning.

She walked on down the block, turning left at Bank Street, which ran behind some small boutique businesses that had sprung up at the west end of town. She passed the remains of Roy Adams's insurance company.

Roy was unrelenting and hard-nosed, but it was obvious he had the best interests of Silver City at heart. Of course there were folks who were sore about their insurance claims. She shook her head. There just wasn't enough evidence to come up with a clear suspect, one that connected to every fire.

Other than Jake.

She was turning back to Main Street when she saw a shadow flitting from the back of Evelyn's Boutique. A jolt of adrenaline made Kate's heart race and alerted all her senses. Holding herself perfectly still, she tried to think through the situation.

Since Evelyn Winn, the owner, was about as petite as Susan Tanner, Kate knew instantly that it wasn't her. The man who slipped among the shadows was big. Not fat, but tall and well built. Or, at least, that's how he looked in the dark.

Kate's hand went to her nightstick and she checked to make sure the flap that kept her gun secure in the holster was free. Heart pounding, she started after the fleeing shadow. Maybe it was nothing, a high-school kid. Or maybe it was someone up to no good. She could feel her pulse, strong and steady, as she crept silently after the man.

Out of the darkness another shadow sprang, this one smaller and close to the ground. Before Kate knew what was happening, she felt her feet knocked out from under her and she tumbled to the street, barely able to clutch a handful of black fur.

The man she'd been stalking heard the noise of her fall and took off at a dead run. Kate sprang to her feet and began pursuit, but he was too far ahead. She lost him in the back of the casinos.

Breathing hard, she stopped. Well, if he was up to attempted burglary, maybe she'd scared him off for good.

She turned back to see if she could spot the dog, obviously Jake's Ouzo. From the back of Evelyn's Boutique a yellow blaze licked out a window.

Kate stared in disbelief. "Fire!" she cried, running toward the blaze. "Fire."

In the deserted back street no one heard her. She quit wasting her breath and ran to the building. Kicking in the door she saw the blaze. It was roaring out of a trash can and climbing the chintz curtains that Evelyn Winn had so carefully color-coordinated with her shop's decor.

Kate didn't waste a moment. She rushed to the counter that held the cash register and began pulling out boxes and clutter until she found the fire extinguisher. In less than a minute she was in the back room, soaking the blaze that had already begun to lick at the ceiling.

Within minutes she had the fire under control, and it wasn't until the ashes were thoroughly soaked that she lowered the fire extinguisher and took a breath. She went to the phone and dialed the fire station. After five rings, the call was transferred to one of the firemen, who answered.

Kate gave the details, assuring the man that the fire had been extinguished. "I need someone to alert Jake Johnson. It was definitely arson," she said, wondering if Jake had gotten back from Denver yet.

"I'll be over to seal the scene," the fireman assured her.

"I'll wait," Kate said, suddenly realizing that she needed to sit down for a moment. At the sight of the suspect, she'd gone into automatic, relying completely on her training and instincts. Now she wanted to think.

She replayed the sequence of events. She'd seen the suspect coming out of the boutique. Or had she? She couldn't honestly say she'd seen him come out the door. He'd simply appeared in the shadows beside the door of the boutique. She'd begun to follow him, and then Ouzo had leapt at her from the alley. Or had he been running from something else?

She couldn't be sure because she hadn't truly gotten a good look at him. One minute she'd been on her feet and moving at a pretty fast clip after the suspect, and the next thing she knew, she felt her legs knocked out from under her and found herself on the pavement. And the shadowy man was gone. But he'd been a big man, and if her suspicions were correct, he was the man who'd started the fire in the boutique.

But why?

How did Evelyn Winn fit into the string of arsons?

Because Silver City was, at its heart, a small town, Kate knew a lot about the people who lived there, including Evelyn Winn.

The thirty-two-year-old woman moved to Silver City not ten months before. She was close to Kate's age, and Kate had hoped to make a friend of her. That was before she'd found out that Evelyn and Jake had been dating.

Lately she hadn't seen them in the coffee shop or their cars parked at Chuck's, a local restaurant and bar that hung off the side of a mountain with a breathtaking view.

Kate didn't like the direction her thinking was taking, so she chose a different path. Evelyn Winn was from Alabama and she'd done well with her exotic bath supplies and her certificate as a massage therapist. Local gossip was that she was earning a hundred dollars an hour giving massages.

The pay was a helluva lot better than what a law officer earned.

Kate glanced around the boutique. Evelyn's taste was ruffles and frills that matched or coordinated with towels and rugs and lotions. The soft lighting in the shop showed off the rich bubble baths and soaps carefully molded into golden nuggets, silver dollars, flowers, stars and jewels. It was the beautiful shop of a very feminine woman.

So who would have it in for Evelyn enough to try to burn her out?

Kate's instant answer was a rejected suitor. She pushed beyond that to a creditor, or debtor. Following a hunch, Kate went to the counter and pulled out the account books that she'd seen while hunting for the fire extinguisher. When she saw the amounts of money folks paid for bath products she whistled softly to herself. She smiled when she saw Susan Tanner's name. Along with her cats, Susan also pampered herself. She continued down the columns and whistled softly under her breath. The hotel accounts were incredibly lucrative.

She flipped the page and hunted for accounts which showed large amounts of red ink. She found one, which seemed insignificant, and another concerning Alexis Redfield that gave her pause. Alexis was the new owner of the Golden Nugget, and she was down for a $60,000 debt. For decorating and design work. And the account was two months in the red.

Kate heard the sound of someone coming and she

closed the account book and shoved it back under the counter. If she wanted to examine it officially, she could get a warrant at a later date. Perhaps it would be best if she asked a few questions without tipping her hand.

She went to the back door and met the fireman who introduced himself as Led Gables. When she asked about Jake, he simply scratched his head. "Jake's lights weren't on, and he didn't answer his door. That crazy dog of his didn't even bark."

"That dog of his is running loose," Kate said darkly.

"No, ma'am, not Ouzo. Jake doesn't let him run free. He gets after Mrs. Tanner's cats and she doesn't like it."

"Trust me, Led, the dog was running the streets, including the one beside Tanner's house. I saw him." When she saw he still didn't believe her, she added, "I touched him. Or let me say he touched me. He knocked me down in the street."

"Oh, no," Led said softly. "Are you gonna sue Jake?"

His question was so unexpected that for a moment Kate didn't know what to say. "Of course I'm not suing him because his dog tripped me." It was unthinkable. Frowning, she began to wonder if part of Jake's problem was the intelligence level of the men he hired to work for him. "You keep an eye on the scene. I'm going over to Jake's and see if I can find him, or at least find a clue as to where he might be. He needs to examine this scene."

Since her truck was still at the sheriff's office, she walked to the firehouse. It was eleven o'clock. Jake should have been home. From the sidewalk she gazed at the firehouse. It was dark, without a single light showing in the upstairs apartment where Jake lived. Kate felt a whisper of warning on her skin. She tried the front door that led to the firemen's area and the garage where the two fire trucks were parked. It was locked.

A tingle of worry nagged at Kate and she slipped around the building to the back. The total silence made her edgy. She pressed herself against the wall, her hand going automatically for her weapon. Something wasn't right. Jake's vehicle was parked under a tree. She left the protection of the wall to slip to the vehicle. Her hand brushed the hood and found it cool. It had been parked for some time.

So where was Jake?

She eased to the back door and found that it pushed open with a touch of her finger. She peered into the darkness but could see nothing at all. There wasn't a sound to indicate that Jake might be home, but something kept Kate from calling out to him.

She crept up the stairs, holding her breath and concentrating all of her energy on listening. At the top of the stairs she found an iron gate and assumed that it was designed to keep the dog in the apartment. The gate swung open at her touch.

Not good, not good. Her mind repeated the phrase as she crept forward in the darkness.

The hands that grabbed her came out of the blackness before she could react. She felt an arm slide to her throat, choking off her air and bruising her neck. She tried jabbing with her elbows, but the man who held her was very strong. His other arm went around her waist and tightened.

Her hat was knocked askew and her hair spilled out across her face. The man's hand moved up to capture a breast, then halted. His grip on her lessened, and she used all of her strength to twist. She'd caught him by surprise, and she could almost taste freedom.

Suddenly she was free, and as she stumbled away from her attacker, the room was flooded with light.

"Kate!" Jake looked at her in surprise.

"Jake!" she answered, just as startled.

"I thought you were breaking in," he explained.

"What were you doing hiding up here in the dark?" she snapped. She could still feel his hands on her, a lingering touch of heat.

"What were you doing sneaking around in my house?" he countered.

"Your dog is running loose all over town." She was rattled, but she was determined not to show it. "And there's been a fire."

"A fire?" Jake snapped to attention. "Where?"

"Evelyn's Boutique," she answered, noticing for the first time that there was a trickle of blood in Jake's hair. "What happened to you?"

"Someone was in my apartment waiting for me when I got home. They hit me and knocked me out." Jake checked his watch. "About forty-five minutes ago." He rubbed his head. "I'd better get over there and check on the fire."

"Led Gables is there."

"You called Gables?" There was a hint of offense in his voice.

"I called here, but no one answered. The phone rang over."

Jake nodded. "I was out cold. I didn't hear a thing."

"Are you hurt?" Kate started forward, her hand reaching out to him before she caught herself.

Jake rubbed the side of his head where a knot was clearly swelling. "I'm okay. The bastard caught me by surprise."

Kate went to the sink and ran a paper towel under the tap. She directed Jake to a chair and kept her expression very professional as she cleaned the blood around the edges of the wound. "You don't need stitches, but an X-ray might be in order. That's a nasty goose egg."

Jake allowed her to continue to dab at the wound, but his face showed he had no intention of seeking medical attention. "I'm really not hurt," he insisted.

"Any idea who attacked you? Or how they got into your apartment? Surely you keep the door locked?"

Jake stood up. "No, no and yes. Now decide whether you're going to play Florence Nightingale or a member of the Inquisition."

"It's my job to ask questions." Kate started out with some heat in her voice until it occurred to her that Jake might be suffering a bit of embarrassment at being knocked out. "But I can save most of them until later," she added.

Jake nodded slowly. "Thanks."

Kate sighed. "If you can stand one more bit of bad news, your dog is on the prowl. I saw him over at Mrs. Tanner's. Jake, I have to warn you, she's upset."

"I know. She's going to shoot him, and I hate to say it, but I understand where she's coming from. That dog is incorrigible. And I don't have time to go chasing after him right now."

"I was going to walk around town. I'll find him for you if you'll give me his leash." She saw something—maybe a flicker of desire in his eyes—that made her uncomfortable and she quickly looked away. "I was walking a beat anyway. I'd hate to see an animal get destroyed."

When Jake only continued to gaze at her, Kate cleared her throat. "I want to send a deputy over here to take some fingerprints, and you need to check and see if anything is missing."

"Nothing's missing."

"Have you looked?"

"I don't have to." Jake rubbed his head. "This wasn't about burglary."

Kate looked at him sharply. He knew more than he was telling, and just like in the past, he wasn't telling anything she didn't drag out of him. Annoyed, she went to the phone and called for a deputy. She gave a brief summary of the facts and hung up.

"You won't find any prints," Jake said. "He wore gloves."

"For someone who was attacked from behind, in the dark, and who didn't see the attacker, you know a lot about him. Are you sure you didn't see him?" Kate felt her patience growing thinner by the second.

"No, but he wasn't the type to make a bunch of stupid mistakes. You won't find any clues."

Kate knew it was time for her to go, or else lose her temper. "The deputy will be here, Jake. Let him do his job." She stepped around him. The hallway leading to the kitchen was clearly lighted now, and Kate saw the cluster of yellow roses that had been cast onto the floor. She looked at them a moment, startled by the pang that came with the idea that Jake had bought roses for someone.

She felt his gaze on her. "I'll check back with you," she said, stepping over the flowers and hurrying down the stairs. At the iron gate she took a moment to check the lock. It hadn't been forced. At the back door she checked the lock there. It was undamaged.

When she turned around Jake was standing at the top of the stairs looking down at her. Silhouetted there, he was about the same size as the man she'd seen running down the back street behind Evelyn's Boutique.

Chapter Four

Dawn was breaking over Silver City, and Kate and the cat stood outside the sheriff's office watching the sky lighten from midnight to the promise of another achingly beautiful day. She leaned down to scratch Familiar's back. He was pretty good company, especially to a woman who'd turned into an insomniac. After scouting the town, she'd returned to the office to find her reports of the fires scattered about her desk as if he'd been reading them. He was a smart cat—he'd found the device used to burn the church—but she wouldn't go so far as to believe he could read a report. Still, he was smarter than the average human.

Now, she was bone-weary and her shoulders ached. She'd found Ouzo and had a deputy take him home. Deputy Clyde Smith had dusted Jake's place for prints and searched for signs of forced entry. He'd drawn a blank on both.

Kate had called the Golden Nugget and discovered that Alexis Redfield was staying there. The prissy guy who'd answered the phone had told Kate to call "during business hours" to make an appointment. Kate didn't really want an appointment; she wanted a shot at Redfield's financial records. It seemed impossible that the

Golden Nugget wasn't making a good profit. It was a gold mine. Or it should have been. Alexis Redfield had brought some major talent into town, and the audience that came to listen brought pockets full of money to gamble.

In recent weeks, the old stage where Kate's grandmother had once sung and danced had been the setting for Elton John, B.B. King, Tina Turner, Reba McEntire and a host of comedians as well as Chinese acrobats, touring musical groups and magicians. The place had been packed night after night, and the roulette wheel, blackjack tables and slot machines had spun, dealt and whirred twenty-four hours a day with bettors waiting five deep in line. It wasn't possible that the Golden Nugget was losing money.

Something wasn't right in that financial department, and Kate only hoped she could make it pan out. If not, her only suspect was the shadowy stranger. The one who had the exact body type as Jake.

Jake *and* a thousand other guys, she found herself arguing. And Jake had an alibi.

Some alibi. He'd been knocked out by a man who didn't force an entry, didn't leave a fingerprint and didn't have a known motive.

JAKE SAT ON HIS SOFA with Ouzo in front of him. The dog's amber gaze looked mournfully into his.

"This is the last warning, Ouzo. You chase Mrs. Tanner's cats one more time, and I'm going to give you to her trussed up like a Christmas turkey. You know it's wrong, and you do it anyway. You gleefully do it anyway."

Jake watched the dog, who appeared to be paying close attention. But Jake knew better. He'd had Ouzo for four years, and in that time he'd learned that Ouzo paid attention only when something he wanted was in the offing. For example, Jake could tell him to go and fetch a packet of steaks off the counter. Ouzo would willingly comply, on the off chance that he might be rewarded with a steak. On the other hand, an order to bring the paper in from the street, or a pair of slippers—hah! Jake had a better chance of waiting for the tooth fairy to deliver either of those things.

"Ouzo?"

"Err-err-err-aarr!" Ouzo lay down and put his paws over his ears.

"Very funny," Jake said. Another problem with the dog was that he wouldn't do any of his crazy tricks, like this paws over ears, if anyone else was around. The end result was that all of the guys in the fire department thought that he, Jake Johnson, made up lies about Ouzo's talents.

"I mean it, Ouzo. I'm not saving your bacon another time. You should be ashamed of yourself. If you'd been here at home, where you belong, you might have prevented me from being knocked in the head. You abandoned me, your master, to a man who could have easily killed me."

Ouzo's amber gaze was slightly glassy.

"Go on, go to your room," Jake said, finally giving up. An idea struck. He flipped open the yellow pages to dog trainer. There were three listed. All wasn't lost. Not yet. The battle had only begun.

With the matter of Ouzo settled in his mind, Jake walked to the window. Kate and the black cat, who, he saw with disgust, heeled perfectly, were coming down the sidewalk with a bag of sweet rolls and coffee from the bakery. It rankled Jake that a cat could behave better than his dog. But it was actually Kate he was watching. She'd returned to his life with the power of a natural element—fire. She could warm him to fever pitch, or she could toast him to a crisp. If he allowed her. He sighed and turned his thoughts to what had occurred at Evelyn's Boutique.

He'd studied the scene of the fire. Someone had tossed a match into a trash can full of paper soaked with kerosene and had then run out of the building into the back street. The fire had been deliberately—and hastily—set. It didn't show the preparation and planning of the five previous fires. But Jake couldn't be certain if the arsonist had actually intended to burn the building down, or if it was some kind of hoax. It had crossed his mind that it was even a setup, an attempt to frame him.

In truth, he had no solid alibi. He'd been knocked cold during the time the fire was started, which might indicate that the fire starter had planned it exactly that way.

Kate and the cat were just across the street, and he had an impulse to walk over and see if she'd discovered any new evidence. He didn't think it through any more than that. If he gave it too much thought, he'd back out. Kate did things to him. She tied him in knots and then walked away. It wasn't something he liked, but it also wasn't something he could turn away from. Like it or not, they weren't through with each other. Their future might be as antagonists, but it would never be casual or passing. At least not on his part.

"Come on, Ouzo."

Just as Jake leaned down to snap on the leash, Ouzo sprinted out the back door. "Ouzo!" he called, but the black dog was only a memory.

Jake hustled around the building just in time to see the Reverend Theodore Lyte step out of his new burgundy El Dorado and approach Kate in a long angry stride. Jake hurried forward with neither Lyte nor Kate aware of his approach.

"Another fire!" Lyte cried, his fists clenched. "Roy Adams assured me that you'd stop this madness. We both know that Jake Johnson is behind this. I want him arrested."

"I want you to calm down, Reverend," Kate said.

"Listen here, I never believed a woman could do this job. You've proven me correct."

Jake felt the blood rush to his brain. He was furious. Out of the corner of his eye he saw a flash of black. Ouzo was behind a car and sneaking straight toward the preacher. Jake halted in his tracks. When Ouzo stood right behind Lyte, he lifted his back leg. There was the sound of liquid striking cloth.

Lyte whirled, his expression stunned. Ouzo took off running in the opposite direction. Across the street, Jake ducked into the doorway of his building.

Lyte's face was a violent shade of red. "Grab that dog. Grab him! I want that dog captured," he huffed, shaking his leg. "He's a menace!" He whirled back to Kate. "I demand that you pursue that dog."

"Sorry, Reverend, that's the animal control officer's responsibility. Since you seem to think I can't manage my own job, I wouldn't presume to tackle someone else's." She leaned closer to him. "My professional advice to you is that you clear out of town, go somewhere and cool off, and don't come back until you can act like a mature adult. You see, running around accusing folks of arson might be considered slander." She brushed past the preacher and walked into the sheriff's office with Familiar right on her heels.

MY OLD DA ALWAYS told me that the best way to calm an angry fever was with a long draught. Ah, Da, did you see the man dance? He was doing a one-legged polka! A sight for sore eyes, it was. I'm sure you never meant the long draught to be anything other than a pint of Guinness, but a dog has to improvise. Indeed, it was a fine and lovely sight.

When my ancestor, Red, first came over from the old country, he used almost the exact same bit of diplomacy on a lawman who'd cornered Billy the Kid. Now imagine, if you can, that Billy was wounded. It was just a flesh wound, but it was nasty and festering and it was in his gun arm. He'd been walking out of a saloon after a bit of blarney with some of the ladies. Without warning a shot rang out and Billy felt the burn of lead in his right arm. The bullet spun him around, and with the instincts of a man who lived on the edge of danger, he dropped to the ground and avoided the second bullet.

It was a one-horse town up in southern Colorado, and dusk was falling. Billy was in the middle of the only street, his bright red blood spilling into the dust of the road. He looked at the saloon and saw there was no help from that quarter. No help from any gun-toting lead-driller in that place.

From his right he heard a deep, "Billy. No sense dyin' over this."

He looked up to see the sheriff, standing there. His gun was holstered but his hand was hovering over it, itching for a chance to draw, even if Billy was wounded.

Billy used his old noggin, though, thinking about the odds. He knew that in a draw-down, speed and accuracy are the only two things that count. Well, with his arm festering, he knew his speed was gone, and from his position in the dirt, accuracy was something only the *saints could determine. Out of the corner of his eye, Billy saw a black shadow detach itself from the side of the saloon. There was a faint whine as Red sauntered into the empty street toward the sheriff.*

"Make a choice, Billy. You can come with me, or you can die in the street," the sheriff said.

Billy didn't do a thing. His fate was completely in the hands of Red, a roving Irish dog.

The sheriff's hand moved down toward the butt of his gun. Just as his fingers caressed the handle, Red cut loose on his leg. The sheriff was so startled he lost his concentration. Billy grabbed for his gun, rolled and came up blasting. He winged the sheriff in the arm and made his escape with old Red gallivanting along at his heels.

Now that's the tale of a great moment of relief, and one that's been completely forgotten in the lore of Billy the Kid.

Ah, indeed. One day I ought to write the history of my family, "Dog Days—Canine Tales of Bold Romance and Adventure." Jack London made a fortune with his White Fang books, and those dogs were savages.

Let me cock my ear to the south. I hear the sound of some cats stirring at the Tanner residence. It's early, and what a wonderful surprise—to spring forth from the bushes and give those lazy pusses a moment to remember.

KATE COULD BARELY control her laughter as Lyte stormed to his car and got in. He was fuming. Beside her, Familiar also looked amused.

"How about some breakfast?" she asked the cat as the minister drove away. She turned away from the window just in time to hear a knock at her door.

"It's open."

She wasn't completely surprised to find Jake standing there. She'd been thinking about him all night. "Your dog deserves a T-bone, my treat," she said.

"He deserves a prison term," Jake couldn't stop his smile, "but I'll let him have the T-bone."

"Is he always so discerning about character?" Kate found that Jake's smile opened the door on a lot of emotions. And memories. He looked so young when he smiled, so much like the eighteen-year-old she'd left behind. Looking at him, at this moment, it felt as if fifteen years had not slipped away from them.

"Ouzo has a knack for puncturing pomposity, particularly mine," Jake said, his smile turning slightly rueful. "Lyte is going to be out to have my head."

"Does he know Ouzo's your dog?" Kate realized that Jake didn't need Lyte any angrier. The minister was already over the line.

"If he doesn't, he'll find out. Ouzo is a hard dog to hide. He's a descendant of Big Red, the dog that ran with Billy the Kid."

"Yeah, right. Familiar here is straight from Salem, Massachusetts. Right, boy?"

Familiar's golden gaze was unyielding.

"Sorry," she said, stroking his back. "Familiar is not amused and neither am I." She popped the top on a tin of smoked shrimp. "Try this, fella." She placed it on the floor.

"It's true. Big Red was a famous Irish setter. He was imported directly from Ireland."

Kate gave him a sidelong look. "If Ouzo is descended from an Irish setter, why is he black?"

Jake paused, a frown settling on his face. At last his eyes brightened. "Because he was a blackguard. He was something of a criminal mastermind."

"Jake, I hate to disillusion you, but Ouzo looks like a black cur. Maybe a cross between a lab and a setter or bird dog, but he definitely can't trace his ancestry farther back than the street corner where his unlikely parents met up. He's black as the ace of spades and those golden eyes, they're wolfish, Jake. Not to mention the long hair on his back legs that makes him look like he's wearing baggy trousers. The Kennel Club would be on you with a lawsuit if you tried to claim that animal as a descendant of some pedigreed setter."

"Kate! Ouzo would be mortally offended. And after he saved you from the attack of the enraged Reverend Lyte."

Kate laughed out loud. Jake's false indignation was over the top. It had been a long time since she'd shared the absolute joy of a good laugh with… She straightened up. "Where *is* Ouzo, that pedigreed dog?"

"Uh-oh." Jake looked out the window. To his surprise, Ouzo was sitting on the street, staring in at them. "He's right there. Let me get him."

"Use the leash," Kate called out. "I've seen him at work with cats, and Familiar doesn't care to be harassed."

Kate found another can of chicken and opened it for the dog. "Don't say I'm spoiling him," she forestalled Jake when he returned with the dog. "It's rude to feed the cat and not Ouzo, besides I do owe him a thank-you."

"Since you're handing out food, how about sharing one of those pastries." Jake pointed at the bag. "Let's see, you got one cheese Danish and one bear claw. You'll eat half of each one, unless I beat you to it."

Kate pushed the bag toward Jake, hiding her sudden

uneasiness behind a smile. "Help yourself." Jake remembered too much about her. He knew the small details, the little crazy things she did that no one else bothered to notice. Jake reached into the bag, selecting the bear claw, as she knew he would. He reached for the other bag and drew out one of the two coffees. She always bought two, just in case she wanted a second cup.

They found themselves staring at each other. The wall clock ticked louder as the long moment continued. Kate stood beside her desk. She knew she should say something, but words were inadequate to help her now. There was only Jake and the emotions that sizzled between them. Hurt, pain, distrust, fear, and ultimately, desire. He was sitting on the edge of her desk, and more than anything in the world she wanted him to kiss her. She'd hate herself—and probably him—when it was over, but it was almost painful she wanted him so much.

Jake lowered the coffee and the sweet roll. He stood, slowly. Kate could see it in his eyes. He wanted her, too. They were both aware how stupidly they were behaving. Their chance had been missed long ago. Kate, better than anyone, knew there was no going back to the past and changing things. And yet...

She swayed toward him as he closed the distance in two steps. She sank into his arms and felt them close around her with a sensation of pure happiness. Nothing else mattered. Not the past, not the future. Kate pressed her cheek against his shirt and held him as tightly as he held her.

"Kate?"

She looked up slowly. His lips were right there, and it seemed lifting hers to his was the only thing to do. How many times had she dreamed of this? But she'd never expected it to happen. Never.

His lips were as sensual as she remembered, and his kiss as tender. She felt his hand move up to her neck, his fingers working into her hair as he slowly tugged it free of the pins that held it. He deepened the kiss, and Kate met him with demands of her own. Her own hands moved up his back, sliding over the muscles that were bigger, more developed than she remembered them.

But his hair was the same. The silky texture of it, the feel of it made her tighten her hold, and he responded with more urgency in his kiss. In the background, Ouzo began to bark, but Kate ignored the dog and so did Jake. His face, unshaven, was slightly abrasive against her cheek as he broke the kiss to explore her neck with hard, hungry kisses.

"Oh, Jake," she whispered, unable to deny him.

His fingers claimed her hair, gently tugging her head back further. His lips trailed down her throat, down to her collar bone and one hand dropped from her hair and began to slowly unbutton the uniform she wore.

It occurred to Kate to stop this madness. It was insane. But it was the sweetest, most incredible lunacy Kate had experienced in a long, long time. Jake's touch had always been magic.

"Katie," he whispered against the top of her breast. "I've spent many a long night thinking of you," he said. He pushed the shirt off her shoulder. "I—"

He blinked with shock at the sudden pain in his leg. Looking down, he saw the black cat, both front paws extended into his calf.

Kate felt the tension in him and looked down, too. "Familiar!"

Kate bent to push the cat away just as the office door burst open and an angry Roy Adams appeared, huffing and red-faced. Still bent over, Kate buttoned her shirt in what she prayed was an unobtrusive manner.

"Well, I'm glad to see you've got Jake," Roy said. "Something has to be done about these fires and done now. Jake, if you can't handle it, you can find another job. Kate, I hate to say it, but if you don't get busy, there's talk of a recall election." He looked at both of them. "Is something wrong here?"

"Nothing," Jake said. He glanced at Kate. "Roy, putting pressure on Kate or me won't change the facts. We're working together on this case, and the best thing that could happen would be for you and everyone else to back off and let us do our jobs."

"You're working together, are you?" Roy shot Kate a suspicious glance. "I never thought I'd see the day when you two worked together. I remember when you tried to run him down, Kate."

"That was a long time ago, Roy," she said carefully. Damn! Was she always going to be haunted by the past? Either hers or her family's.

"What's really going on here?" Roy glanced back and forth between them. "There's something else…"

"You're right, Roy," Jake said, stepping forward. "You'll hear about this sooner or later, so it might as well come from me. Ouzo used Theodore Lyte for a fire hydrant."

Adam's face registered puzzlement, then disbelief, then for a split second, amusement, before he replaced it with a scowl. "That man has been a bane ever since he took over that church last year. Jake, did you tell that dog to do that?"

"You should know by now that Ouzo doesn't do anything I tell him to do."

"That's true enough." Adams glanced at the dog who

was sitting beside Familiar. "What a duo. Where'd you get the cat?"

"I'm keeping him for a friend," Kate said quickly.

"I believe there's some law against keeping animals in public buildings." He eyed Kate suspiciously. "There's really something going on here between you two and I can't figure it out."

"I was trying to figure out what charges to file against the dog," Kate said, sending Jake a glance that begged for help. "There ought to be a law against doing what he did, but I couldn't find one on the books."

"Well, book him as a public nuisance and fine Jake." Adams stomped back to the door. "I don't care what you two have to do to get results, I want results. Remember, Jake, you've got a report to give tonight at the meeting, and I want to see the officials of Dandy Diamond Casino leave here with big smiles on their faces about the prospect of putting a new casino here."

"No promises," Jake said, holding his ground. "Roy, nobody would be happier than me to put the arsonist behind bars. You, of all people, should remember how much my ranch meant to me. Solving these arsons has become personal, and the only promise you'll get from me is that I'll do everything I can to find the person or persons responsible for the fires."

Roy snorted. "So far, that hasn't been good enough. Now get busy and quit wasting time."

He walked out, closing the door behind him. Kate went to her desk and fidgeted with the coffee, now cold. She didn't want it anyway. She also didn't want to have to meet Jake's eye. They had stepped off the world and into a fantasy of madness. It could never happen again.

"Kate," Jake said softly. He walked over and lifted her chin so that she had to look at him.

"Don't, Jake," she said. She stepped back. "That was crazy. We both lost our minds for a minute. That's all it was, so let's forget about it."

Jake followed her, his hand brushing her cheek. "Can you forget it?—because I can't."

"I have to," she said. She looked up at him. "I came back here because I finally realized that running away wasn't a solution to anything. No matter where I went, I was still Kate McArdle's granddaughter. I was still the sixteen-year-old whose mother ran away with a gambler and left her all alone. I was still the girl who slept with her boyfriend and then discovered that a hardscrabble ranch meant more to him than she did." She put her finger over his lips to stop his protest. "That's the way it felt, Jake. I've grown up enough to understand that maybe, just maybe, that wasn't exactly the way it was. But don't you see, it doesn't really matter now. That's the past. We had our chance and we blew it. Or I blew it. I was too...damaged to be whole enough to be the woman you needed." She shrugged. "I may still be too much of a mess." She faced him again. "But at least I'm trying now. And getting involved with you will only mess me up worse."

Kate's words were like a slap. Kate had been doing her own thinking, and it wasn't running parallel to his.

"What we had was something special, Kate. I'm not willing to write it off and say we made a mistake so now it's finished. You're here. I'm here. There's a chance for us, if you're willing to take it."

The memory of their kiss made her skin burn with desire. There was no denying the power of their attraction for one another. But attraction was one thing, love was another. That was the wisdom she should have learned from Kitty McArdle. Desire was like the flame of a candle. It glowed beautifully in the right setting. But a strong gust of wind could extinguish it. Or in the wrong setting, it could start a devastating fire.

Kate shook her head. "Not now, Jake. There's no chance for us now." Even as she spoke the words her body betrayed her. She wanted to go to him, to feel his arms wrap around her in an embrace that made her feel safe and loved.

"You always think you're the one who calls the shots, Kate." Jake had grown angry. "When you roared out of town that day you never gave me a chance. Now, once again, you're in total control. Maybe it's because you can't allow anyone else to be in charge, not even of your desires." He reached over and picked up Ouzo's leash. "That's always been the problem here. You and your obsessive need to be in total control. And I guess you're right. That's something that I can't deal with. No man would be able to."

Jake walked out and left the door open behind him.

For a moment Kate remained perfectly still. She felt as if he'd knocked the breath out of her lungs. The first sensation that returned was a kind of sickness. She had the terrible feeling that it truly wasn't over with Jake, despite her brave words to the contrary. Coming back to Silver City might have been the worst mistake of her life.

Especially since so much evidence suggested that Jake could actually be an arsonist.

Chapter Five

Kate stood at the door of the Golden Nugget. Even though it was nine in the morning, the place was hopping with activity. It was true that no matter the hour, there were always gamblers eager to test their skills against lady luck.

Kate had done no more than glimpse inside the old theater since she'd come back to town. Seeing the changes would be hard. Kitty McArdle always had a taste for the flamboyant in her clothes and decor, but she hadn't had neon lights and rainbow-hued tiling and carpet to toy with.

Kate pushed through the door. She took a look around, absorbing the addition of gaming tables, slot machines, and roulette wheels. At least Alexis Redfield had kept the flavor of the place as a saloon and theater. The old stage was just as it was when Kitty walked off it for the last time, except now there were expensive lights and plush curtains. The stage floor, once worn by the dancing feet of Kitty's Kittens, was polished. Nearer to the bar, the floor was covered with plush carpeting patterned with a full-house poker hand.

The crowd was solid and boisterous, and Kate walked up to the bar where her grandmother's likeness stared down at her. Kitty McArdle had been a beautiful young woman, and the artist had captured every curve and even the glint of mischief in her green eyes. Kitty had never married. It was a family tale that she'd been in love with the U.S. Marshal who was in charge of the Colorado territory at the time. He was a man who kept company with Kitty, taking her and a bottle upstairs to her private apartment at the end of a long evening. But Kitty had never talked about her personal romantic encounters. Never.

The bartender glanced at Kate, then looked again. He turned so that he could look at the picture behind him, and then back at Kate. "You could be her ghost," he said.

"I'm her granddaughter," Kate answered evenly, "and I'm also Sheriff of Gilpin County. I'm here to see Ms. Redfield. I have an appointment."

He pointed to the staircase. "She's up there."

Kate knew her way around. She'd spent her childhood running through the old building, playing hide-and-seek. It had been a wonderful place then. An air of secrecy hung about the entire building, and especially Kitty. And Kate had loved secrets.

As she walked up the stairs she put the past aside. At a door marked Office, she knocked.

"Come in," a sultry voice called out.

Kate entered. The room's color scheme was of mint and orange sherbet, and everything was painted or printed in stripes, dots and stars—the pillows, curtains, rugs, walls, blinds, and even the furniture. Kate instantly felt suffocated. There was at least fifty thousand dollars' worth of ruffles in that room alone.

"Whatever it is that you want, state it and then get

out.'' Alexis Redfield stepped out from behind a pastel plaid screen.

Kate blinked. Alexis was wearing an orange sherbet dressing gown with a mint green boa collar. A matching fuzzy green turban covered her head. Unable to take her eyes off the strange outfit, Kate managed to say, ''Hello. I'm...following through on an investigation, and need to ask a few questions. What's your relationship with Evelyn Winn?''

Alexis went to a small antique desk against the wall and picked up an orange cigarette holder. From a silver case she withdrew a mint green cigarette and put it in the holder. At Kate's open stare, she twisted one corner of her flaming orange mouth and said, ''I have them specially made. They're menthol.'' She lit up and blew a gust of smoke at Kate.

''Did Ms. Winn...decorate this room?''

''It was the only thing she did right,'' Alexis said, crossing the room with long steps.

Kate had a mental image of a pastel Cruella DeVille. ''Have you and Ms. Winn concluded your business dealings?''

''That woman will never step foot in my establishment again. This room was her masterpiece. With my taste and inspiration, Evelyn achieved the pinnacle of decorating. And then when we moved into the dressing room and bath, she decided that we should shift the color scheme to white.'' Alexis's eyebrows rose and were lost under the fuzz of her turban. ''White! What kind of color is white? The woman completely lost her mind. I had the bouncer escort her out and told her never to return!'' She threw her hands into the air in a dramatic gesture. ''White!''

Kate had absolutely nothing to say to that. "Then your parting wasn't amicable?"

"Amicable? Are you serious? The woman had the taste of a Stepford wife. Our parting was not amicable. I have no use for someone with such boring taste." She eyed Kate's uniform with a suddenly critical eye. "Take a tip from a professional and change that color scheme to navy slacks and a kiwi top. Much better for your eyes and complexion."

"Thanks," Kate said lamely. Whatever else Alexis Redfield was, she was a woman with a forceful opinion.

"What exactly are you investigating? And why are you so interested in Evelyn?" Alexis asked suddenly. Her eyes widened. "She's trying to collect on that bill, isn't she? She actually turned me in. I can't believe it. I made her take all of that wallpaper and material back. I cancelled the plumber and carpenter that she hired. I owe her nothing. Not one red cent."

Kate smiled. "I didn't know you owed her money," she fibbed, "but that's a very interesting fact in light of what happened last night." Kate had her now. Alexis had talked herself into a corner.

"What happened?" She stepped forward, all eagerness.

"You tell me," Kate replied. "Where were you about ten o'clock last night?"

"Here, darling." Alexis smiled. "Having a drink with Bobby Bojangles, the piano player. He was here until…quite late. Now, tell me what's happened." Her eyebrows drew together in a V. "Evelyn wasn't in a car accident or something, was she?"

Kate already knew that if Alexis was involved in the arson attempt, she would have hired someone to do the dirty work. "Ms. Winn's business was almost destroyed last night. Someone set a fire."

"Another fire." Alexis dropped some of her theatrical gestures. "That's terrible. If that firebug isn't stopped, I might be next." She stubbed her cigarette out.

Kate was instantly alert. "What makes you say that?"

"Nothing, nothing at all." Alexis slunk across the room. "Let me make us some tea."

Her sudden hospitality was another tip-off. Kate halted her with a cool sentence. "Forget the tea, Ms. Redfield. I want some answers. What makes you think you might be a target of arson?"

"Why, darling, my establishment is the biggest draw in Silver City. There are other casino owners who are jealous of me. So jealous they'd love to see my place reduced to a pile of ashes."

The Golden Nugget wasn't in Kate's family any longer, but the idea of it burning to the ground was distressing. Even if it would get rid of an ocean of awful orange and green.

"Has anyone threatened you?" Kate asked.

"Not in so many words."

Kate checked her watch. She'd wasted enough time. She walked to Alexis, put a hand on her shoulder and pressed her into a chair. "If you know something, Ms. Redfield, now's the time to tell me. If another business burns and I find out you held back information, I promise you that I'll charge you as an accessory to arson. That's a serious crime."

"I'm not an accessory," Alexis argued. "You can't do this. I'm a prominent businesswoman. I won't be bullied by a...a...a female law person."

"I won't be stonewalled by a person who is guilty of abuse of pastels." Satisfied by the woman's look of alarm, Kate leaned closer. "Now I have to get over to the boutique and investigate the scene. I want some answers. Who threatened you?"

"Well, it wasn't exactly a threat." Alexis reached for another mint green cigarette. "It was Evelyn. She threatened to pull my hair out."

"And what prompted this threat?"

"I asked that handsome fire chief Jake Johnson over for dinner." Alexis's long eyelashes brushed her cheeks in fake demureness. "And he accepted."

"You mean your falling out with Ms. Winn was over a man?" Kate wanted to shake her until her capped teeth rattled. Because the dispute wasn't over any man—it was over Jake.

"Yes. Evelyn had him, and I wanted him." Alexis looked up at Kate. "And whatever I want, I get."

SO THIS FROU-FROU boutique is the latest arson scene. Pretty shoddy work after the thoroughness of the fire at the church. This could be the work of a, pardon the pun, copycat.

Which brings to mind another complaint I want to register against the human species and their inadequate linguistics. Cats are the most unique and original of all creatures. How is it that we got stuck with a derogatory term such as copycat. Truthfully, have you ever known one cat to copy the behavior of another? I rest my case. It is humans who seem intent on dressing alike, talking alike, eating alike, etc. etc. I mean how many Pamela Lee blondes have you seen lately? Or surgically induced pouts? Humans have an absolute obsession with owning, wearing, or looking like the rich and famous. I shall, in the future, use the term "copyhuman."

Back to the mystery at hand, though. A true copyhu-

man would have taken more time to study the technique and patterning of the original arsonist and made a more sincere attempt to replicate the crime exactly. That's the challenge—to do the same crime the same way with the same results.

In the fire at Evelyn's Boutique, this is not the case.

Kerosene was used as the accelerant, and the fire was hastily thrown together in the garbage can. As I wander around this boutique I clearly see that a good fire would have helped to clear out some of this highly scented clutter. I'm a little dizzy from so much stuff packed into so little space.

My deduction here is that another firebug was at work. And one who didn't really intend to burn the boutique to the ground. So the question any good sleuth would ask is why?

Kissable Kate is following a financial trail, but unless Evelyn Winn owes a ton of money to the bank and can't pay it off, money doesn't seem to be the motive for this fire. It looks more personal. Hastily done, poorly exe-cuted—the work of someone who hopes to gain some-thing. Hmm. Revenge, perhaps.

I can see that Kate shares my theory. She's been standing in that corner of the room as if she'd been hypnotized by those odd-shaped candles. I think maybe she's just trying to stay out of Jake's way. They had their own fire going this morning. I thought I was going to have to get that black fuzz-ball of a dog to help me get out the water hose. Yep, there's a definite spark between Jake and Kate. I do find it slightly depressing that Kate is attracted to a man who owns a dog—and a dog with some kind of lilting Irish accent. After all, he's only been in America for what, twenty generations? What a crock!

If Ouzo comes from lyrical Irish stock, I'm the Wizard of Oz.

Uh-oh, speak of the devil, here comes that boot-licker as I speak. He's signaling me to meet him outside. As if I could be deceived by his innocent and eager demeanor. He wants to get me out there so he can chase me up a tree. No can do, big boy. No can do.

JAKE WATCHED KATE out of the corner of his eye. She and the cat were at the fire scene when he arrived, and he felt a jolt of pure desire at the sight of her. But she'd been elusive. Probably as confused as he was about the current of passion they'd switched on earlier that morning. But in the split second his lips had touched hers, the past fifteen years had disappeared. It was as if they were the same two teenagers who'd been so deeply in love and assumed they'd share their future. That's where the trouble had started. They'd both assumed.

She felt his gaze on her and turned away, her attention on the notes she was making. Still, when he approached, she was acutely aware of the intense look he cast at her neck. She could almost feel his lips there.

"Penny for your thoughts," he said.

Kate nodded at the notepad she held. "I spoke with Alexis Redfield. At first I thought she might have been involved in this fire, but now I don't think so."

"Alexis? She doesn't seem the firebug type to me."

"What type is she, Jake?" Kate couldn't help the sharpness of her question.

"The pastel type," he said, chuckling. "If you'd ever seen her apartment at the Golden Nugget, you'd have an idea of what she's like."

"I've seen her apartment." Kate frowned. Jake had obviously seen her apartment, too. If he'd stayed vertical long enough to notice the place. The thought rankled. "A fetish for pastels doesn't prevent someone from having a criminal nature. Why, I'm sure Ted Bundy loved pastels. He probably only selected victims who *wore* pastels."

"But you said you didn't think she was involved." Jake was obviously baffled by her anger. "I was only agreeing with you."

"Naturally," Kate snapped, unable to contain her jealousy. Had Jake been responsive to Alexis's come-ons? "I have to get back to the office." Kate took off without a backward glance.

Jake stood for a moment trying to digest what had just occurred. Only an hour before, Kate had been melting in his arms. He hadn't imagined it! It had happened. And now? She acted like he was lower than a snake's belly. Jake had no clue of what had transpired between the kiss and the kiss-off. But he was going to find out. Talk, conversation, intercourse, debate, argument—whatever route Kate chose—they were going to speak of whatever it was that had gotten under her skin.

He checked with his firemen and made sure they'd gathered every shred of evidence—pathetic though it was. He whistled up his dog and took off for the sheriff's office.

KATE CLIMBED into her truck. "Come on, Familiar. I think we need to pay a visit to Evelyn Winn, another in the long line of conquests that our fire chief has left with smoldering embers."

If Jake wasn't directly responsible for the Gilpin County arsons—and Kate didn't really think he was—maybe his tomcatting ways had provoked some otherwise sensible women. Or maybe all of Jake's rejects had formed a club—the Flamethrowers, or the Abandoned Arsonists. Kate felt her own temperature rising. She knew she was being ridiculous, but she couldn't stop herself. The kiss she'd shared earlier with Jake had opened the door on a lot of emotion. And it was damned uncomfortable to discover she was jealous. Especially when she knew intellectually that she didn't have a right to be.

She pulled the truck up to Evelyn Winn's house and held the door open for Familiar. "While I question her, you snoop around." Kate had already gotten into the habit of talking to the cat as if he were a partner. Sometimes she felt a little foolish, but the truth was that Familiar acted as if he understood every word she said.

Evelyn Winn came to the doorway, her eyes still red from crying. She took one look at Kate and her uniform and burst into tears again. "Who would do such a thing?" she cried.

"How much insurance do you have on the business?" Kate countered in a no-nonsense voice.

The implication was not lost on Evelyn. She dried her sniffles. "Surely you don't think I set that fire hoping to collect insurance. I've put my heart into that business. I love every item in the store."

Kate took a deep breath. Her anger at Jake was making her far too hard on the woman. "Sorry, Ms. Winn. Who would want to see your business destroyed? Is anyone out to get you or make trouble for you?"

"I can't think of a soul," Evelyn said. As she motioned Kate inside the house, Familiar slipped inside undetected.

Kate stopped in the foyer. To her left was a formal drawing room crammed with antique furniture. Pewter photo frames and candles were on every flat surface, the velveteen-covered furniture was large and dark, and long draperies pooled on the floor. There seemed no room at all for oxygen. But at least the color scheme was a dark hunter green and burgundy—not pastels.

"Have a seat," Evelyn said. "Would you care for a cup of tea?"

"That would be nice," Kate answered, surveying Evelyn. She was slender and pretty, her dark hair cut to frame her face and large brown eyes. Kate suspected that her distress about the fire was more than a little put on. Out of the corner of her eye, Kate saw Familiar take off around a corner. Probably headed for the kitchen. But he would also scope out the rest of the house. She had to give him enough time. Besides, Kate wanted to find out everything she could about Evelyn and Jake. If only—Kate told herself—because Evelyn and Jake were suspects.

Evelyn reappeared with a magnificent silver tea service and what appeared to be fresh baked scones, cucumber sandwiches, and a plate of cookies. Kate checked an antique pendulum clock, which confirmed that it was almost lunchtime. Not even twelve and Evelyn was serving a full tea.

Evelyn poured and chatted about the tea service and how she'd found it at an estate sale. Kate listened, noting the slight tremor in Evelyn's hands as she poured.

"I spoke with Alexis Redfield this morning." Kate was not displeased to see that Evelyn almost dropped the tea pot. There was something going on between the two women. But what?

"How is Alexis? I'm afraid we don't see each other very often any more."

"How long have you known Ms. Redfield?" Kate asked.

"We both came to Silver City about the same time. Less than a year." She finished pouring Kate's tea. "Did she tell you we were friends?"

"No, not exactly. What made you decide to relocate to Silver City?"

Evelyn's hands continued to tremble as she replaced the teapot on the tray. "I don't know. It was a fluke. My boutique needs a big tourist trade." She shrugged. "I always adored the West." She picked up the pot and started to pour her own cup, concentrating on the dark golden stream of tea.

Kate decided to change tactics. "Ms. Redfield said she owed you money."

"She did?" She looked completely panicked.

"I suppose I stated that incorrectly."

"I should say so! She gave me free rein to decorate her apartment above the Golden Nugget. She wanted all of that sherbet and green, which can be refreshing if done with a light touch. But my goodness—" Evelyn opened her eyes wide. "I couldn't even go in there after we were done. It felt as if the room had come to life and might eat me."

Kate couldn't help laughing. She knew exactly what Evelyn was talking about.

"Anyway, I thought Alexis and I had developed a certain...understanding. That our friendship could survive the truth. That apartment of hers was so overpowering that white was the only answer. And if you've talked with Alexis, I'm sure you know that white, or gray, or beige, or even ecru are all considered vile. The world should be a place of pastels, or so she believes, even if it makes all of her friends ill to visit."

"So you ordered the materials to decorate—"

"And she cancelled the job. I told her she owed me for the material, the part of it I couldn't send back."

"Which would be how much?"

Evelyn shrugged. "I have a good relationship with many of the suppliers I do business with. They bent a few rules and took a great deal of it back. It left about three thousand dollars that I had to eat."

Kate didn't want to reveal that she'd snooped into Evelyn's books. The amount showing in the red for Alexis Redfield was far larger than three thousand dollars. Either Evelyn was lying, or perhaps she'd simply never corrected her bookkeeping after the merchants had accepted the materials back. Perhaps Evelyn's only fault was poor bookkeeping. That—and the fact she'd dated Jake. So, why was someone trying to either frighten her or burn her out of business?

"Where were you last night?" Kate asked. She knew Evelyn wasn't the person she'd seen leaving the boutique. There was no way the slender woman could have been the figure she'd seen in the alley.

"I was here, reading a book." Evelyn's expressive eyes showed worry. "Why? Am I really a suspect in my own fire?"

"This isn't the first fire in Gilpin County, but it was the most sloppily done." Kate set her teacup back on the tray and stood. "As far as I'm concerned, until the arsonist or arsonists are caught, everyone is a suspect."

"That's outrageous. I refuse to be a suspect. I'm an innocent victim. Anyone with eyes can clearly see that I'm the one who's suffered here. That's why law officers don't get any support anymore. You treat the victims like suspects."

"I'm sorry." Kate walked to the door, holding it open a crack for Familiar, who'd appeared in the hallway.

Evelyn had never even noticed the black cat. "I'll be in touch," Kate promised her as she closed the door. One thing was certain, both Evelyn Winn and Alexis Redfield would bear watching. Those two women were neck-deep in something, and Kate wanted to know exactly what it was.

Chapter Six

Kate held the door of the sheriff's office open for Familiar. The grilled tuna she'd ordered for him was in the carryout container. On the drive back from Evelyn's, the cat had been completely uncommunicative—until he'd seen the restaurant that specialized in seafood delicacies. Now Kate eyed him, wondering if he really was a detective cat or just a gourmet freeloader.

"Meow," Familiar demanded, gaze fixed on the styrofoam container.

"I'll bet you'd prefer it on bone china," she said as she put the food on her desk for him.

Ignoring her, he started to eat.

"Kate."

She whirled around. Her office was off-limits to the other members of the sheriff's department—unless she'd asked them in. She found herself face-to-face with Jake.

"What were you doing at Evelyn Winn's?" he asked.

"Investigating. How did you know I was there?" She knew the answer as soon as she asked. "She called you, didn't she?" It instantly burned her that Evelyn Winn had called Jake to complain about how she was doing her job as sheriff.

"She was upset. She said you treated her like a suspect instead of a victim."

"I'm not altogether sure which one she is," Kate said hotly. She didn't like the spark in Jake's eyes. Not one little bit.

"And Alexis, too? She's also a suspect?" A grin teased the corners of his mouth.

"Maybe. I haven't ruled anyone out. There's motive there, except I'm not certain exactly what it is," she admitted. She glared at Jake. "Why are you grinning like a gambler on payday?"

"When you left the fire scene this morning, I was one confused man. Now, though..." His grin widened. "You're jealous, aren't you?"

Kate started to speak, then clamped her mouth shut. She took a breath. "I am no such thing."

"Yes, you are," he said, nodding.

"You are an egotistical fool," Kate said slowly. "If you're twisting all the facts on the fires in this way, it's no wonder you haven't solved any of them."

Jake's expression spoke volumes.

"Don't patronize me," Kate warned.

"I wouldn't think of it." He took a step toward her. "In fact, I'm willing to forget this entire conversation. Let's just pick up where we left it this morning when Roy Adams interrupted us."

Kate backed up a step. "Jake..." She'd given their kiss a lot of thought, and it wasn't going to happen again. No matter how tempted she was. "Stop." She lowered her chin slightly. "I can't explain how that happened this morning." She decided to risk the truth, or at least a smidgen of it. "I can only tell you that it scared me." She saw that she had his attention. "I thought I'd grown up, that I'd matured and become more...

controlled.'' She could hear the tremor in her voice and she wanted to curse her weakness. Even after all these years, she wasn't truly done with Jake Johnson. But that was something he didn't need to know. Not ever.

"Kate, we have to talk about things. We were kids fifteen years ago. We acted rashly. And we both assumed too much. But we can talk—''

"No.'' Kate spoke the word softly, but its impact was like a slap. She met his gaze. "We can't talk about this. Not now.''

"We have to talk about this.'' Jake's amber eyes were compelling. "We have to talk about a lot of things.''

Kate felt as if the past were rearing up behind her and snatching at the back of her heels. There were too many mistakes in the past. Too many bad decisions and bad behavior. And she could tell that Jake wanted to pull all of it out and examine it.

"I can't,'' she said.

Jake took a long breath. "Okay. Now isn't a good time for this. But later, Kate. You can't run forever.'' He turned and walked out of the sheriff's office.

JAKE'S MIND WAS CHURNING as he hit the streets of Silver City. He didn't care that Kate had hassled Evelyn and Alexis. A little hassling was probably good for both of those women. Though they weren't on his list of suspects for the arsons, he knew they were both capable of troublemaking. He'd had some casual dates with Evelyn. Mostly, she'd initiated the meetings by calling him up to discuss sprinkler systems, which she obviously hadn't installed. He'd had dinner once with Alexis. She was, after all, an interesting woman. But when he'd discovered that neither of them made his heart rate increase or his curiosity kick in, he knew he was wasting his time. They had been women to spend a few hours or share a meal with, nothing more.

Jake sighed. How was it possible that two women were chasing him, and the one woman he wanted was running as hard and fast as she could in the opposite direction?

The look on Kate's face troubled him. The prospect of a talk had simply frightened her to death. The emotions that he evoked frightened her. In the future plan he'd been sketching in his head, this was not a good thing. The whole plan depended on his ability to get Kate to talk about the past. Their past and any other thing that might bear on their future.

In truth, he didn't have a clue of what her life had been like for the years she'd been away from Silver City.

The more he thought about it, the more clearly he saw that her life had been a series of traumas in her teenage years. Kate had loved her grandmother with the pure love of a child. From the bits and pieces Jake remembered of the old lady, she was a pistol, one of the proverbial night ladies with a heart of gold—except that no one knew for an absolute fact that Kitty McArdle had ever sold her pleasures. She had run a cathouse, that was a historical fact. She'd been a singer and dancer and had entertained men with a stage presence and a flair that showed she loved her work.

But no one, not even the men in town known for their bragging, even hinted that they'd shared Kitty's pleasures. Still, people in Silver City remembered her as a bawdy woman.

Kate had carried that stigma. Then her mother, Anne, disappeared with a gambler.

Kate was left alone. Left with a legacy her classmates were more than willing to throw in her face.

And Jake's response had been to blithely assume that Kate would want to spend the rest of her life in Silver City because he was there.

It was a remarkably self-centered view, and now that he was aware of it, he wanted to talk. He had to make her understand that it was youth and that single-minded ability to focus on one thing that had made him so pig-headed—a character trait they shared. She had assumed that leaving was the answer to her problems. Jake had finally learned that staying or leaving didn't matter. There wasn't a simple solution. Not for him and not for Kate. And no one was solely to blame.

He could tell by Kate's expression only moments before that she blamed herself for many things in the past. Well, Kate was going to have to share that blame. Whether she liked it or not.

He deliberately walked past the Golden Nugget. Alexis Redfield had done a good job with the place, but the thought of Kate in Alexis's lair made Jake grin. At least until he saw Cal, one of his firemen, rushing toward him. Jake's heart sank.

"Jake! Jake!" Cal was calling when he was still fifty yards away. "You'd better get to the firehouse and fast. The animal control officer is there and he's going to take Ouzo. He has a warrant!"

"A warrant!" Jake had never heard of a warrant for a dog's arrest. "For what?"

"It's that minister, the one whose church burned. He said Ouzo assaulted him."

Jake could see that Cal was truly upset. Even though Ouzo had stolen Cal's dinner—more than once—the fireman seemed to have a soft spot for the black thief. "Lyte?"

"That's the one," Cal said, drawing abreast of Jake. "He came up like the wrath of God. I know the animal control officer, Colin. He didn't want to come for Ouzo, but that reverend wasn't going to let it go. I finally said that I didn't have a key to your iron gate. They got all the way up there and Ouzo met them, fangs bared."

"Great." Jake had never seen Ouzo growl at anyone, but the dog would pick that particular time to show a little assertiveness toward humans. Ouzo had the most unique sense of timing—when to do exactly the wrong thing.

"Colin didn't want to push the situation once I pointed out that the fire station was public property but that you paid rent on the apartment, which made it private property."

"Good thinking," Jake said. He and the fireman had begun to walk quickly toward the station.

"He said he'd be back with a court order to get in the apartment." He looked at Jake. "What are you going to do?"

For a split second, Jake didn't have a clue. But the answer came to him, crystal clear. "I'm going to take Ouzo to a hideout."

"I was already thinking along those lines. How about my place?"

Jake considered it. "No, they might think to search the houses of all my firemen, and if they found Ouzo there, it might get you into trouble."

"I don't mind getting into trouble. Not when a dog's life is involved."

"Did they say they were going to kill him?" Jake couldn't believe this. It was a nightmare.

"That minister said he was going to make certain Ouzo was destroyed. He called him a menace to society and a danger to anyone walking the streets." Cal hesitated. "What exactly did Ouzo do to him, if you don't mind me asking?"

"He peed on his leg."

"He...peed?" Cal's eyes were wide. "He actually peed on the minister's leg." A slow grin spread over his face. "I like that, Jake. I like that a lot. If anybody ever deserved a free watering, it's that Reverend Lyte."

They turned the corner and Jake ducked back. Theodore Lyte was standing outside the fire station as if he were guarding the place.

"He thinks you're going to try to spring Ouzo," Cal said.

"And I certainly am," Jake admitted. "As soon as I think of a plan."

"Times a-wasting, Jake." Cal checked his watch. "If they find Judge Harvey, they could get that court order and be back in the next fifteen minutes."

Glancing up and down the street, Jake saw the black cat in the window of the sheriff's office. "I know who can help. Stay here and make sure no one gets Ouzo."

Jake rushed into the sheriff's office. "I need your help," he said to Kate. "It's Ouzo. He's in trouble for what he did to Theodore Lyte."

Kate didn't hesitate. "We can hardly let Ouzo take the fall for something that needed to be done a long time ago."

Jake grinned. This was the old Kate. The girl who'd stolen his heart.

"Familiar," Kate said. The cat instantly hopped from the desk to the ground. Kate lifted him and held him at the window. "See that bad man over there? Do you think you can distract him a bit while we get Ouzo over here?''

''Meow.''

Kate put him down and watched as he hurried across the room and out.

''That's amazing,'' Jake said. ''I never would have believed a cat could be trained to do anything, much less such a complicated task.''

''The first thing you've got to learn about felines in general, Jake, is you can't train them. They do whatever they want. You just have to figure out how to make them want to do what you ask.''

''And how, exactly, did you do that?''

Kate laughed. ''I don't have a clue. Let's go.''

By the time they got to the street, Familiar was already circling the minister's legs.

''Scat!'' Theodore Lyte snarled. ''Get out of here. I hate cats.''

Familiar moved between his legs, rubbing and purring.

''Get away!'' Lyte stomped his foot, but Familiar paid no heed.

''Get away from me, you furry rodent.'' Lyte drew back his foot and kicked. His shoe hit only thin air. Familiar was already circling his other leg, purring loudly.

I don't like this guy. Not a bit. I always thought that religious practitioners were supposed to love the creatures of the world. I thought it was in their creed to show tolerance and kindness. Kicking a cat—or at least trying to—doesn't fit in with any religious doctrine I've learned about.

But, for a cat of my consummate skill, it is quite enjoyable to toy with this clumsy humanoid. Though he snarls and kicks, he's too slow and dumb to be able to hurt me. Hah! I'll bet he has trouble getting into his pants. He probably has to sit down so he won't fall over. I mean this guy has no sense of balance.

I can't believe I'm dodging flying feet to save the hide of that renegade Ouzo, though. That pretentious, troublemaking mutt. The irony of this situation is that Ouzo IS a menace to society, and he delights in chasing my fellow felines up trees. I can only justify helping him by noting that I never met a cat who couldn't use a little exercise. And Ouzo, like the good minister here, isn't smart enough to catch a cat. So he's a nuisance, like the minister, but no real danger to the felines of Silver City.

Oops! he almost caught me with that kick. I swear, I can't believe this! Cars are beginning to stop! I know it must look like he's dancing on the sidewalk. Yeah, that lady in the blue Volvo is stopping. She's getting out, and her face is white with anger. This is getting better and better.

How about if I dodge left, then fake right. Heh! He kicked his own leg! Here comes the Volvo lady, and she's about to puncture the sidewalk with her high heels she's so mad. Man, dig those plaid green-and-orange leggings!

I think my job is almost done. I saw Kate and Lovelorn Jake sneak across the street and head to the back of the firehouse. Another ten minutes and they should have Ouzo on the road to freedom.

"Heh! You!" Alexis Redfield had left her car in the middle of the road and traffic was beginning to pile up behind it. She stalked toward the man who'd blatantly been trying to kick a poor stray cat to death. "I'm talking to you," she said, poking a long, orange-sherbet-tipped fingernail into his chest.

"That cat was trying to trip me." Theodore Lyte squinted his eyes against the glare of Alexis's outfit.

"That cat was trying to get some affection. I could hear him purring all the way out to my car." She whipped a notepad out of her matching sherbet patent-leather purse. "Name, address and phone number."

"What?" Lyte glanced at the cars where at least twenty curious people were now watching him. Some of them wore very angry expressions.

"Your name, address and phone number. I'm going to report you for animal cruelty. You are a blight on this community."

"I, madame, am a minister. I am the Reverend Theodore Lyte," he said, drawing himself up to his full height of six feet.

"Yeah, and I'm Princess Grace of Monaco. Ministers don't mistreat animals or children. It's in the codebook." She looked up at him. "I should know. My father was one."

"I'm in the middle of important business." Lyte glanced at the firehouse. There was no movement there. Any moment now the good-for-nothing animal control officer would return with the court order and that mangy black bane would be taken off and exterminated.

"Okay, Reverend Lyte," Alexis said, tucking the notepad back into her purse just as the stalled drivers began to blow their horns in impatience. "I'm filing charges against you." She walked over to where Familiar had found a place to sit in the sunshine. He gave a meek meow as Alexis approached. She scratched his head and tickled under his chin. "Sweet boy. You want to come live with me?" she cooed.

Familiar gave her a purr, brushed against her leg and took off running around the corner of the fire station.

"Not the grateful kind, are you?" Alexis spoke softly. "Surely you're a male." She went back to the minister. "You'll get your court summons. And you can count on me to be there. If it takes a heavy fine and a few days' jail time, you need to learn that you can't mistreat helpless animals." She walked back to her car and drove away.

KATE GLANCED behind her just as Jake and Ouzo were disappearing from sight. Jake had the dog on a leash, but it looked as if Ouzo was directing their path. Under all that fur, Ouzo surely had the canine equivalent of Sly Stallone's body. She grinned at the thought.

Turning back to the scene on the sidewalk in front of her, Kate didn't even try to suppress her chuckle. Theodore Lyte had unknowingly waded into battle with Alexis Redfield, and the woman had won, hands down.

Kate watched as Alexis drove away. Theodore Lyte remained on the sidewalk as if he'd just been blasted by a laser beam and turned into a zombie. Knowing that she was adding insult to injury, Kate sauntered over to him.

"How's it going, Reverend Lyte?" she asked cheerfully.

"What's the statute on animal cruelty?" Lyte asked, still obviously frazzled.

"Depends." Kate frowned.

"Depends on what?" Lyte twitched as he asked.

"Depends on who brings the charges, how much they care to make them stick, which judge you get and how many eyewitnesses there were to the event." She smiled.

"You wouldn't be worried about trying to kick that cat to death, would you?"

Lyte's eyes widened. "I did no such thing. No such thing at all. I was simply trying to make it get away from me. It was diseased. It was foaming at the mouth. I was terrified it had rabies. I was only defending myself, and that's not a crime."

Kate let her gaze shift to the street and linger on the place where at least twenty cars had stopped and witnessed the event. "If that's the case, I'm sure you'll have plenty of witnesses to verify how the cat was actually foaming at the mouth and how it attacked you. I couldn't see any odd behavior in the cat from where I was standing, but I'm sure that of the forty or fifty people who witnessed the incident, a few will be able to verify what you say. Of course, there will be those who saw it the same way Ms. Redfield did."

Lyte was speechless.

Kate continued in a pleasant conversational tone. "You know, I never realized that Ms. Redfield was such an animal lover. She has all that money, too. I think, Reverend, that you'd better change your attitude toward animals, and fast. Might I suggest a check to the local humane society. I mean it would show good faith and concern and all of that. A substantial check." She nodded and started across the street to her office just as Colin, the animal control officer came driving up.

"Sheriff McArdle, hold up a minute," he called. He waved a document at her.

Kate turned back. "Yes?"

"I've got a warrant to search Jake Johnson's apartment to take his dog." Colin looked downright miserable. He cast a disgusted look at the minister.

"What's this about?" Kate asked innocently.

"The Reverend, here, wants Jake's dog destroyed. He said the animal was vicious and shouldn't be allowed to live."

Kate turned disbelieving eyes on the minister. "Another animal attacked you? This is incredible. This time a dog? I've never heard of such a coincidence in all my life, Reverend. It makes me begin to think that maybe you're doing something to these animals to make them want to attack you." She gave it a full ten seconds for the implications to sink in. She turned to the animal control officer. "As unbelievable as it sounds, Reverend Lyte was just attacked by a cat. Right here on the street with at least fifty witnesses."

Colin looked at the minister with obvious contempt. "Maybe the problem isn't the animals."

"That is enough." Lyte glared at the man. "I won't be criticized by you," he turned to Kate, "or you. I have a right to protection. I want that dog removed and now." He snatched the court order from Colin's hand, checked to make sure it was signed and handed it to Kate. "Do your duty," he said.

"Certainly." Kate grinned. She reached into her pocket and pulled out a quarter. "Colin, call up Buster at the newspaper. I think he'll want to cover this story."

"What?" Lyte was furious. "No newspaper. That is completely unnecessary. Are you trying to crucify me in the press?"

"A person sure of his case wouldn't be worried about a newspaper story," Kate said silkily. "You've got a right to have the dog taken, and the public has a right to know about it. I'm certain Ms. Redfield will want to organize a campaign to save this dog. She is such an animal lover."

Lyte crammed the court order into the pocket of his

suit coat. "Never mind," he said to Colin. "I want to think this through. The dog will be there." He stalked away.

"Good work, Sheriff," Colin said. "I didn't want to take Jake's dog. Ouzo has always seemed harmless enough to me. He's conniving. Anyone with a brain can see that, but he isn't mean."

"I couldn't agree with you more," Kate said. "Thanks, Colin." She strolled across the street to her office. She hadn't felt so effective in a long while.

Chapter Seven

Kate walked into the meeting of Silver City merchants and elected officials and took a seat against a wall. Glancing around, she saw that everyone who was anyone in town had come. Evelyn Winn and Alexis Redfield were seated side-by-side in the front row. Seemingly, they'd gotten over their argument about Jake and the interior decorating. In concession to Alexis's passion for pastels, Evelyn was even wearing a powder-blue skimmer with a buttercup-yellow scarf. They were exquisitely color-blended.

Kate watched them bend their heads together and whisper. She could tell by the nodding of Alexis's tiny mint green pillbox hat and Evelyn's dark curls that each agreed completely with whatever the other was saying. After the venom they'd spewed at each other, their making up was curious and Kate made a note of it.

Jake was nowhere in sight. He'd called her from a house near his old ranch. He'd taken Ouzo out there, hoping to track down one of the Double J's previous ranch hands. Jake was hunting for someone he could trust to care for Ouzo for a few days until the heat blew over and the minister realized how foolish it would be to pursue his vendetta against the dog.

Almost as if she'd conjured him up, Reverend Lyte entered and stood at the back of the room. His gaze swept everyone there, halting for a moment on the oblivious Alexis Redfield.

Kate was closely watching Lyte as the door swung open and several men she didn't recognize entered. They were dressed like high-powered executives, from their tailored suits to their hand-cobbled shoes. They exuded power and money, and she leaned back against the wall to watch the show. These were the men from Dandy Diamond Casino. They were all dark-haired and olive-complected, and Kate admitted to herself they were walking stereotypes of mafiosi.

Roy Adams banged a gavel to bring the room to order. The city council was seated in a line at the front of the room, and the strangers took seats, flanking the council on the left. "We're here to talk with the representatives of Dandy Diamond Casinos," Roy said. "This company wants to come into Silver City and they're offering some mighty fine incentives to get the city to agree to work with them. And, as we can attest, the gambling business has been good for Silver City. Real good." He paused. "Now I'll let Bobby Cochran, the legal representative for the casino concern, tell you a little about their plans for Silver City."

The man who stood up beside a slide projector and giant flip chart was darkly handsome and well versed in his presentation. Kate listened as he flawlessly presented a strong case for the city to embrace the new casino concern. Still, in her mind, the town had enough casinos. More than enough. Silver City was becoming a mockery of what it once had been.

On the other hand, it had been slowly going bankrupt, she reminded herself. Once the silver rush wore off and the thick veins had been tapped out, Silver City had begun to fade. The glory days were over, and in the late 1970s, the city had been in dire shape. The historic buildings were abandoned and rotting into the ground. That was when the first casino had opened.

Kate's mother, Anne, had hung onto Kate's grandmother's saloon and dance hall as long as she could, but she'd been forced to sell it. Kate remembered how her mother had cried as she signed over the deed. And Anne had promised Kate that the sacrifice would be worth it, that they'd have a life where they could find happiness. And then Anne had up and disappeared. With all the money. Except for ten thousand dollars she'd left on the kitchen table. But what was a girl of sixteen to do with ten grand?

Kate had managed.

Now she almost jumped out of her skin when she felt a hand on her shoulder. She looked up to see Jake, his amber eyes drawn with concern. "You okay?"

"Yeah," she said. "You?"

"I'm fine. Ouzo's over at your office. I put him in one of the holding cells for good measure."

"What?" Kate lowered her voice instantly as several people turned to look at her. "He's in jail?"

"I had to, Kate. It's just for the meeting. I couldn't find any of the ranch hands and there was no one else I trusted to manage him. To be honest, I don't trust that dog at all. He senses that there's trouble brewing, and I swear he relishes the idea. I think he's up there now planning a way to make things worse for me."

"I can't keep a dog locked in jail," Kate protested.

"Sure you can. I took his dog food over. Besides, it may do him some good."

"Jake, you honestly can't believe that dog is capable of connecting the punishment to his crime."

Jake was deadly serious. "Kate, that dog is capable of anything. He can solve these fires, if he gets a mind to. And he can also send me to the insane asylum. Either you keep him or I...I don't know."

Roy Adams's gavel banged on the desk and he pointed it at Jake. "You're report is next, Chief Johnson. Until that time would you show our speaker some courtesy."

Jake slipped into a chair behind Kate. She felt his fingers on her neck, a soft, easy massage at just the place where the tension was the worst. She wanted him to continue forever, and she also wanted him to stop. Why was it that everything about Jake put her in a state of conflict?

She listened to the casino lawyer begin to sketch the Dandy Diamond Casino's future plans for Silver City. The DDC wanted to build a theme park and a discount shopping mall. Not to mention at least two golf courses. As the man flipped through the architectural plans, Kate began to grow alarmed. Soon nothing of Silver City would be left. Nothing. It would all be one big gambling theme park. It sounded as if the DDC even had its goals set on acquiring existing historic properties.

"You can get over any idea that you'll ever buy the Golden Nugget." Alexis Redfield was on her feet. "I own the Nugget, and I have no desire to sell. Not for any amount of money. Not now, not ever."

Cochran, the DDC lawyer, gently put his pointer down and glanced at Roy Adams. The mayor shrugged. Kate felt Jake's hand grow slack against her neck. He was caught up in the tension that suddenly filled the room. She leaned forward to better see Alexis's expression—stubborn and unrelenting. The lawyer's face was a guarded mask. Roy Adams had gone beet red. Kate felt a glimmer of intuition.

"It isn't prudent to discuss the details of a real estate sale before such an...interested audience," the lawyer said to Alexis. All of the other DDC representatives remained completely impassive.

"We aren't discussing details, because there won't be a sale!" The mint green hat that sat atop Alexis's blond chignon bobbed dangerously.

"As I said," the man replied smoothly with a dark glitter in his eyes, "this isn't the place, Ms. Redfield. I'd be delighted to speak with you after the meeting."

Kate was about to stand up when she felt Jake's hand on her shoulder.

"Be still," he whispered.

"He's threatening her," Kate whispered back.

"No, he hasn't uttered a single threat."

"But he is. I see it clearly."

"I do, too," Jake answered, "but he's done nothing overt."

It was the truth, but Kate's every gut instinct screamed at her that the lawyer was a dangerous man, one who would do whatever it took to get his way.

"What are your plans for the Golden Nugget?" Kate asked.

"What business is it of yours?" Alexis responded, rising to her feet again.

Roy Adams intervened. "Kate's family owned the place a long time ago."

The lawyer gave Kate a brilliant smile that never touched his cold eyes. "Our plans aren't definite, Ms...." His eyebrows shot up. "Sheriff."

"I see," she said. "You want to acquire the property,

but you don't have any plans for it?'' She let the question float. ''That doesn't strike me as very sound business.'' She leaned back in her seat, content with the dart she'd hurled.

The other members of the DDC were whispering together. One of them wrote something on a pad.

''I think you're on their blacklist, Kate,'' Jake whispered.

''I hope I'm at the top,'' she answered. There was something about the representatives of the DDC that made her believe they were little more than common crooks. Or uncommon crooks who did their dirty deeds with such sophistication that they were hard to catch. Suddenly the series of fires began to make sense to her. The pattern that had pointed so clearly at Jake could also perfectly fit the future plans of the DDC.

Roy Adams and Betty Cody were both members of the city council. Perhaps the fires had been used to intimidate and influence them to vote to accept the DDC's offer. If the DDC was trying to influence a real estate deal, it might be smart to implicate Jake first, so that his credibility would be shot.

Lester Ray sat on the far side of the room, and ever since the fire in his saloon, he'd been very subdued. He was a blustering man who liked to pick public fights and who had vowed to block any attempts to bring more casinos into Silver City. The big casinos with their free liquor were eating him alive.

And the Reverend Theodore Lyte was the biggest opponent of gambling in Gilpin County.

Kate heard Lyte clear his throat in the back of the room and prepared for a fifteen-minute sermon on the evils of gambling.

"Reverend?" Roy Adams said, acknowledging him. "Make it short. We aren't in church."

"And neither am I," Lyte pointed out. "I can't be there, because it's burned to the ground. Are the DDC investors aware that Gilpin County has an arsonist on the loose?" He smiled. "So, do you really want to invest in a city that seems to be burning to the ground, day by day?" He glared at Jake. "Maybe it's time we heard from the man who claims to be our fire chief."

Jake stood up. "What is it you want to hear, Reverend?"

"Oh, a list of suspects would be nice. You don't have that for us, do you?"

Jake's hands tightened at his sides, and Kate briefly closed her eyes. The worst thing would be for Jake to lose his temper. That would be the very worst.

"I don't have a list of suspects. And there's no common thread to link the crime scenes."

"Except that—" Reverend Lyte shut up when Kate stood up beside Jake. She didn't say a word, but her eyes dared him to accuse Jake in public.

"My investigations show that the arsonist or arsonists are very sophisticated," Jake continued. "The state lab has examined all of my evidence. In the three fires in which a timing device was used, all of the devices were extremely complex and required a great deal of knowledge. Whoever set those fires knew quite a bit about the process. Our biggest hope is to trace the pieces of the timing device to the manufacturer. We're in the process of doing just that."

The entire room had grown completely quiet. Kate watched the faces of those she considered the key players. There was every chance that the arsonist was sitting in the room. It was an opportunity she had to use wisely.

Roy Adams was staring at the top of his desk. Betty Cody was fighting back tears. Across the room, Lester Ray was looking at the ceiling. Only Reverend Lyte was willing to meet her gaze, and she locked with him in a battle of wills.

When no one else spoke, Jake continued. "The gasoline fires would appear to be the work of a different arsonist, but I'm not so certain. I think it's the same person and he or she is merely trying to cover their tracks.

"As for the fire at Evelyn's Boutique, that was started by a different arsonist."

Roy Adams leaned forward. "You're sure of that, Jake?"

"Very sure," Jake answered. He glanced at Evelyn. "Whoever started that fire didn't intend for the building to be destroyed. It was set as a warning."

Evelyn Winn's breath drew in sharply. "What kind of warning?" Tears sprang into her eyes. "Who's warning me? About what? Oh, this is too much. Too much."

Jake shook his head. "I haven't a clue, but I hope to soon."

"What about my church?" Lyte demanded. "Who would burn down a house of the Lord?"

Jake shook his head. "Perhaps the fire was directed at you, Lyte, not the church."

There was a split second of silence.

"But you are making progress?" Roy's tone urged Jake to agree. "We are on the road to solving these crimes?" Roy glanced at the DDC representatives. "Up until this arson spree, Silver City was one of the safest communities in the United States. We have the lowest crime rate in the West. Sheriff McArdle has been able to deal with our criminals in a personal way." He beamed at Kate. "We are a terrific little community."

"Quit fawning on those businessmen, Roy," Reverend Lyte said. He looked them over one by one. "Has it occurred to anyone else that these fires started when the DDC became interested in moving to Silver City?"

Kate almost gasped. Lyte had followed her exact thinking. She looked at him with new respect. He'd not only thought it, he'd said it out loud.

The DDC lawyer pointed at Lyte. "You, sir, had better watch your mouth. That statement borders on slanderous."

"Isn't it true that a string of arsons will depress property values? You can hold that over the heads of every single Gilpin County resident whose property you want to buy." Lyte's tone shifted to something dark. "I can see you saying, 'Oh, yes, your property is worth a million, but since no one wants to live in a place where they could be burned to the ground any night, we'll give you half a million and you should thank us.'"

Roy Adams's gavel nearly split the table as he slammed it again and again. "Enough. That's enough. Theodore, either sit down or Sheriff McArdle will escort you from this building. This is uncalled-for. Sit down!" He banged again.

Silence descended over the room. Kate waited to see what would happen next.

"Gentlemen, I can only apologize," Adams said to the DDC committee. "This is an emotional issue, as you can see. There are those who oppose gambling on religious grounds—"

"Amen!" Lyte shouted from the back of the room.

Roy glared at him. "There are also property owners involved who want to keep Silver City the way it is.

Change is always difficult. Let me hold a town meeting tomorrow night and present the positive sides of what the DDC could do for Silver City. I'm sure many of the citizens have no idea of the amount of money that would be funneled directly into our school system and our parks and library.''

The DDC men rose in a single motion. Their faces were as blank as if they'd just awakened from a long nap.

Adams stood. ''Thank you all for coming. This is something that needs a lot more discussion in the community. Meeting adjourned.''

I am descended of ancient Irish kings, and where am I? Sitting in a jail cell like a lowly criminal.

One of my ancient cousins, Baoh the Wolf, was incarcerated in the far reaches of Dublin Castle, along with his owner, a member of a noble Irish family who was forced to work as a highwayman to feed his starving family.

The trial of Black Jack O'Flaherty and his dog Baoh drew the people from miles around. There was feasting and drinking and many a sad ballad written for Black Jack and his dog. It was not generally the custom to behead a man's dog with him, but it appeared that Baoh the Wolf was a true accomplice, not just a canine sidekick. In fact, there are those in MY family who would say that Baoh was the brains behind the entire scheme. Baoh went to his death with all the dignity of his blood while the crowds sang a dirge praising his finesse at tormenting his English overlords.

'Twas a historic moment. My point is this. Baoh lived a life of risk and adventure, and left many offspring behind in small villages all over Ireland. But in all of his years, he was never detained in a cement cell with a

cold floor and not even a sofa to curl up on. When Jake returns, I shall make him pay, and dearly, for this indignity.

JAKE CHECKED THE CELL, afraid for a moment that somehow Ouzo had pulled a Houdini act and escaped. But the tip of a black tail peeked lifelessly from beneath the bunk.

"Come on out, Ouzo," Jake coaxed.

The dog refused to acknowledge his master's presence.

Kate walked in beside Jake and watched. "Is he okay?"

Jake spied the empty foam container. "What's that? I didn't give him anything except dry dog food."

Kate walked into the cell and picked up the container. It had been licked clean. "This was something I bought for Familiar." She frowned. "It was on my desk. The only way it could have gotten here was if Familiar pushed it."

"A cat? Giving his meal to a dog? I'd have to have it on videotape to believe it."

"There's no other way," Kate answered, "unless someone sneaked in here and poisoned him. Let's get him out from under the bunk."

"Ouzo!" Jake called the dog's name in a commanding voice. "Ouzo!"

The black form beneath the bunk didn't respond at all.

"Jake, pull him out. I'll call Dr. Weathers and tell him we're bringing Ouzo right away." She started toward the telephone when Familiar blocked her path.

"Meow!" he said.

"Not now, Ouzo may be in terrible shape," she said

as she distractedly pushed past the cat and made her way to her desk.

Familiar whipped past her and rushed into the cell. He extended a front paw, claws out and obvious, then swatted Ouzo's black rump as hard as he could.

"Arrr-ar-ar-ar!" Ouzo leapt to his feet, ignoring an astounded Jake completely, as he took off in pursuit of the cat. Familiar, hardly breaking a trot, whirled into Kate's office and jumped on the windowsill, far out of reach of the dog.

Kate stood, telephone in hand, as Jake walked out of the cell and into her office. His eyes met hers. "I told you he was smart."

Kate replaced the receiver. "That dog was punishing you. And me." She pointed at Ouzo. "You, mister, are too smart for your own good."

Chapter Eight

Jake sipped his coffee and stared across the desk at the woman who seemed imprinted in his mind. Kate's green gaze held his, and the tiniest smile touched the corners of her lips. God, but he'd dreamed about that smile. There had been nights when the memory of her lips had been more real than anything around him.

Kate's eyebrows drew together briefly. "I probably shouldn't ask, but my curiosity is killing me. What are you thinking about, Jake? You're staring at me almost as if I were an inanimate object—a painting or something."

Jake didn't answer immediately. "This is one of those conversations that could delve into the past. Are you sure you want to open it?"

Kate shook her head. Her voice was suddenly husky. "The problem with you is that *every* conversation seems to head back to the past. I've put my bad memories behind me, why can't you? If we're going to try some type of relationship again, the best thing for both of us would be to put the past aside. To start fresh."

The fact that she'd even mentioned the possibility of a relationship made Jake's heart rate increase. This time, though, he wasn't going to mess it up. "It won't work," he said softly.

"Why not?"

"Trying to ignore what happened between us isn't possible, Kate. Most men my age are married with children. Most women your age are, too. Something happened in the past that prevented either of us from following the normal course of life." He held up a hand at the angry expression that stormed over her face. "I'm not saying that women who don't marry aren't normal, I'm just saying that the past played a key role in *our* evolution to adulthood."

Kate's lips compressed into a thin line. "Lots of kids have it tougher than either of us dreamed. They get over it and they don't go dragging it around behind them like some badge of honor. The past is over. Kitty is dead. Mother vanished into the night. You and I made our mistakes too, and they're behind us—where I intend to keep them. If you can't move forward without digging up moldering old bones, then I guess we can't move forward together."

Jake waited for her to cool down. "You asked why I was looking at you. Because I see my youth in you. I look at you and I remember the day when you were in the eleventh grade and I was a senior. Remember the big spruce tree out behind the high school?" He waited for the memory to register with her.

When he saw her green eyes soften, he continued. "That was the first day I kissed you, and it was like falling through the looking glass into a magic world. I'd kissed other girls, and I was expecting that same sort of charge that made kissing them a pure torment and an absolute delight. With you, it was so different, Kate. It was as if I'd found a part of me that I never even knew was missing." He reached across the desk and brushed his hand over her cheek. "I know it was like that for you, too."

He saw in her eyes that she remembered.

"If we throw away the past because of our mistakes, we throw all of that away, too. I'm not willing to do that. I remember the clean smell of the spruce needles and the light filtering down on us. It was spring and the sky was so blue. When I touched your face, like this, I'd never felt anything so wonderful in my life."

Jake allowed his fingers to brush along her face, to float through the silky red hair that hung to her shoulders. His impulse was to pull her into his arms and cement the past and present in the most intimate of ways. But he saw the flicker of fear that flared in her green eyes. He lowered his hand. "I know you're afraid, and I won't push you. I may not be as smart as my dog, but I am smart enough to know that what we have, the potential of what we can be together, is worth waiting for—until you want it too."

He lowered his hand and stood up. His body ached for her, for the feel of her against him. It was time to leave.

"I'm going to stake out the hotel where the representatives of Dandy Diamond are staying. I got a bad feeling from those guys."

Kate braced her hands on the desk and stood. "Jake..." She let the sentence fade.

"All I'm asking is that you think about it, Kate. Take it slow and try to get back to the place where we both knew that our futures were destined to be together. Once you remember that, we can work out all the rest."

"You're asking a lot of me," she answered.

"I am. But it was something we once gave each other

without even thinking about it. We have to get back there before we can ever hope to go forward.''

"And what if you're wrong? What if going back to the past makes me bolt and run?''

Jake felt a smile touch the corners of his mouth. "This time I'll go after you. I won't be a fool twice in a row. Whatever the Double J once represented in my mind, it's not nearly as important now as you are.''

He walked to the doorway and turned back to look at her. "I believe we've both learned enough hard lessons to be able to see what a gift we've been given.'' He snapped a leash on Ouzo's collar. "He's a poor substitute for you, but I'll keep him by my side.''

Kate's smile was wry. "You'd better. He can cause you a lot more heartache than I ever could.''

"That's where you're wrong, Sheriff.''

KATE AND FAMILIAR sat in the pickup outside the tidy home of Reverend Lyte. Looking at the well-maintained two-storey home, she realized she knew very little about Lyte. Like Alexis and Evelyn, he was a newcomer in Silver City.

Kate had done a background check on the minister, which had turned up a series of churches where he'd ministered, and finally a request to move to the West. His record of service was without blemish, and he had no family that Kate had been able to determine. In fact, none of the background checks she'd run, on several suspects, had given her any useful information.

With a little more time, Kate could have had more specifics on the minister, but Lyte was probably nothing more than a victim. She'd decided to stake out his house because she feared the members of the DDC might attempt retribution for his vocal stand against them. If the

DDC was behind the arsons, then Lyte was a logical target. If they were the perpetrators—and that was still a big if—they'd already gotten his church and it had failed to quiet his protests. Would they try a home fire?

Jake was trailing the DDC members, but he couldn't follow four men at once if they decided to take separate paths.

"Me-ow." Familiar's cry ended on a low growl.

"What?" Kate picked up the binoculars with special night vision capacity and focused on Lyte's back yard. A dark shadow crouching low to the ground crept through the bushes.

She was too far away and the yard was too filled with shrubs and foliage for her to get a clear look at the person. "Damn," she whispered to the cat. "I can't even tell if it's human." The shadow flitting through the shrubs could easily be an animal. Maybe a deer.

"Meow." Familiar hopped out the open window of the truck before Kate could stop him.

"Familiar," she whispered. "You're going to obedience school with Ouzo if you don't get back here."

Familiar paused to give her a golden gaze, blinked once, then disappeared into the shadows of the lawn.

Kate's hand dropped to the revolver on her belt. She was an expert with weapons and better than fair at martial arts. Coming back to Gilpin County, though, she'd hoped the time would never come when she had to draw her weapon against another person. Throughout her childhood there hadn't been a single incident of violence that she could recall.

"Welcome to the nineties," she said to herself as she crept out of the truck and began to follow the route the cat had taken.

Lyte's yard was bigger than she'd thought. She moved

from shrub to shrub, using the glasses to check the area around her. Familiar and the shadow had completely disappeared. Maybe she'd been a little too hard on Jake about Ouzo's disobedience. It was obvious that when Familiar decided to take off, he was not going to listen to anyone.

Up ahead she caught a flicker of movement and crept toward it. Familiar purred and kept his attention focused on the back door of Lyte's house. The evening was mild and the door was open, golden yellow light spilling out into the yard.

In a moment a dark shadow shifted into the light.

"Damn," Kate whispered as she recognized Ouzo. "Where did that dog come from?" Before she could move, he pawed the screen door open and entered the minister's house.

Kate rocked back on her heels and waited for the night to explode. If Lyte caught the dog, then he would certainly have a right to demand that he be destroyed.

Kate held her breath, counting the seconds. A minute slipped away, then another. Just as she was considering going to the front door and knocking as a diversion, Ouzo slipped through the screen and headed straight for them. He was carrying something in his mouth and his leash was dragging behind him. As soon as he got to her side he dropped the shoe, his tail wagging with pride.

"Let's go," Kate commanded. She picked up the shoe simply because she wanted no evidence that the dog had been in the house. Together the three of them slipped back across the yard. Ouzo jumped into the truck behind Familiar without any urging.

Kate started the vehicle, going a full block before she turned on her lights. When she finally felt safe, she glared at the dog. "What in the world do you think you're doing?"

"Arf!" Ouzo wagged his tail. "Arf! Arf!"

"You're going straight to Jake and he can leave you in the jail cell if that's what it takes to keep you out of trouble. I hope you know Theodore Lyte would have taken great pleasure in holding a public lynching if he'd caught you in his house."

"Arf!" Ouzo said, pushing the black cat aside as he went to the open truck window and stuck his head out, ears flapping in the gentle breeze.

Kate gave the dog an exasperated glare. He was completely without remorse. Scolding him was a waste of breath.

Kate pulled in at the fire station, intending to shut Ouzo up in the apartment until Jake returned. She'd barely had time to shut off her motor when she saw Jake pulling in beside her. At the sight of Ouzo in her truck, he shook his head.

"That rascal took off about an hour ago."

"What about the DDC?" It wasn't like Jake to leave a job half finished.

"They're playing poker at the Golden Nugget. They were deep in a game and I left Led and one of your deputies to watch them."

"At the Nugget?"

"They're in their shirtsleeves. It looks like a long game ahead of them. Of course, if they're behind the fires, they may have hired someone to do their dirty work."

Kate nodded. That was the problem. If the DDC wanted something burned, they'd never get caught red-handed. She held up the shoe. "Your charming canine has been breaking and entering and burglarizing Theodore Lyte's house." Instead of the anger she expected, Jake's face brightened. "What?"

"I could wring his neck, but the dog was working." Jake hurried to the passenger side of the truck and caught Ouzo's head in both of his hands. Looking into the dog's eyes, Jake frowned. "It's good work, Ouzo, but if you had gotten caught…"

"What, exactly, is this about?" Kate demanded. "He could have gotten himself killed. Not to mention the fact that both Familiar and I were in danger."

"It's the shoe," Jake said. "Now I can see if Lyte's matches the print from the church fire. There was no legitimate way I could have gotten Lyte to agree to give me a shoe. Ouzo just skipped a few technicalities and got one for me."

Kate looked from Jake to the dog and back. "He retrieved a shoe because you needed it?" She'd accepted Familiar's brilliance, and she was well aware that Ouzo was a very smart dog, but was he that smart? She was skeptical. Besides, what he'd done, if he was cognizant of what he was doing, was illegal.

"I told you Ouzo helped me with my cases," Jake said, slightly defensive. "He's as much help as that cat."

Familiar drew up one corner of his mouth and hissed at Jake.

"The difference between Familiar and Ouzo is that Familiar is helpful and Ouzo is…a criminal," Kate blurted.

Glancing at her and the cat, Jake burst out laughing. "Perhaps you're right. But sometimes the forces of good need a little assistance from a master criminal." He patted Ouzo's head and opened the truck door so he could get out. "Let's see if this shoe is a match." He reached beside Familiar and picked up the wingtip.

Together they trooped up the stairs to Jake's apartment where he now had crime photos and assorted lab reports on the different arsons. "I've got the print here," Jake said. "And I should be hearing from the lab on the timing devices..." He checked his watch. "Soon."

"The print." Kate eagerly pointed to the carefully packaged mold that had been taken from the wax print. Even before Jake matched them, she knew Lyte's shoe size was smaller. "No match," she said.

Jake compared the two, his head shaking. "Well, it was a long shot. I really didn't think he was crazy enough to burn down his own church just to try and make me look bad."

"No," Kate sighed. "I keep going over the evidence, Jake. The fires are connected, and though they could be connected to you, they also go nicely with the motives of the DDC. But would men with that much money be so unsubtle? If Lyte could put their actions and motives together, so could everyone else in town."

"But what do they care if they are suspected of burning people out as long as no one can pin it on them?"

"You're right. They don't pretend to be nice guys. They're businessmen. The kind who find the most efficient means to achieve their end."

"Exactly why this community doesn't need them."

Kate looked at Jake, her eyebrows raised. "You're opposed to the DDC coming into Gilpin County?" She'd never heard him express an opinion one way or the other.

"Enough is enough, and I think we have enough. How many more tourists do we need? How many more hotels and motels and restaurants? Pretty soon we won't be a community any longer, we'll be a strip mall with transient owners. No one will know anyone else." He shrugged in a gesture meant to downplay his sudden outburst of passion.

"What about Roy Adams?" she said. "He seems awfully eager to have the DDC come in."

"Roy's got the heart of a land developer. He sees more concrete and buildings as better. The natural beauty of the land has never touched him. He doesn't have a problem destroying the environment, but I've never considered him a criminal."

"And does he stand to benefit from the DDC?"

Jake nodded. "He owns about a hundred acres out where they're proposing the theme park. It's range land about like the Double J. Not good enough to really support cattle. It would be a financial coup for him to sell it to the DDC."

"And you?"

"They've approached me, too." Jake grinned. "Hell, I never made a profit off the Double J, so I don't intend to start now. I told them it wasn't for sale."

Kate's eyes sparked. "But what if they decided they wanted it, and the easiest way to get it was to put the blame for these fires squarely on you?"

Jake tensed. "So far I have been the best suspect. At least everyone in town, except you, seems to think so."

"Give me your shoe," Kate said.

"What?"

"Give me your shoe!" She pointed to his foot.

Jake slowly slipped his foot out and handed the shoe to her. She held it to the mold of the print. It was a perfect match.

"Check and see if any of your shoes are missing," she said. "Any left shoes."

Jake went to his bedroom and she could hear him rummaging around. In a moment he returned with a worn black shoe. "The mate is missing." He stared at the print. "Whoever did this intended for you to find the print, not me," he said.

"Exactly. That's why they were so eager to put me on the arsons." While she was duty-bound to view this evidence objectively she simply didn't believe Jake was involved in the crimes.

"Maybe whoever is doing this knew about our past," Jake added.

"He thought I'd be burning to put the blame on you." Kate thought back to the day when she and the cat had gone out to the church. If they'd started at the opposite side of the area, she would have found the print. Once she'd had the print, things could have gone in a very different direction.

"Roy Adams knew our history," Jake said softly.

"So did Betty Cody," Kate added.

"Anyone could have told the DDC."

"Anyone who was working with them."

"Then we're agreed that someone local is involved in this?" Jake said.

Kate nodded. "Someone could have innocently mentioned our past," she pointed out. She bit her bottom lip as she looked at Jake. "I hate to say it, but Roy Adams seems like our best suspect."

"I find this hard to believe of Roy." Jake began to pace the room. "I can't deny that he looks guilty, though."

"Who has access to your apartment?"

"Roy has a key. Since it's attached to the fire house. He's the mayor. But anyone on the city council could get hold of the key."

"Maybe it's time we began checking on Roy and

Betty's alibis, just to play it safe. I've already spoken to the other two suspects about their alibis."

"Other suspects?" Jake gave her a curious look.

"As much as it flattered your ego to think that I questioned Alexis and Evelyn only because I was jealous, I did consider them both suspects. They have alibis for the night of the church fire, though." She lifted her eyebrows. "Which doesn't mean they couldn't have hired someone to do it."

"The damnable thing about this is we still have the same list of suspects we had a week ago, only with more additions," Jake said. "We need some way to narrow the field."

"I'm afraid the only way to do that is to wait for another fire and hope the arsonist makes a mistake," Kate said.

"Don't—"

Before he could finish, the alarm bell began to clang. It startled both of them, but Jake reacted by picking up a leash and throwing it at Kate. "It's a fire. Keep Ouzo out of trouble for me, please." With that he disappeared down the firepole. Kate could hear him throwing his gear onto the truck as the station doors opened and the volunteer firemen began pouring in.

Kate snapped the leash to Ouzo's collar before the dog could think of making an escape. "Come on, Familiar," she called as she raced down the stairs with the dog.

She jumped into her truck and was ready when Jake and the firemen who'd hurriedly assembled took both engines out into the night.

Even as she pulled behind the fire trucks she had a sinking feeling in the pit of her stomach. Ahead of her the orange flames licked the night sky. The fire was downtown, in the heart of the old historic city.

Kate knew that most of the buildings, though updated and refurbished, were made of wood. If the fire got out of hand it could quickly spread.

Heart pumping, she followed the trucks far enough to see that one of her worst nightmares had come true. The Golden Nugget was in flames. The building that held so much of her childhood was in danger of burning to the ground.

JAKE STEERED the first truck through a street crowded with panicked pedestrians. His only thoughts were of fighting the blaze that had turned the main street into an inferno. Had all of the gamblers escaped? Alexis? His mind was racing.

As the second truck pulled in behind him, he saw that the firefighters were functioning as a highly trained unit. The ladders were out and the hoses soaking the wood that was burning as efficiently as kindling.

"I'm going in," he called and saw that two firemen clad in protective gear fell in behind him. He pulled down the visor of his fire mask and walked into the burning building.

The interior of the casino was a smoke-filled inferno, but it appeared everyone had escaped. He and the men made a hurried search of the first floor while the fire hoses sprayed the building.

"Looks clear," one of his men called. "Let's get out of here!"

But an overhead beam snapped. Roofing dropped not three feet from Jake's shoulder. The ensuing rush of heat made him stagger backwards, stumbling against a slot machine.

"Help!"

Jake stumbled to regain his balance as he tried to pin-point the feminine cry for help.

"Help!"

"It's a woman," one of the firefighters said. He pointed through the smoke and flames. "Look! she's there, at the top of the stairs."

Jake saw Alexis standing at the head of the staircase that led to her private apartment.

"Go to the window, Alexis!" he cried. He knew there was no way she could make it across the casino, which was blazing. At any moment, more of the roof could collapse.

"Jake!" There was relief in her voice.

To Jake's horror, she started down the stairs toward him.

"Go back!" He waved at her. "Go back! Go to the window and jump. We'll get you."

"Jake!" she shrieked as part of the staircase fell beneath her weight. She barely managed to catch herself. "Jake, I'm scared," she called, looking around as if she expected help to come.

Jake waded through the flames that licked at his fire-proof clothing. Even though he was protected, he couldn't take the heat. He had an oxygen tank, but the air in the building was quickly being consumed by the fire, and the danger grew with each passing second.

"Jake, I'm afraid," Alexis wailed.

"Don't do it," the fireman warned Jake. "Either she goes out the window or she doesn't. You can't get to her."

Jake looked around. The casino bore a strange resemblance to what he imagined hell would look like. There wasn't a choice. He was the fire chief. It wasn't in his job description or his nature to leave someone to burn.

He ducked beneath a large burning beam then headed for the stairs.

Chapter Nine

Kate watched the smoke billowing out of the Golden Nugget and felt a pain as sharp as if she'd physically been stabbed. No matter that she'd accepted that the building no longer belonged to her, it was always there, always a reminder of the relative she'd loved...

And finally come to view as an embarrassment.

The emotional fire that licked at her heart was more devastating than the sight of the old saloon and stage in flames.

Jake's words came back to haunt her. She couldn't escape the past by trying to forget it. There was no running from what she'd felt and what she'd done.

The truth was, there was no more running at all. She'd come to Silver City to take her stand, and she wasn't going to buckle. She'd lost her family and everything that tied her to it—except the old saloon. And now it was going, too.

Dazed by the enormity of her loss, she got out of the truck and walked closer to the fire. Firemen shouted orders as they fought the fire hoses off the spools and struggled to hold the torrents of water onto the flames.

"I think we can save some of her," one of the firemen shouted at Kate.

She stared at the flames that leapt into the night and felt as if she, herself, were burning.

Suddenly she remembered the portrait of her grandmother that hung over the bar. No one would think to save it. No one cared. It was a piece of decoration to Alexis Redfield, but it was family history to Kate.

History she had turned her back on, Kate reminded herself.

But what if Jake was right? What if stepping into the future required an acknowledged peace with the past? And once the portrait was burned, there would be no recovering it.

If the fire destroyed the casino and the portrait, there would be nothing of Kate's family history left. Kitty's portrait was virtually all that was left.

She made sure no one was paying attention as she slipped down the alley to the back entrance that opened under the staircase.

She felt a tug on the back of her leg and looked down to see Ouzo gripping the hem of her denims. That darn dog was everywhere.

"Grrrrrr!"

"Let go." She shook her leg.

Ouzo refused to yield.

"Let go!" She shook harder.

Ouzo hung on for dear life.

"I'm going for that portrait," she told the dog in no uncertain terms. "I'm going now." She jerked free. Before she could take a single step, Familiar flashed by her and headed in through the back door.

"Familiar!" Kate cried as she ran after him, Ouzo hot on her heels.

Immediately Kate's eyes began to burn and tear. The smoke was so thick she was afraid she wouldn't be able to breathe, but closer to the floor there was a draft of air. Crouching low, she allowed Familiar to lead her forward. The fire was contained mostly in the front of the casino, but Kate had no intention of surveying the damage. She moved forward as Familiar and her memory helped her inch ever closer to the portrait. Ouzo brought up the rear, as if he could protect her from the fire.

Familiar leaped at her. "Meow!" he cried, dodging a piece of the staircase that almost fell on top of him as he pushed her aside.

Kate managed to twist and avoid the burning wood. When she looked up, she saw that a portion of the staircase was gone. Disappearing from the edge of what was left was the unmistakable boot of a fireman. Someone was actually climbing the burning stairs!

Beside her, Ouzo began to whine.

It took Kate an instant to connect the two. "Jake!" She started toward him only to be driven back by a timber that fell from the roof. Shaken, Kate drew the cat and dog to her side and held them. Ouzo was determined to go after his master, but Kate firmly held his collar. There was nothing the dog could do.

The roar of the fire was like a cyclone in her ears, but it seemed as if the flames were diminishing in intensity. She could hear the shouted orders of the firemen, their voices grim with determination.

Jake would be safe. He was doing what he had to do. She ran those words through her mind like a mantra. They would be fine. In another minute she'd have the portrait and be out in the fresh air.

Beneath the sound of the fire and the firemen, Kate heard another noise. The overhead timbers were groaning. For a split second, the significance didn't strike her. When it did, she was terrified—for herself and Jake. He was on the second story. If the flooring gave, he might tumble into the flames.

"Jake!" She darted forward again, the cat and dog with her. As she looked up the staircase she saw Jake disappearing into Alexis's apartment.

So, Jake was risking his life to save Alexis. Kate might have been jealous in the past, but she was proud now. Saving people was Jake's job, and if he had to put his life on the line, he would. Just as she would in performing her duties as sheriff.

"Come on, Ouzo," she said, holding firmly to the dog's collar. "The best thing we can do for Jake is to get out of here safely. Once he has Alexis out, he'll be okay." She tugged the dog after her as she started back the way she'd come. Familiar was more than ready to lead the retreat. The firefighters might be able to put the blaze out before it got to Kitty's portrait and it might escape water damage. She'd have to hope for the best.

Kate looked back once. Kitty McArdle stared at her from above the bar. So far the flames and the water hadn't damaged the original bar or the stage. Kate stared at it, trying to commit every detail to memory.

In a split second she remembered sitting with her grandmother at the piano. Kitty had turned to her, her face wrinkled beneath the mass of her bright red hair.

"I was a beautiful young woman once," she told Kate. "When you want to see me in my prime, go to the opera house. I'm hanging there in all my glory."

The stab of memory galvanized Kate forward. She wanted her grandmother's portrait. She needed it. The past wasn't dead and buried after all.

Kate pushed Ouzo and Familiar out the exit, then slammed the door behind them. She was across the space in a flash, and to her surprise, the portrait came down from the wall easily. It had hung by a wire, as it always had.

"Come on, Kitty," she said, hefting the big canvas and heavy frame.

Above her she heard the loud crack that signaled trouble. She sprinted, half carrying, half dragging the canvas. She was almost safe when the fire-weakened beam came down. The end that struck her head was not on fire, but it knocked her to her knees. For a moment she braced against the picture frame.

Out of the corner of her eye, she saw movement. She knew she was losing consciousness, though she fought hard not to. A figure loomed up out of the smoke and flames, and she instinctively reached a hand out to it. Jake had come back to rescue her. Somehow he'd known she was in trouble.

She saw him, his face covered by the fireman's hat and the mask that he wore. "Jake," she said on a breath so soft that she couldn't be certain if she'd spoken aloud or not.

She saw another piece of lumber coming at her head, but she was too befuddled to duck. The shadowy figure reached out and delivered a blow that struck her temple. Slowly she toppled forward, her hair only inches from the flames that crept slowly along the burning beam.

"OKAY, ALEXIS." Jake scooped the woman into his arms. She clutched an armful of pastel calico cushions, sobbing into them as she let Jake lift her.

"I'm terrified of heights," she said, burrowing deeper into the cushions and his arms.

"Don't look," he said as he approached the window with her.

"Boys! Are you ready?" He called down to the firemen who held the tarp.

"Let her rip," one of the men said.

"Please, Jake, don't do this." Alexis clung to him.

Beneath his feet Jake felt the floor shift. It was impossible to tell how extensively the fire had damaged the support structure of the casino, and he had no intention of waiting around to find out. It was only a one-story drop, and Alexis would be fine. He held her out the window and felt her nails dig into his fire-coat.

"You're fine," he said. And then he let her go.

She hit the tarp with a resounding thud. The men tossed her to her feet on the side and held the tarp for Jake. He didn't waste a second as he went out the window and landed safely.

"Oh, Jake," Alexis said, almost swooning toward him.

Jake sidestepped, easing her into the arms of another, very willing fireman. He walked to the fire truck to talk with the men.

"Good thing you went after her," a sandy-haired fireman said. "The smoke would probably have gotten her if the flames didn't."

"Yeah," Jake answered as he rubbed his eyes, which burned from the smoke. Ouzo and Familiar came tearing around the side of the building. The dog barked and the cat meowed as if they were reporting important news.

Jake bent to scratch Ouzo's ears. "What's going on?"

The cat grasped his hand with a none-too-gentle paw, and Ouzo snagged his coat and began pulling at him.

"I've had about all I can take for one day," Jake cautioned them. He looked around, hunting for the flash of Kate's red hair. In the crowd he saw no one who looked like her at all. Kate was, indeed, uniquely herself. Even as a teenager she'd stood out in a crowd.

Ouzo tugged and growled deep in his throat. The premonition hit Jake hard and with a feeling of near panic. Kate would never have allowed Ouzo to be free on the street...unless something had happened to her.

"Jake, we're about to get the fire under..."

Jake didn't wait to hear the fireman's statement. He took off running, pushing his way through the bystanders with fear in his heart. When he saw that Ouzo and Familiar were headed to the alley entrance, he knew that his worst fears had been confirmed. For whatever reason, Kate had gone inside the casino. She was in there now, more than likely injured.

JAKE KICKED THE DOOR IN with one hard blow of his boot. He still wore his protective coat, pants and boots, but he'd removed his helmet and mask after he'd rescued Alexis.

Before he dove into the blaze, he waved three firemen over. "Did you see Sheriff McArdle go in here?"

"No, sir," they answered in unison. One frowned. "We wouldn't have allowed anyone to enter a burning building, even if she is the sheriff. We've got more training than that."

Jake reached down and snatched Ouzo's collar. He motioned the young fireman over. "Don't let go of this dog no matter what he does, okay?"

"Yes, sir," he answered, his fingers twisting around the collar.

Jake didn't waste any more time. He rushed through the door and into the hottest fire he could remember. The blaze at the front of the building was almost under control, but the residue of heat and smoke was like a furnace. As soon as he adjusted to the smoke, he began a frantic search. Almost instantly he noticed that Kitty McArdle's portrait was off the wall.

He strode over burning embers and smoldering braces, dodging flaming pieces of the ceiling as they fell to the floor.

"Kate!" It was useless. If Kate were in a position to answer, she'd be outside with the portrait. Something had happened to her.

He made his way to the bar. Had she gone back to the alley entrance? He couldn't count on that. And he didn't have time to make a mistake. A layer of thick smoke hung in the air. Had Kate found a niche to hide in where she was protected and able to breathe? Kate was a smart woman. Very smart. He couldn't allow his panic to make him underestimate her ability to cope.

"Kate!"

Only the determined roar of the fire answered him. He ran forward into smoke so thick that he couldn't see anything. He felt his way along, establishing a grid pattern in his head. He'd have to do the search systematically, like a blind man.

He was near the stairs when something brushed his leg. It was Familiar. The cat seemed unsteady on his feet, but he struggled as Jake attempted to capture him.

"Familiar!" The feline eluded him.

"Meow!" Familiar headed away from the stairs.

"Dammit, Familiar, I don't have time for this." Or was Familiar attempting to lead him to Kate?

"Meow!" Familiar called from another two steps away.

Jake followed the cat. After only three yards, his boot nudged something on the floor. Kneeling, he felt the obstacle. He knew instinctively that it was human and more than likely Kate. His hand moved over the soft flesh and he felt a hip and then the curve of feminine buttocks. She was on her stomach. For one heart-stopping moment, Jake thought she might be dead. In the dense smoke, he couldn't see her. But he could feel her, and there was a slight rise and fall as her lungs worked.

"Kate," he whispered. "Kate."

He felt her stir beneath him. Turning her gently, he lifted her into his arms, away from the trail of fire eating slowly along the beam on which she'd fallen. Another moment or two and it would have reached her thick, glossy hair.

"Easy, Kate," he whispered. "Easy." The weight of her in his arms was unbearably sweet.

"Arf! Arf!" Ouzo's excited bark came from the doorway.

Kate's face was smudged with soot but undamaged. A trickle of blood oozed from her right temple. She was breathing lightly, but a quick examination showed no other obvious injuries.

"Let's get out of here," Jake said. Familiar darted toward the door, and Jake cradled Kate in his arms, protecting her with his chest as they rushed out of the building.

As he came out the alley door, Jake was blinded by the explosion of television lights and photographers. The news media were hot on the story now. Though he attempted to negotiate the pack without revealing Kate's identity, her brown sheriff's uniform gave her away.

"Is Sheriff McArdle injured?" the reporters called.

Jake ignored them as he carried Kate to a waiting ambulance. Just as he was about to place her inside, she started coughing. Her eyes opened and she looked around as if she had no idea where she was or what she'd been doing. Looking up at him, her eyes narrowed.

"What happened?" she asked.

Jake sat her on the back of the ambulance. "Catch your breath and get your groundings," he said. "You almost got yourself killed. What on earth were you doing in that building?"

Kate's last image was of the fireman—the man she'd assumed had come to rescue her, but had instead attempted to leave her unconscious in a burning building. In her heart she could not believe it was Jake—yet that was who she called out to, that was who she'd thought it was.

For the first time in her career, Kate couldn't trust her own vision, or her judgement.

"Kate, can you understand me?" Jake's voice was panicked.

Was it sincere or a ploy? The memory of her actions came back to her and beneath the soot and dirt she knew her face was flushing. What she'd done was incredibly stupid. She'd gone into a burning building not to save a life but to retrieve a picture. Jake had talked to her about the past, about how she had to confront it, and it had almost cost her her life.

"Get a doctor over here, fast!" Jake called out.

"I'm okay," she finally answered. She didn't look at him. "Really, Jake." She put a hand to her temple, feeling the knot. It had happened. Someone had tried to kill her. "I'm okay," she said.

"Sheriff McArdle, what happened?" A newscaster thrust a microphone at her.

"I was making a last check of the building to be certain everyone was out. A beam fell and struck my head."

Kate's hand went involuntarily to her temple where a major headache had set up housekeeping.

"Was Sheriff McArdle assisting the fire department?" the reporter asked Jake.

Kate knew the reporter had gone to the heart of the matter. As sheriff, she had no authority to clear the building. It was a job for the fire department. If Jake actually knew what she'd been doing, he'd have good cause to publicly humiliate her.

"We're cooperating on the arsons," Jake said, his curious gaze never leaving Kate's.

"Wouldn't that chore have been better left to a trained firefighter?" the reporter pressed. A small crowd of additional reporters had gathered behind him. They were eagerly listening.

"We had our hands full," Jake said carefully. "The Sheriff was a big help. Now the building is clear and the fire is under control. I think you've got enough of a story."

Kate waited until the reporters were gone. Jake's face showed his relief at seeing her safe, and his words confirmed it. "You scared me half to death." His hand cupped her face. "When I couldn't find you, I had a terrible vision of you in trouble." A scowl crossed his face as he looked more closely at her temple. "I wasn't far from the truth. What happened?"

Kate brought the image of the masked fireman into her mind. He'd worn a yellow coat, a mask. He could have been any fireman at the scene. She thought back to the dark figure escaping Evelyn's Boutique after the fire was set, the footprint that had been so conveniently left at Lookout Church. She'd believed Jake in the past. Before she thought of what she was doing, she placed her hand over his. "Someone attacked me, Jake. He struck me. I think he was trying to pin it on you."

Her words startled him to silence. When he finally spoke, it was to insist that she allow the paramedics, at least, to check her. He waved one over and as Jake watched, the medical expert examined Kate's injuries.

"One very lucky lady," the paramedic proclaimed. "Minor smoke inhalation and a nasty knock on the head. Other than that, she's going to be okay."

Jake thanked the man and when he was gone, Jake turned to Kate. His anger, which had been carefully concealed, shone clear in his eyes. "When I find whoever did this, Kate, he'll be sorry of the day he was born."

"If I had died in the fire, it would have put you in a position where you would appear incompetent." Even as she spoke she realized how her actions had jeopardized Jake's career. "If I didn't die, then the attacker assumed that I might blame you. He was about your size. He wore a mask that completely covered his face. As best I can remember, his hair was dark, like yours."

"This has gone beyond arson to attempted murder. My question is why?"

"A good question," Kate agreed. With each passing moment, she felt better, though her head throbbed painfully.

Jake slowly shook his head. "The first thing we need to check is the fire equipment. We keep an inventory."

Kate thought of something. "How did you know I was in the building?"

"I wouldn't have known to go after you if it wasn't for that cat and Ouzo."

"Familiar?" Kate had a moment's anxiety until she spotted the black feline who sat by the ambulance cleaning his fur.

"He's fine and so is Ouzo. They alerted me to where you were." Jake caught sight of several reporters still lurking on the scene. Stepping so that he blocked Kate from their view, he frowned down at her. "Let's get out of here."

"How bad is the damage?" Kate looked behind him at the old building. It was still standing. She thought of the portrait and then forced it out of her mind. Listening to Jake and all of his drivel about the past had almost gotten her killed. That was exactly what the past was—a death trap. For those who weren't smart enough to avoid it. And she was smart. Whatever the future held, she would never let Jake lure her back to the past.

"It could have been a lot worse. The guys did a terrific job." Some of the anger was gone from Jake's voice, and he looked around to see that his men were still busy putting out the last smoldering remains.

"And Alexis?" Kate kept her voice neutral.

"She's fine." Jake shook his head. "The woman would have burned to death rather than jump out a window. With these old buildings so tight and close together, we couldn't get a ladder truck in there. It was jump or burn."

"And you?" Kate looked up at him. "Are you okay?"

Jake's smile reflected the worry he heard in her question. "Fine. You're the one we had to pull out of the building."

Kate sat up straighter. A bit of color had returned to her face and she brushed her tangled hair out of her eyes. "I think I owe Familiar something special." She eased out of the ambulance and stood, shaky for a moment but quickly regaining her balance. "And I think I want to go back to the office, shower and change. I feel like an

Oscar Meyer, the kind that's cooked and ready for a bun.''

Jake took her arm to steady her as they began to walk away. "Do you want my preliminary observations?"

"Can't wait," she answered.

"The fire started in the front, and there doesn't appear to have been a chemical accelerant, which makes sense. With people gambling, it would have been hard to drag something like gasoline in."

Kate frowned. "The front is a strange place for a fire to start. I mean there's nothing in there except tables and chairs. There's not any electrical equipment or..." She shook her head. "I was hoping maybe this one would be an accident. I can't believe someone would deliberately try to burn down a building so much a part of this town. Of the West."

"Believe it," Jake said. He turned to the firemen gathered around the truck. "Make sure the fire is dead and then file an initial report with me. I want you all back at the fire station as soon as possible." As Jake faced the men one by one, his tone softened. "You did a great job, guys."

"Yes—" Kate's voice caught with emotion. "I want to thank you all."

From twenty yards away, a female voice called out. "Jake, darling, there you are. How can I ever thank you." Alexis came toward them, a mint green cigarette in a holder.

"Alexis," Jake said carefully. "I see you've recovered from your fright."

"Jake, you absolutely saved my life." She completely ignored Kate. "Those flames were practically licking at my heels. And there you were. My knight in shining armor." Her eyelashes fluttered. Suddenly she stumbled slightly. "Oh, my," she said. "I thought I was over the shock, but I feel a little...dizzy." She put the back of her hand to her forehead. "Do you think you could take me some place where I could get some tea and compose myself?" She smiled shakily at Jake.

Out of the corner of his eye, Jake could see Kate. Hell, he didn't have to see her, he could almost feel the laughter she held inside. Her lip was curled in a perfect Elvis sneer.

"Alexis, it's late and I have a fire to investigate. I'm sure you'd rather I spent my time trying to discover who set fire to your casino—"

Alexis waved a hand. "Don't be foolish, Jake. Let one of your peons do the grunt work. I need someone to help me recover." She sighed. "I was nearly frightened to death."

Jake gave Kate a sudden, inspired glance. "Alexis, Kate has some questions for you."

Without fumbling, Kate pulled a slightly damaged notebook from her pocket and a pen. "Ms. Redfield, do you have any idea why someone might want to burn down your establishment?" she asked.

Alexis gave her a withering look. "Why are you always nipping at my heels like a little dog? I don't have any enemies. Everyone likes me."

"What about Evelyn Winn?"

Alexis fixed a glare on Kate, then caught herself and dismissed the idea with a wave of her hand. "Oh, Evelyn wouldn't hurt a fly."

"But you said—"

"Fiddle on what I said before. I was angry at Evelyn. But after someone set fire to her boutique, we made up." Her eyes narrowed. "Evelyn said you'd been by to talk with her. She said you harassed her."

Jake took Alexis's arm. "I think Fireman Wells will take you over to the Brass Kettle for a cup of tea. Unless you'd prefer something stronger. I have some business with the sheriff."

Her bottom lip trembled. "I was hoping you'd have time to take me. I might be able to think of something that would help solve the arson. You know the representatives of the Dandy Diamond Casino were gambling in my casino last night. I was down there with them for a while, until the game got tedious beyond belief. You'd think casino corporate heads would know a little bit about gambling, wouldn't you?"

"Are you suggesting they started the fire? Do you have evidence?" Kate asked.

"Don't be a fool," Alexis snapped. "They were sitting right at my best poker table. If I'd seen them start a fire I would have made them put it out." She turned to Jake, pouting. "I could think better if I had some tea, and I need you to escort me."

Kate's expression was carefully blank as she looked at Jake. "Maybe you should ply the lady with tea and learn her secrets," she suggested.

Jake didn't need an interpreter to hear the sarcasm in Kate's comment. "Are you sure you're okay?" he asked.

"Positive," Kate replied. "Go on."

"I'll check back with you as soon as I'm done here." He searched her face for understanding. For a split second he thought he saw a glint of humor in Kate's eyes, but then it was gone. "Will you keep an eye on Ouzo?"

"My pleasure, and good luck," Kate said.

Pistol-Packin' Mama needs a lesson in handling a man. You never let the competition walk off the playing field with the prize. Especially not if she's "just going to borrow him for a few minutes." Right. Alexis may say she wants a cup of tea but that woman wants to blend ole Jake into the fabric of her life.

This calls for a drastic step. One that may even require a partnership with that canine furball. He was somewhat helpful during the fire. And he did take care of quenching the Reverend Lyte's anger. The problem with Ouzo is that he's over there scratching out an epic poem about his role.

Why is it that dogs seem to think that every thought they have, every deed they do, should be immortalized in a song or poem? I swear, if he starts blathering poetry, that's the end.

Kate called Ouzo over, relieved to see he actually obeyed. But as soon as he saw Familiar, he began to bark. The cat, unperturbed, gave some low growls and hisses.

So, 'tis that black devil cat's plan to enlist me. I'll have him kissing the Blarney stone and reciting limericks. But even a blind man can see that Jake is being led to the slaughter by the woman in the bad plaid. That shade of green would be a killing crime in the old country. And Jake appears to be as goofy as a newborn lamb, bleating along in her wake. Why is it that the man can't find a sensible woman to keep the hearth warm, dinner on the stove and a pint in the house? Aye, that Alexis Redfield is not the type to let a man keep his dog close at hand by the fire. No, she's the kind who'd put one of those igloo doghouses in the back yard with a plaid pillow and a bowl of gruel. My future is at stake, so therefore I must act.

Kate was just about to snap Ouzo's leash to his collar when the dog bolted. She darted right, instinctively assuming that Ouzo was headed for Susan Tanner's and the joy of chasing cats. Instead, Ouzo lurched around Kate and headed straight for Jake. Just when it seemed the dog would bowl into Jake and Alexis, Ouzo cut a sharp right and snaked toward the smoldering building.

"Jake!" Kate cried, getting his attention and pointing to the fleeing Ouzo.

"Dang that dog," Jake said. He started after Ouzo.

"Jake, it's only that old black stray. He'll be fine," Alexis said with some impatience. "I'm the one who's been traumatized and frightened. I'm the one whose livelihood has just been burned beyond repair. I'm the one..." She faded to a stop as she realized Jake wasn't staying around to listen.

"Kate, please escort Ms. Redfield to have a cup of tea," Jake called over his shoulder, his grin almost unbearably smug as he ran into the Golden Nugget after Ouzo.

Chapter Ten

The Brass Kettle contained more checks than chintz, and Kate figured that Alexis would feel perfectly at home among the matching tablecloths, napkins, curtains, rugs, aprons and placemats. Homes and restaurants where everything under the sun either matched or complemented each other had somehow become a craze. It was a little scary, Kate thought.

The owner had been about to close—the late-night crowd not thick in an establishment that catered to young mothers and the older population. Kate prevailed on the young woman behind the counter to give her a few moments with Alexis. It was more the soot and dirt on Kate that won the day than her powers of persuasion.

Kate sat with her back to the wall and watched as Alexis riffled through the different types of sweeteners, finally settling on lemon only. Alexis was obviously not happy that Jake had failed to accompany her. She had no use for Kate and didn't bother to try and hide her sentiments. Kate was mildly amused. She sipped her tea and waited while Alexis entertained herself preparing hers.

Although the fire had been horrific, Alexis seemed curiously undisturbed. The woman's business was a total loss. Even if the shell of the old opera house could be saved, it would be months before the place could be renovated and new slot machines installed. Not to mention lighting, sound equipment—the expense was overwhelming, even to Kate.

A dull pain throbbed in the region of Kate's chest, and she realized that she didn't want to think about the fire. What she'd tried to do by leaving Silver City fifteen years before, the fire had accomplished in a few hot hours. Her family's past was totally erased. And though she recognized and accepted the real danger of sentiment, she still couldn't help the sense of loss.

Watching Alexis stir and sip her tea, Kate decided then and there never to mention the portrait or why she went back into the burning building. Never. Jake was wrong. One thing she had learned about mistakes—it was better to let foolish behavior fade. And her rescue attempt of the portrait was more than foolish. It could be considered irrational.

It had put her in a position where someone had almost killed her.

"Are you going to stare a hole in me or are you going to interrogate me?" Alexis asked, scowling.

Kate composed her thoughts and asked her first question softly. "You mentioned that the DDC representatives were in the casino during the evening," she said. Alexis focused on her tea cup. "Do you honestly think they might be responsible for the fire?"

Alexis finally looked at her. "I don't think anything. They were there. There were five of them. Five cheap men who wouldn't go over a twenty-five-dollar bet." She shrugged. "I have no idea what they might have done."

"Alexis, they all but threatened you in the meeting. Is that so easy to dismiss?"

"I'm not hurt, am I?" Alexis stared pointedly at Kate's temple.

Alexis's cool demeanor baffled Kate. The casino owner had suffered a partial loss on a multimillion-dollar business—and nearly her own life. After all, she'd been trapped in her apartment when the fire started. Which made Kate wonder why none of the staff had made any attempt to warn or save the woman.

"I have to say I find your lack of concern for the casino fire to be more than a little suspicious." Kate put it on the line. "That was your place of business and your home. I find your attitude strange."

Alexis gave her a look. "*You* would find that strange. You find everything strange, don't you?"

Kate decided to let the barb pass. "The fire at the Golden Nugget is the sixth in Gilpin County. It's *strange* that both you and Evelyn Winn should suffer an arson attack." She saw the first glint of apprehension in Alexis's eyes, but it was quickly covered. "Don't you find it *strange?*"

"No," Alexis snapped. "Not in the least. We're local businesspeople and the fires are directed at local businesses. I'm one in a *long* list of unfortunate victims. As far as I'm concerned, that's the end of that."

"Betty Cody's house wasn't a local business. Jake's ranch wasn't a local business. Lookout Church isn't exactly a business." Kate waited.

"In a way, they all do have connections to Silver City businesses." Alexis wasn't about to back off her point. "Even the church. If Silver City doesn't grow and thrive, the church won't grow. It's simple economics. And before you go off on Evelyn again, we've patched everything up. In fact, she was thinking of helping me do some minor redecoration in the casino. We had a lovely visit yesterday. And Evelyn doesn't gamble, she's a businesswoman.''

Kate followed her gut instinct and kept playing the line. ''A case for business-relatedness could be made for each fire, but in some way all of the fires also have connections to gambling.'' She leaned forward. ''Especially the Golden Nugget.''

Instead of the denial she expected, Alexis nodded in agreement.

For the first time Kate saw how tired Alexis was. Her skin, normally a healthy golden color, was pale and sallow. The mint green suit, which had once been lovely, was now wrinkled and dirty.

''Who's setting the fires?'' Kate asked.

Alexis sipped her tea before she answered. When she did look at Kate, her gaze was direct. ''I honestly thought it was Jake. I really did. Until this one. But he'd never burn the Golden Nugget. He's too much of a history buff to even consider it. He loves all of the old buildings in town and that one in particular.'' Her gaze sharpened momentarily. ''I've often wondered why, but then...'' She shrugged in her nonchalant way. ''There's no accounting for taste, is there?''

Kate sipped her own cup of tea. ''Why do you think Jake would burn anything?''

''He's opposed to more gambling coming into town. I thought maybe he was trying to frighten the DDC out of Silver City.'' She lifted one eyebrow. ''Or perhaps that he'd taken a payoff from another gambling interest. Someone who wanted to make the DDC think that Gilpin County wasn't a good place to locate.'' Alexis's gaze didn't waver. ''Some of the casinos that are here already don't want to see more competition. Jake's got a lot of friends in town. He's not a stranger. Good old hard cash can be a tremendous motivator.''

Kate nodded. Alexis Redfield was no dummy. "Jake and I have thought of those angles." She made it clear Jake wasn't a suspect in her mind. "But why aren't you more upset by the fire?"

"Oh, it's down to the tedious truth." Alexis made a face. "I wanted out of that business. It's a dreadful bore, and the casino wasn't making the kind of money I wanted. It was very lucrative, don't get me wrong, but it was...boring. The fire was actually a blessing, and I know you'll hear this from Roy if I don't tell you myself. Because of all these fires, I went in last week and had the insurance increased. The amount I'll collect will pay my debts and give me a nice little nest egg to pursue a new line of work.''

Kate was amazed at the total innocence with which Alexis made her confession. "Don't you realize this will make you the prime suspect in the fire?"

"I'm sure it will," Alexis said reasonably, "but I didn't do it. I loved my apartment. It was the most perfect place I've ever lived in. I would never have burned it. Never." She shrugged again. "It just so happens that whoever decided to burn me out did me a big favor. But then that's your problem, not mine." She stood up. "I'd better go by and see Roy. I'm sure he's up, wringing his hands and wailing. I want to get my claim going as fast as possible.''

She walked away leaving Kate at the tiny table staring after her.

Kate paid the tab and left the tearoom, wondering if she could find Jake at the fire. He was going to be truly amazed by Alexis's latest revelation.

She hurried along the street. For a time, the fire at the Golden Nugget had slowed the gambling in the other establishments, but now everything was back in full swing. Music, the clanging of the machines, the cries of winners and the moans of losers came out from the open doors as she walked past the Ruby Slipper and Red's Roulette Wheel.

Folks young and old poured in and out of the casinos, never looking around, never once seeing the backdrop of the beautiful old western town that was more than a page out of history. The gamblers were eager only to get back to a machine where they could play the slugs they carried.

The fire was out, the danger was past, and the tourists and gamblers were back in their own worlds.

The loss of an old building didn't touch them. They were mostly people from out of town. They came to Silver City not for the rich history of the past but to gamble.

She walked along, wondering for the first time in a long while what life must have been like back in the early days, when Kitty McArdle ran a saloon and theater and house.

As she drew near the Golden Nugget, the smell of the fire was all around her. Though the building still stood, it was blackened and burned. It would take a while before the true damage could be estimated. There was a good chance it would have to be torn down completely if it was a hazard. Only Jake would be able to determine that.

The temptation to dash in and see if, by some miracle, the picture of Kitty had been saved grabbed hold of Kate. She resisted the urge and walked faster, easing through the gawkers who remained on the sidewalk.

"Kate!" She heard Roy Adams's voice and braced herself for a confrontation.

She turned to face him. "Roy," she said.

He shook his head. "Terribly sorry, Kate. I know this is a tragedy for you."

She turned back to view the old building. "It is. I guess I'd fooled myself into believing that the old opera house was out of my family and therefore out of my heart." She was startled by her own words. Something had snapped inside her, some constraint that had always made her deny that she even cared.

"It isn't that easy, is it?" he asked.

Kate was baffled by the sentiment in Roy's voice. "No." Before she'd even thought it through, the words came to her lips. "Alexis wants to get out from under the building. Once the damage is assessed, I'm thinking maybe I'll buy the place."

Roy's mouth opened. "You? Get into the casino business?"

Kate shook her head. "No, but maybe a community theater. Something along those lines."

Roy's brows drew together. "Now that's not a bad idea. If there's anything left of the building. I saw Jake and he said he'd have to do a detailed examination. In fact, he's in there right now." Roy drew closer. "I heard the DDC men were in there gambling this evening. Do you think they were somehow involved in the fire?"

Kate smiled. "What I think and what I know are two different things. I'll check with Jake. As soon as there's something concrete, you'll be the first to know." Kate hadn't forgotten that Roy was on the list of suspects. Sometimes the smartest thing to do was play along.

"I suppose you know that Alexis just upped her insurance.'' He glanced beyond Kate as he said it, his gaze roving over the building.

"She told me."

"As my mama said, 'I don't believe in coincidences.' I want some evidence in this fire, Kate. Something concrete. Alexis had this place insured to the max. Either she's responsible for this, or—"

"I'll keep that in mind, Roy," Kate said as she stepped around him and entered the casino.

The place was a shambles. Water covered the floor, sogging the carpet that had once been so bright and colorful. The old stage remained, but the expensive curtains and the sound and lighting systems were a twisted wreck. Even the old piano, which Kitty McArdle had played, was burned into a knotted mass. Kate saw that the bar had not been severely damaged, but the portrait of her grandmother was gone. She remembered taking it from the wall and getting halfway across the room. Perhaps if she'd left it hanging...

"Kate!"

It didn't take her long to locate Jake. He waved to her from a ladder halfway up the back wall where he was examining the wiring. From a safe distance she watched as he traced the wires, following them over beams. "The fire didn't start in the wiring," he called out to a fireman who was making notes in a pad.

"Then how?" the fireman questioned. "There wasn't anything else in the game room to start it, and we know that's where it originated."

"I wish I knew," Jake said. He caught Kate's attention and waved her to his side as he climbed down the ladder. She looked pale, exhausted. He had to get her out of the burned building, because no matter how much Kate denied it, she cared. A woman didn't run when she didn't care. Jake's hand on her arm was light. "Let's get out of here."

She felt the aggravating pressure of tears that she blinked away. That Jake understood only made it worse. She met his concerned gaze. "I'm okay. I think I'll go take a shower." The night had lasted an eternity, and she was bone-tired. "Alexis had some interesting revelations. Maybe we can talk in the morning." She knew she had to get out of the building. Fires were always tragic. Even when it was a place that held no memories, no past.

"Kate?"

She knew she hadn't fooled him. "I'm tired," she said, turning away. "I need a shower."

Jake's hand brushed her back, a gesture of comfort and support.

"Chief, we've got something over here." The fireman spoke cautiously.

"I'll be there in a moment," Jake answered before he turned to Kate. His voice was quiet, caring. "I haven't had a chance to check the fire equipment. There were eight men here, counting me, Kate. I have enough equipment to fully suit eleven men. Could you stop by my apartment and count the equipment that's left? Probably the sooner that's done, the better. If someone took something, they might try to put it back. Besides, I had one of the men take Familiar there. You can feel free to take a shower at my place, too, if you want."

Kate was more than grateful that Jake had given her an out that also bolstered her dignity. The moment of teariness passed. There were a million things to do, and her job was to get busy. "I'll take care of it," she said, stepping out of the ruins and onto the street.

"Chief Johnson!" The fireman called. "You've got to see this."

"I'm coming." Jake walked to the far end of the building where one of his firemen stood, a shovel in his hand and an unreadable expression on his face.

"What have you found, Grayson?" Jake asked. He walked to the edge of a shallow depression the fireman had obviously been digging. Ouzo sat only a few feet away, quiet and obedient for once.

"I was trying to move that timber," he pointed to a huge beam that still smoked, "when your dog started barking. I looked closer and found that." With the tip of his shovel he eased more of the burned flooring back.

Jake knelt, uncertain what he was looking at but with a strange feeling that it wasn't wood. He used his fingers to brush away the timber and dirt.

"Looks like a femur," he said after a moment's examination.

"It looks human," the fireman said. "I didn't want to touch it until someone else told me what to do."

"You did exactly the right thing," Jake said. He more closely examined the bone, brushing carefully at the dirt to reveal more of the skeleton.

Ouzo moved up beside Jake and began to whine deep in his throat. With one paw, he gently pushed at the ground. "Easy, there," Jake said. The body had been buried in a shallow trench, and Jake worked with quick efficiency to reveal the entire skeleton, except the head.

"Wonder who it could be," the fireman said.

Jake had a real bad feeling, but he only shook his head. This time he would assume nothing. This time he would have the facts before he spoke. For everyone's sake, but most particularly for Kate.

"Rope off this area. I don't want anyone near here," he said. "And keep this quiet."

He stood up. Whatever tragedy had resulted in a body buried beneath the new curio shop of the casino, Jake intended to have an answer. He was no expert on bones. He knew the body Ouzo had found had not been embalmed. The body could belong to a time long ago—possibly even back in the days when Kitty McArdle ran the house. It might be some gambler who'd pulled a fast one and met his fate. Alexis had built the curio shop some eight months before. It was possible that she'd done that to cover up the body. It was also possible that she didn't have a clue the bones were there. There was another possibility, and one that only forensic testing could answer. Jake was a fireman, not a detective, and he couldn't begin to estimate the age of the bones. But one possibility he couldn't get away from was that the skeleton Ouzo had discovered might be Kate's mother, Anne McArdle.

"I'll call the coroner," he said.

He went to the fire truck to radio the coroner, glad that Kate had left. The one thing she didn't need on top of everything else was a body. Especially this body. It was almost unbelievable, Jake thought as he made his request and made arrangements for the coroner to make an examination.

As he replaced the radio, he had a sudden image of Kate alone. It was startling in its intensity—the clear picture of her in the shower—and for the cold that swept over him at the thought.

Someone had tried to kill her. If she was in the shower, would she be able to hear an attacker? His apartment had stout locks, but it wasn't safe. Someone had already gotten into it once, and without even breaking a lock. That someone had knocked him in the head and had left no trace of his identity.

Sending Kate there hadn't been his most brilliant maneuver.

He looked around. It was still several hours until dawn. Silver City was up and running. It seemed that gamblers never tired of the game. They were out on the streets, moving from casino to casino. For some reason the activity gave him no sense of security.

He hurried back into the old opera house and left instructions with the firemen. They were highly trained, and for a few seconds he watched them work before he walked out and headed for the station house. He couldn't get Kate out of his mind, nor could he leave behind the seed of worry that had begun to nibble at him.

KATE WENT THROUGH the lockers in the fire station. She found three pairs of fire boots, two coats, two hats and two masks. The conclusion she drew was that someone had stolen a coat, hat and visor.

She climbed the steps, hearing Familiar's welcome. As she opened the wrought iron gate with the key Jake had given her, she stooped to sweep the cat into her arms. Sitting on the landing, she cradled the cat. "I hear you saved my life," she said.

Familiar rubbed against her, purring. She went to the refrigerator and pulled out milk and cheese, cutting off hunks to feed him as she prepared a bowl of milk.

"This is a poor reward, but there's nothing else in here. I promise, as soon as I have a few hours' sleep, I'll order something from the finest restaurant in town. For Ouzo, too, when he gets here."

She stroked the cat and stood, stretching. "I've got to have a shower. Stand guard, Familiar," Kate instructed,

unbuttoning her smoky uniform as she walked to the
shower. On the way she stopped by the door to Jake's
room. His clean laundry was folded on top of his dresser.
He wouldn't mind if she borrowed a T-shirt. She picked
one up and went on to the bathroom. In a moment she
had the hot spray jetting on her face, completely oblivious to the sound of the downstairs door opening, followed by the iron gate swinging wide.

"Oh, what a handsome kitty," Alexis said, bending
to pet Familiar. "And Daddy's in the shower, isn't he?
How perfect. Perhaps I'll just knock on the door. Oh, no
answer. Too bad! I'll have to go into the bathroom and
get Jake out of the shower myself."

Alexis opened the door. The bathroom was clouded
in a layer of hot fog, but she walked to where the outline
of a body could easily be seen against the pale blue
shower curtain. "Hello, darling," she said, pulling the
curtain back.

For a moment, Kate stared at Alexis in disbelief. She
saw her own amazement reflected in Alexis's face. For
a split second, neither of them could say a word.

Kate snatched the shower curtain which had dripped
all over Alexis's expensive pistachio flats. "Get out of
here," she said.

"Gladly," Alexis answered, backing away. Shock
still registered on her face. "How dreadful. I think I've
been scarred for life!"

Kate pulled the curtain back. "On second thought,
you're under arrest." A hive of bees couldn't have stung
Kate more. She was boiling angry, and water dripping
from her hair down her face only made it worse. "Have
a seat at the table in the kitchen, Alexis, I'm not done
with you." Kate grabbed a robe and herded Alexis into
the kitchen.

"You can't make me stay here." Alexis started to turn away.

"Oh, can't I? For starters, you're going to tell me where you got the key to Jake's apartment."

Alexis dropped the key to the floor. "There. You can have it."

"Where did you get it, Alexis?"

"I borrowed it from Roy."

"Borrowed it?" Kate wasn't about to let her off the hook. "When?"

"It was on his desk. I met him in his office just before I came here. I told you I was eager to get the insurance claim started, and Roy," she shrugged, "was agreeable. When he went to get a file, I sort of...borrowed the key."

Chapter Eleven

The first thing Jake noticed when he unlocked the gate to his apartment was the wet footsteps that came out of the bathroom, went to the kitchen and then returned down the hallway to the bathroom. There was the sound of his shower going. He checked his watch. Surely Kate hadn't been in the shower the whole time. Obviously not, he thought, remembering the footprints. She'd gotten out to get something to eat? In the middle of a shower? Well, if she was hungry she was feeling better, and food of any description was an excellent idea. Maybe it would keep his mind off Kate in the shower. He was all too susceptible to imagining how she would look, sleek and wet.

He bent to pet Familiar and moved on to rummage in the refrigerator, selecting cheese and some crackers. He was ravenous, but he took time to cut slivers of cheese for the cat. Ouzo had taken off from the fire scene, and though Jake had combed the town, the dog had disappeared. "I'm too tired to chase him. If he gets caught doing something illegal, he'll have to pay the consequences. I've decided to initiate a program of tough love where that dog is concerned."

"Meow," Familiar replied, in perfect agreement, Jake thought.

Putting the plate in the sink, he felt it slip from his fingers and clatter. "Clumsy me," he said to the cat. He was so tired he felt punch-drunk. And he had the additional worry of what he'd discovered at the Golden Nugget.

The sound of the shower changed, and Jake imagined Kate stepping back from the spray to soap herself. It was a picture that made him groan. Maybe a drink would help keep his mind off subjects it had no right to roam to.

He leaned down into the refrigerator in search of a beer. When he looked up, he was facing the bore of a deadly-looking pistol.

"Jake!" Kate lowered the gun slowly. "You scared the life out of me."

Jake's hand went to his heart. "You haven't done much for my ticker, either." He pointed to the gun, doing his best to ignore the all-too-obvious fact that she was naked and dripping on his kitchen floor. Little drops of water sliding down her skin, all over.

He had a lot of memories of Kate, but none were nearly as impressive as her in the flesh. He cleared his throat. "Do you always shower packing heat?"

Kate lowered the gun. "Only when your ex-girlfriends break in on me."

Jake didn't really register the answer. He was far too busy taking in Kate in her entirety. Parts of her had rounded, growing into the lush curves that had only been hinted at when she was a teenager. Where once she had been a young girl, now she was all woman.

"Kate," he said, finally looking up at her. He still

held the beer in his hand. The refrigerator door remained open and neither of them moved.

"Your floor," she finally said, stepping out of the puddle that had accumulated around her feet. She felt incredibly awkward. She'd come out of the shower at the sound of someone in the house. She hadn't even bothered to think about clothing. Her only concern was the gun and to get the intruder before he got her first. She put the gun down on the counter. "I feel like such a fool."

"I don't care about the floor." Jake reached out and lightly caught her wrist. "Don't go," he said.

"I should go and get dressed." But she didn't move. She knew what would happen if she didn't, and she also knew she was tired of running away from it. She wanted Jake. There had never been a time when she didn't— even those long years when she wouldn't admit to it. Now, she could see that he wanted her, too.

As if he read her mind, Jake closed the distance between them. His hand slid over her shoulder, the water still warm on her skin. Her hair was like wet silk teasing him as it brushed across the top of his fingers, a whisper of the promise of pleasure she held for him. "You're the most beautiful thing I've ever seen," he whispered.

Kate expected to feel the old fear pushing up in her, the need to run, to flee before she found herself in a place where she could be hurt. Instead, her body melded to his. "I didn't intend for this to happen." And she hadn't. Not consciously, at least.

"I did." His arms encircled her and drew her closer. The water from her skin was absorbed into his clothes, damp and cool. But Kate's warmth was far more penetrating.

"The shower's still going," she whispered.

"Good," he said. Together they began to walk to the bathroom. Jake's fingers fumbled with the buttons of his shirt. When it was undone, he left it on the hallway floor. As they stepped into the bathroom, he walked out of his pants. In a moment he was as naked as she. Pushing back the shower curtain, he stepped under the water. He held her hand and drew her in beside him.

In the steamy warmth of the shower, Kate let go of the last vestiges of restraint. Jake was everything she'd ever wanted, though she'd never fought so hard against anything else. She reached up to him, kissing his chest and neck and face, working slowly to his lips. She felt his arms around her and knew at last that if there was such a thing as coming home, she'd finally found her way.

The water was hot and fast, and Jake found it an arousing contrast to Kate's smooth, soft warmth. Her breasts slid against his chest, and he could feel the sudden hardening of her nipples. He looked into her eyes and felt as if he'd jumped from a cliff. It occurred to him in the moment that he bent to kiss her that perhaps she was right. Perhaps the past did not matter a whit. Nor the future. If only the moment mattered, then Jake was truly in paradise.

HAND IN HAND, Jake and Kate walked the main street of Silver City waiting for dawn to brighten the horizon. For Kate, the town was brand-new and alive with an energy she'd never seen before. Jake's hand in hers was a connection she wanted to cling to, though she held him lightly.

Their lovemaking had unlocked her emotions, and she realized that for too many years, she'd held herself in reserve with such discipline that now, it was as if the doors of a prison had been opened. Freedom, though exhilarating, was also terrifying.

Still, she could not escape the memory of Jake's kisses, the slow, lingering way he touched her. They had moved from the shower to the bed, and though both were exhausted by the events of the night, they'd found new energy, new ways to touch and express what they felt for each other. Layered beneath the moment of magic was the past, the long-ago days when they had learned from each other what it meant to make love.

Holding Jake's hand, Kate found the strength to acknowledge, at least to herself, what the past twenty-four hours had brought her—the good and the bad.

The destruction of the old opera house was a wound in her heart. The loss of Kitty's portrait, now ground into the embers and the water, was the symbol of all that she'd either walked away from or lost. Things she'd run away from because they were too painful to confront. She knew Jake was right, that she'd eventually have to face those things. But they were too fresh and painful to speak of, even to Jake. All she knew was that while he held her, while he kissed her and whispered of the past, she was strong enough to face it.

"I have a pretty good idea where that black rascal has gone," Jake said.

Ouzo had failed to return to the firehouse—not a surprise to Jake or Kate. But instead of sleepy, their lovemaking had left them unable to sleep. It was as if they didn't want to lose each other even for a few hours of rest. They'd decided to hunt for the dog.

"We'll find him." She listened for the tiny clink of the dog's tags as they rounded the corner by Susan Tanner's. Even though she searched for the dog, she was still half in the past. Dawn was breaking, and everywhere she looked, she remembered something of her childhood. As a young girl she'd walked this same route from school, going to the old opera house.

"Listen," Jake whispered, squeezing her hand. "I think I hear him."

There was the tinkle of aluminum tags, and Kate felt her body tense in preparation. If they could only catch Ouzo before he got into serious trouble, they could go back and sleep. Even an hour or two would be better than nothing.

Sleeping in Jake's arms was something she wanted to experience. In their youth, they'd never had the luxury of truly spending the night together.

"Ouzo," Jake whispered.

There was the sound of a low growl.

"Cat," Kate interpreted. She'd learned a lot from Familiar in the past few days.

"That dog," Jake said with exasperation. They'd just drawn parallel with Susan Tanner's house. Two black cats perched on the steps and another white one sat on the sidewalk. There was no sign of the dog.

The house was dark as pitch, and Kate silently hoped that Susan was a sound sleeper.

"Ouzo!" Jake called, a little louder.

The front porch lights came on, and Jake cursed softly under his breath. "We're caught now."

"Indeed," Kate answered before the door opened and the petite woman stepped out onto the stoop.

"Looking for your dog?" she asked in a pleasant voice.

"I apologize, Mrs. Tanner," Jake began. "He slipped out. There was a fire— Whatever damage he's caused, I'll pay for it."

"I was sorry to hear the Golden Nugget burned, yes,

I know." She came out onto the steps, her yellow chenille robe flowing about her petite figure. "I have your dog."

Instead of anger, Kate heard a certain fondness. She felt Jake tense.

"Whatever he's done, I'll make it up to you. I know he's a terrible pest, but you see, I'm quite attached to him."

"No need to explain." She motioned them into her yard. "I caught him when Billy Boy cornered him in the yard. My first thought was to call the dogcatcher and have him hauled off to the pound. You know he's been a terrible nuisance to the cats."

"I know, and I'm so sorry. I promise you that I'll keep him on a leash or contained in some fashion. He's a dog with a long past and—"

"Oh, quit trying to explain him." She motioned them up the steps. "In fact, we've had quite an evening together, and I've become fond of the black rascal."

Kate stopped in her tracks. She exchanged a glance with Jake. "You're fond of Ouzo?" She must have misunderstood the woman.

"Well, you see, once Billy Boy turned on him and decided to take a stand, it was all over. The dog came running to the door, begging to get inside to escape the cat. When Billy Boy and I realized he was such a coward, there was no reason to fear him. I let him inside and discovered that he has a charming array of tricks. He's a very smart dog."

"Tricks?" Jake looked at her as if she'd lost her mind.

"Of course. I'm sure you taught them to him."

"What tricks?" Jake was confused and didn't hide it well.

"Oh, don't be so modest. The dog is a master of imitation. He can do any of the television commercials featuring animals. I really think, Chief Johnson, that you should take him to Hollywood.''

"Hollywood?" Jake was in a daze.

"Absolutely. Why, we've been up for several hours channel surfing for commercials that feature animals so he can imitate them. The dog is a genius."

Kate was about to laugh out loud. Jake looked exactly like a parent who'd been told his wayward child was a prodigy. "Where is Ouzo?" she asked.

"Why he's in the kitchen eating. He seems to favor spicy food, doesn't he?''

Jake groaned. "Not jalapeños," he said.

"Oh, he adores them. And those little green chili peppers. I do believe the dog has some Mexican blood, though he sniffed out a book of Yeats's poems and seemed absorbed by them." She chuckled at the absurdity of a dog reading poems. "You've done a remarkable job with him, Chief Johnson. If I didn't know better, I'd swear he was reading that poetry."

"I doubt that," Jake said under his breath.

"What kind of dog is he? Ouzo is Greek, but he doesn't look like any Greek breed of dog I've ever heard of.''

"He's—"

"Black Irish," Kate supplied. "That's why he's fond of Yeats. And James Joyce. Why, that dog is a fool for *Ulysses*."

"How fascinating. You know I used to teach high school literature. It's a shame to say it but that dog is smarter than many of my students." Susan Tanner was beaming.

"I really don't know what to say," Jake replied.

"Shut up," Kate whispered under her breath.

Susan sighed. "Now, I suppose it's time to take him home."

"I can only thank you for looking out for him," Jake said. Together he and Kate walked to the door. Behind the screen door, Ouzo wagged his plumed black tail.

"Any time. He's a charming dog," Susan answered. "By the way, do you have any leads on who burned the Golden Nugget?"

"None," Jake said as he readied the leash for Ouzo.

"You'll catch them, I'm sure. If you get too stumped, put the dog on it. I'm sure he'll turn something up." She held open the screen and Ouzo ran to Jake, licking him and barking as if he'd been separated from his master for months.

"Thanks," Jake said.

"Any time." Susan closed the door and Jake and Kate remained staring at each other.

"*Ulysses?*" Jake asked.

"I was at a loss for an Irish book. It was the first thing that came to mind."

"I never understood that book."

Kate grinned. "As the lady pointed out, Ouzo is a very smart dog."

"Ouch," Jake grinned in return. "You know how to pierce a man's ego." He turned to the dog. "You, sir, are in a heap of trouble. I'm not sure what punishment I'll mete out, but you can't continue to escape and run rampant over town. One day you're going to get hurt."

"Arf." Ouzo wagged his tail for emphasis. In his golden-brown eyes there wasn't a shred of remorse.

KATE SNUGGLED back into the pillow and sipped the coffee Jake had made. Though they'd only had two hours of sleep, both were wide-awake.

"You haven't a clue about the man who struck you?" Jake pressed.

Kate shook her head. It was a point Jake had not been able to turn loose. Kate had told him again and again the details she remembered. Except for the missing equipment and the knot on her head, she might have believed she'd made the incident up. It was almost impossible to believe someone had actually tried to kill her—had left her alive in a burning building.

"He was my size?"

"Yes. Or it seemed that way. The smoke and the heat... My vision was blurry." No matter how hard she tried, she couldn't remember a truly clear image. "I'm sorry."

Jake leaned over to kiss her forehead. "So tell me everything Alexis said." He pulled her close against him. "If I could work every case this way..." He kissed her forehead.

"Nothing really. The most memorable thing was that she had your key and she wasn't upset about the fire. She'd just increased her insurance."

"Why would she have been dumb enough to tell you that?" he mused aloud.

"She was nuts to come in here like she did. I might have shot her, but she's smart enough to know that I would have found out about the insurance, eventually. Something like that is a smoking gun. At least by telling me it looks more aboveboard."

"True. I've got—"

The ringing of the telephone interrupted him. He put down his coffee and picked up the receiver by the bed. It was not yet eight o'clock.

"Chief Johnson here."

"This is Chip, at the lab in Denver. We've got some reports ready for you."

Jake gave Kate a thumbs-up sign. "What are the results?"

"We've determined the maker of the timing devices. It's a company here in Colorado. There are some reports you might want to compare and contrast," Chip said.

"I'll drive over to pick up the results." He thought a minute. "Or better yet, why don't you send them by special courier. I've got a lot of things to do today."

"Sure thing," the lab tech said.

Jake put down the phone and gave a rueful look at the clock. "Time to hustle," he said.

"Don't I know it." Kate put a hand on Jake's chest. "There's so much I want to tell you. So many things that need to be said."

Jake kissed her softly. "We'll have a chance to say them all. There are some things I want to tell you, things about the past." In the golden light of morning, Jake was having second thoughts about withholding the information concerning the skeleton he'd discovered. Kate was the sheriff. By not telling her, he was, essentially, subverting her authority. But on the other hand, he was also protecting her. At least until he knew something more concrete.

He'd been seventeen when Anne McArdle had disappeared with a man named Johnny Goodloe and the proceeds of the sale of the old opera house. It had been a substantial sum of money. Jake's concern had been Kate. Though she'd shown a cool, composed exterior to the world, the abandonment had hit her hard.

Jake had been so focused on Kate that he hadn't even given Anne a thought. But what if she hadn't really walked out on her daughter? If the body in the casino somehow happened to be Anne McArdle, he didn't want Kate to see it. He wanted to spare her that memory.

"Hey, Jake, are you going to talk to me or just stand there with your socks in your hand?" Kate threw a pillow at him. "Are you okay?"

"Sorry." Jake sat down and pulled on his socks. "I was thinking about the fires."

"A clue?" Kate crawled across the bed and kissed him on the ear. "Tell me."

He turned to her and pushed her long beautiful hair back from her face. She looked maybe twenty, her eyes sparkling in the morning light and her skin lightly tinted a soft rose. She was right not to trust happiness. It was so precarious.

"Not exactly a clue. A hunch. But I want to think it all through before I talk about it." What he wanted was solid proof.

"I didn't know you were superstitious." She kissed his chin and then his lips.

"Not superstitious, just cautious." More than anything, he wanted to pull her back into bed and stay there with her.

"Tell me today at lunch," Kate pressed, her voice light and coaxing.

"Maybe," Jake said, wondering when he would be able to get Mortimer Grell's report. Maybe the coroner had already done his work. Whoever turned out to be buried at the Golden Nugget, he wanted to know before Kate did.

"We'd both better get busy." Kate swung her feet to the floor and almost hit Familiar. "What's this?" she asked, bending down to pick up a map the cat held in his mouth. She unfolded it on the bed. "Look at this

Jake, it's your property map of the Double J. Familiar found it.''

"I wonder where." Jake reached across the bed and picked up the map that was tattered and worn at the folds. "I haven't seen this thing for years and years. I didn't even know it was still around." He lowered the map so he could look into Kate's eyes. "The Double J doesn't mean what it once did to me. Land is no substitute for love and a family."

Kate knew what he was referring to, but it wasn't that simple. "Loving the Double J wasn't the problem, Jake. It wasn't," she added when she saw the skepticism on his face. "My problem wasn't the ranch, and it wasn't you. It was me." Now wasn't exactly the time, but she had to make a point. "There's a lot about the past that I need to unravel. You've given me the desire to do that. But I have a lot of work to do before I can go forward in a relationship. I want you to know that up front. I have to get myself in order. That's work that only I can do."

"*We* have a lot of work to do." But Jake's face showed his concern. If the body at the casino was Anne's, he had to keep the door open between him and Kate. This time, he'd be there to help her through the shock and grief. This time they'd weather whatever came, together. Jake dropped the map on the bed. He wanted to reach out and grab her, but he knew he couldn't hold her if she chose to run. There was also no use in trying to corner her. He had to do it right. He had to trust her to want to stay. There would be doubts and fear. Kate couldn't overcome a lifetime of running in one night. "You take whatever time you need, Kate. I'll wait."

Kate shook her head, a slow smile lighting her face.

"You know, you're too good to be true. Even when I feel the first jitter, you hold steady." She picked up her boot. "Let's go find an arsonist."

"Meow!" Familiar jumped on the bed. He patted the map with his paw. "Meow."

"That's good," Kate said as she dressed. "Good kitty."

"Meow!" Familiar grew more strident.

"Good kitty." Kate scratched him behind the ears.

"Me-owww!"

"Maybe he's hungry," Jake suggested.

"Damn!" Kate looked guiltily at the cat and then at Ouzo asleep at the foot of the bed. "I promised them something wonderful to eat for saving my life. I dropped the ball on that one."

"We'll bring them something back." Jake checked his watch. "In fact, why don't you take care of your promise, and I'll grab a chat with Roy. He may be more open with me alone."

Kate's brow furrowed. She started to say something, then changed her mind. She nodded. "Okay, if that's what you'd prefer."

Jake smiled as he walked to her and kissed her forehead. "I'd prefer that you never leave my side. But I know you, and that would chafe you worse than hobbles on a wild pony. So I think we should maximize our time and talent and get this case solved." He intended to talk to Roy—after he spoke with the coroner.

"Okay," Kate agreed. She scooped Familiar in her arms. "What'll it be today? Caviar? Peking Duck? Name it, cat."

"Me-owwww!" Familiar leaped from her arms onto the map. "Meow!" he demanded.

Chapter Twelve

Mortimer Grell was a somber man who wore the title of coroner as if it were the most important job in the world. Jake entered his office with a heart full of serious concerns and took a seat in a straight-backed wooden chair across the desk from him.

"Good morning, Jake." Grell spoke in a clipped, to-the-point tone.

"Have you had a chance to examine the body?" Jake asked, equally direct.

"Yes. I collected the remains and they're down in the morgue. The bone you first discovered led me to believe that the victim had been buried for some time. After a more thorough examination, I have my doubts."

Jake did not question Grell's expertise, but the man seemed to talk in riddles. "How old, exactly, is the body?"

"It's fairly recent," Grell said.

Jake felt a bubble of relief rising straight from his heart to his brain. "How recent?"

"Well, even without the official lab results, I'd say within the year. And to further ease your mind, the body is male." Grell looked over his half glasses. "You certainly seem relieved."

"I am," Jake admitted.

Grell pondered Jake, and when he spoke it was in a softer voice. "Why didn't Sheriff McArdle bring this to my attention? I would think that mysterious remains are more in her line than yours?"

It was obvious to Jake that Grell had his own set of suspicions. "I found the body, and..." He couldn't think of a truly plausible excuse except the truth. "I was afraid it might date back farther in time."

"You were afraid it might be Anne McArdle, weren't you?"

Jake was surprised at Grell's dead-on guess. Grell was a quiet, private man who never seemed to notice his neighbors or anyone else around him. He'd always seemed to be in his own world. "Yes, that was exactly my concern."

"It crossed my mind, too." Grell took off his glasses and looked at Jake. "I never believed Anne ran off and left Kate. Never. Anne loved her daughter more than life itself. She was smitten by that gambler, but she wouldn't have left Kate. In fact, I tried to track down Goodloe and Anne after they left. They vanished. They simply disappeared. And no one in Charleston, where Goodloe claimed he was from a prominent family, knew him. It was very suspicious."

Jake was more than a little curious. He looked at Grell with new interest. He'd always known the coroner as a tall, quiet man, self-contained and rather standoffish. "Why were you so interested?"

"I was in love with Anne." He smiled. "I don't think she reciprocated my feelings, but that didn't stop me. As a result, I got to know her pretty well, as a friend. I know she was devoted to Kate. So, when that body turned up, I was afraid my old suspicions were about to be resolved.''

"And you're certain it isn't Anne?"

"Quite positive.''

"Who is it?"

"That, Jake, is another question. Without the skull, identification may take a long time—if we ever find the identity of the man. There's very little to go on. But now that you know it isn't Anne McArdle, Kate's got to examine the scene. This man hasn't been dead that long, and someone is guilty of murder.''

"Right,'' Jake said. He reached across the desk and shook Grell's hand. "Thanks, Mortimer."

JAKE WALKED BACK to the Golden Nugget. Several people who had stopped on the street to examine the damage nodded to him.

"Bad business," one man said as he shook his head. "Bad luck for Alexis."

"Sure is.'' Jake eased past them, feeling the lack of sleep from the night before. He wanted to check out the crime scene and then he'd have to track Kate down and tell her about the body. This was going to be delicate. Grell didn't know the half of it. If Kate felt that he'd deliberately held back the information about the body, then she'd be mad as a hornet. What could he say—I thought it was your mother? That would only make matters worse. Yes, it was going to be a very delicate matter to tell Kate so as not to rouse her anger. Mortimer Grell was right on target.

Stepping through the mess that was what was left of the casino, he went back to the place where he'd found the bone. Weak sunlight filtered in through holes in the roof, and he took a moment to assess the damage. He'd have to do an intensive examination, but the part of the old opera house that contained the stage and bar seemed to be salvageable. The pleasure he felt at that thought was partly for the sake of history, but a lot for Kate. He'd seen the expression on her face when she'd realized the building was burning out of control. Deny it as she might, she loved the old place.

The staircase to the second-floor apartment was gone, but if he had to guess, he'd say the upstairs—Alexis's haven of pastels—was probably still in pretty good shape. The whole building would need a new roof, and everything in it was a total loss, either from the fire, smoke or water. Still, it was a historic site, and Kate, or someone, might be able to save it.

Pleased at that thought, he went to the spot where the skeleton had been discovered. To his surprise, there were signs of recent excavation. About fifteen feet from the place where the femur had been found was a deeper hole. Peeking out of the earth was what appeared to be white bone.

"Holy smoke," Jake said, kneeling down to examine it. In the dirt he could see traces of sharpened claw-marks. "Ouzo," he said under his breath. So the black rascal had actually done some work before he went over to Susan Tanner's and conned her.

Jake carefully brushed at the earth and rocked back on his heels with a smile of satisfaction. Ouzo had discovered the skull.

He turned to leave and took a sharp breath. Familiar stood not three feet from him. "Meow," the cat said.

"Hello, Jake," Kate said from three feet behind the cat. "Who's your friend?" She looked at the skull, then looked at him.

Jake rose slowly. "I was on my way to find you. Ouzo found the skeleton last night—"

"You knew about this last night?" Kate's eyebrows drew together. "And you didn't bother to mention it to me? Jake, I can't believe this."

He could see the hurt in her eyes. "I know you might not see it my way at this moment, but I was trying to protect you." This was the thin ice he knew was treacherous.

"Protect me?" Kate's voice still registered more hurt than anger. "How? I thought we were working this case as partners. I thought we were a team." She waved her hand at the skull. "I find you hunkered over a skull buried in Alexis Redfield's casino. Alexis, who along with Roy is one of the top suspects in the arsons. Alexis, who has a key to your apartment. There's a body, which I don't know a thing about, and there's the guy I just spent the night with—" She broke off as the full extent of the betrayal touched her. "We made love, and the entire time it was a lie. You knew about this and you didn't tell me." She stepped back from him.

"Kate, give me a chance to explain this." Jake stood slowly. "If you listen—"

"I'll contact the coroner and have him come for the skull." Kate stepped back further. "I have work to do." She whirled and was gone.

Familiar edged over to Jake and brushed against his knee, purring. He absently stroked the cat as he looked at the space where Kate had stood. She was so angry, so unwilling to listen to reason—to listen to anything at all. He loved her. That was simple enough. But did that count for much if every day was going to be a struggle of basic communication?

What he'd done was the right thing. Maybe the way

he'd handled it hadn't been the smartest way, but he'd accomplished his goal. Kate had been spared a lot of painful speculation, even if she didn't appreciate that fact.

"Meow," Familiar cried, rubbing against him.

Jake stroked the cat with a sigh. He was too tired to pursue Kate, too sore to try. Only an hour before he'd been so positive of their future together. Now he didn't know if he'd ever have a chance to explain to her. Maybe he was too old for the roller-coaster ride that was Kate's stormy emotional life. "Let's go to the courthouse and check on building permits," Jake said out loud.

"Meow," Familiar agreed.

JAKE RIFFLED through the sheaves of paper as he sat in the close confines of the Gilpin County record room. Permission to build an addition had been applied for by Alexis only a few weeks after she'd bought the Golden Nugget. He already had that date, July of 1996. That was just about the time frame Grell projected for the body to have been buried.

He considered what he knew of Alexis Redfield. She'd never struck him as a woman capable of murder. Then again, what did he really know of her? The answer was nothing. And she'd had a key to his apartment, which meant she also had access to the fire suits, and she was strong enough to have knocked him out.

He'd also discovered another interesting fact. There had been another buyer interested in the Golden Nugget before Alexis purchased it. A man named Black. But Alexis had outbid Black for the casino. So, where did Alexis come from and why had she decided on Silver

City? That was something he intended to chase down, with or without Kate's help.

Even with his mind focused on Alexis, he couldn't help thinking of Kate. He wanted to find her and tell her this latest information. Well, he'd be damned if he was going to her. She had a right to feel betrayed, he'd give her that. But she owed him a chance to explain. And it was up to her to find him and give it to him.

"You need some help, Jake?" Meryl Jones asked as she eased up beside him. She was in her sixties and had never missed a day of work in the records department.

"Do you remember a man named Black, James Black?" Jake asked.

Meryl's brow wrinkled. "No, not really. I've been clerk here a long time, and I know that was the name of the fella that wanted to buy the old opera house last year. But as far as I know, he never came to Silver City. He had folks who worked for him."

"No one in town ever saw him?" Jake wondered if the body belonged to James Black. Perhaps Alexis had outbid him, or perhaps she'd simply gotten him out of the picture, permanently.

"Not to my knowledge, and you know how hard it is to keep a secret here in Silver City." She chuckled softly, but her eyes held worry. "I'm surprised you haven't found that firebug, Jake. Folks in town are getting worried."

"I'm worried, too, Meryl, but I'm working on it. And Sheriff McArdle, too."

"I know that tore at Kate's heart."

"It did." Jake rubbed an eyebrow. "Who all has owned the old opera house? I know after Anne sold it that it changed hands several times."

"Oh, it went first to some California movie star, Clay

Cobar, who thought he was going to do something with it. Bring back Wild West shows or something. Then Cobar sold it to a developer, and then the town had it, and the last to buy was Ms. Redfield.'' Meryl shook her head. ''It's a pity, isn't it? Alexis had that place up and running, and I'll tell you, her slot machines paid off better than any in town.''

Jake couldn't help smiling. ''While we're talking old times, Meryl, do you remember when Anne McArdle left town?''

''Lord, like it was yesterday. That was a shock. No one ever imagined Anne to do such a thing. She was one pretty woman. A brunette in among all those McArdle redheads, and she stood out. I believe she was from Maryland, but I can't say for certain. Miss Kitty's son met her when he went east to study. You know Miss Kitty never wanted him to come back here. She must of had a premonition because he hadn't been back in Silver City for ten years before he died.''

''I was just a kid then.''

''Yes, you and Kate turned out to be sweethearts, didn't you?'' Meryl gave him a sidelong look. ''You been stoking old coals?''

Jake just smiled. ''After her husband's death, Anne stayed on here in Silver City, right?''

''She did. She was the bookkeeper for Miss Kitty. If she knew what was going on there, she never showed it. She and that red-haired baby girl would go from the old opera house on Sunday morning to the church.''

Jake felt a need to push, but he knew his purpose would best be served if he took his time and let Meryl get around to the story. ''Do you remember the man that Anne left with?''

''His name was…Johnny. Johnny something.''

"Johnny Goodloe."

"That's it." Meryl smiled. "He was dark and handsome with a mustache. And that man could dance. Why, at the spring dance, he waltzed Anne all the way down Main Street until they just ran out of music."

"Where'd he come from?"

"Charleston, I heard. He had a Southern drawl, too, so I guess it was the truth. He was supposed to be from a family with money, but I heard they'd fallen on hard times."

"How'd he end up in Silver City?"

"He was traveling through on the way to Hollywood. He was in a show, one of those actors who played at Kitty's from time to time. He and his friend, I can't recall the man's name, but they were quite popular for a time. They could recite poetry and talk about their travels. It was fun for the town. Johnny, of course, was the handsome one of the two, but the other one wasn't bad. 'Course he went on with the show when it left. It was Johnny who stayed behind with Anne."

Jake gave a few *uh-huhs* to keep Meryl talking.

"Johnny played the part that Cary Grant played in *Arsenic and Old Lace*. He had a bit of talent, but he was better-looking than he was an actor. Anyhow, he was traveling with the show to Hollywood where he hoped to become a film star."

"Big dreams," Jake commented.

"Oh, Johnny Goodloe was a big dreamer. And he put some dreams in Anne's head. I still can't imagine her running off and leaving Kate. Why, they were as close as close can be."

"I know."

"I thought that girl would grieve herself to death, until

she seemed to latch on to you.'' Meryl leaned back. ''I thought you were going to marry her.''

''I tried,'' Jake said. ''Kate wanted to leave Colorado. She wanted to start a new life.''

''That's not hard to understand. She'd lost everything she ever cared about. I'd want to move, too.'' Meryl drummed her fingers on the counter. ''Look, I've got to get busy. If you need anything else, just call out.''

''One more thing.'' He held her gaze. ''Did anybody check up on Johnny Goodloe? I mean, do you know if Anne really knew much about him before she left with him.''

''I suppose she knew all she needed to know.'' Meryl shrugged but her eyes brightened. ''You know, I accepted the fact that Anne left with the man. But the way you're asking questions has got me to wondering.''

Jake stood up. ''Keep wondering, Meryl, but don't say a word to anybody. If you happen to run across an address or anything that might help me track down this Goodloe fellow, give me a call.''

''What about Kate? She's the sheriff.''

Jake patted Meryl's shoulder. ''Don't mention it to her. If I'm wrong, it will only bring up a lot of old pain for Kate. If I'm right, I'll tell her when I have the evidence to back it up.''

''I always figured you for a smart man, Jake, even when I saw that dog leading you around by the nose.''

KATE SAT AT THE COMPUTER keyboard, but she didn't punch the keys. Her mind was on Jake. The night before had been so intense. For the first time in a long, long while she'd felt as if she were connected to someone. Once again, she'd had to learn how very dangerous those feelings could be.

Determined not to dwell on her wounds, she keyed in the information and began the background checks on all of the potential suspects in the arsons. On her list were Alexis, Evelyn, Reverend Lyte, Roy Adams, Betty Cody, Lester Ray, the head honchos of the DDC...and Jake Johnson.

She'd always assumed that folks she'd grown up with wouldn't have criminal records. Well, the old saying about not assuming anything was true. The DDC members were her *only* out-of-town suspects. She'd quit assuming and started checking facts.

It would take a while to get back the answers to her queries, and she had an appointment at the bank. She had to stop by the judge's house and pick up the orders to open financial records to her scrutiny. The fires were based on financial matters—of that much she felt certain. Perhaps there was something hidden in the records that would give her the motive she sought.

She also initiated an insurance check on Alexis Redfield to see if any prior businesses had gone up in flames. Sometimes an arsonist made a living by burning and collecting insurance.

Even though she held little hope of finding solid evidence or even motive, it made her feel better to get busy. She'd allowed her mind to become preoccupied with Jake, and with the past. Now she was determined to focus on the case at hand. Either she would solve the arsons or she would turn in her badge. Coming back to Silver City hadn't been such a good idea. Not personally or careerwise.

She picked up the phone and dialed the coroner's office for the third time. Grell was busy working on his report, but she couldn't wait for him to call. The phone rang five times before the secretary answered and assured her that Grell had no definite report on the remains and that in all likelihood, a positive identification from dental records would have to be done by the state lab, which might take up to twenty-four hours.

"Can't Grell get them to put a rush on it?" Kate asked.

"Dr. Grell is doing all he can," his secretary said with a sniff of aggravation. "But he did ask me to give you a message."

"Yes?" Kate asked eagerly.

"He wants to see you. In person. He said he'll be finished here in three or four hours. Would that be convenient?"

"Sure. I'll be there." Kate replaced the phone, wondering what Mortimer Grell needed to see her in person about. She'd always liked the man, though he was very reserved. She could remember meeting him on the streets when she was a little girl. He always had a piece of candy or some unusual trinket for her. He'd always hand it over to her with a grave smile and a look at her mother to make sure Anne didn't mind. He'd been strange, and courtly. And Kate knew suddenly that he'd been in love with her mother. The revelation left her a little breathless. How was it that she'd never seen it before? Perhaps because she'd never looked.

At the sound of a knock on her door, she looked up to see a courier dressed in a brown uniform. He held a special delivery letter in his hand.

He nodded. "Special delivery for the fire chief, and one of the firemen over at the station said to bring it here. Would you sign for it?"

Kate hesitated only a fraction of a second. This was Jake's report. But then he already knew the rudiments of it. What would it hurt for her to see it? They were both working on the case, even though they'd decided to work separately. Or at least she'd decided to work alone. "Sure." She signed the label and took the flat envelope. As soon as the delivery man left, she ripped it open.

The reports on the devices used to start the fires were technical and extensive. The gist was that the timing devices were all of the same make and manufacture, created by a company in Denver, just as the lab tech had told Jake over the phone. There really wasn't much new information included, but there was a lead.

She noted the manufacturer's address down on a piece of paper. It wasn't a long drive to Denver, and she had photographs of most of the major suspects. It was a real long shot, but she had little else to do.

"Meow!"

She looked down to see Familiar standing by her desk. She pulled him into her lap. "Want to ride to Denver?"

Familiar struggled out of her arms. He jumped onto the desk and began knocking the paperwork around with his paw.

"I know you're mad, and I don't blame you. But we're a team, and we're going to solve this crime."

Familiar batted the report on Lookout Church over to her.

"You think we need to go back to the crime scene?" It was a wild guess, but she remembered the property map of the Double J Familiar had brought to the bed. Lookout Church had been on the map, as well as Jake's burned-out ranch.

The cat placed his paw squarely on the location of the church.

"Okay, we'll run out there on the way to Denver."

She picked up the photos and the information she'd

written down. At the main desk she stopped one of the deputies. "Take this over to Jake," she said, handing him the packet. "Tell him I've gone to Denver to follow the lead on the manufacturer of the timing devices." Jake might withhold evidence, but she was more professional than that. She checked her watch. "I should be back in plenty of time for the citizens' meeting tonight, and if I run across anything significant, tell him I'll call."

The deputy took the letter and left.

"Meow." Familiar swatted at the deputy's leg.

"Come on, cat, we don't have time to play games." Kate headed out into the sunshine of another perfect Blue Sky day.

Chapter Thirteen

By the time Kate pulled the truck around, Jake was standing on the sidewalk waiting for her. At the sight of him an old hurt rose up and seemed to take up all the space in her chest. Whatever his reasons for withholding the facts about the body, Kate didn't know or care. He'd betrayed her—both personally and professionally—and that was all that truly mattered. Her first impulse was to hit the gas and drive by, but that was too reminiscent of how she'd left him in the street when they were eighteen. This time she angled to the curb and waited. Jake held the documents she'd sent over in his hand.

"You're going to check out the timing devices?" His voice was strained.

"It seems like the best thing to do now." She found it difficult to meet his gaze. There was so much pain between them. And there had been such intense pleasure. But that only made the pain worse.

"Kate, can we talk first?"

It was what she dreaded most. "What's there to say, Jake?"

Her offhand tone angered him. She'd been able to walk out fifteen years before, and it seemed she was just as capable of turning her feelings off now. He'd thought of a way to explain his actions to her, as gentle a way as he possibly could come up with. But her attitude struck a deeper emotion. "Do you deny that you feel something for me?"

She considered lying, but that had never been her way of dealing with problems. Avoidance was her preferred mode, but if Jake was going to push it... "No, I don't deny it."

"Then at least let's talk. I can explain."

"Can you? And even if you can, will it make a difference?" How could she explain to him that every time she felt strong and safe enough to admit her feelings for him, something happened to send her scuttling back into her shell. This was simply too hard. For fifteen years she'd managed not to put herself in line for heartbreak. Maybe running wasn't such a bad option after all.

At the sound of someone clearing his throat, Jake and Kate both turned. Kate was surprised to see the coroner standing on the street.

"Kate," he said, nodding.

"Do you have the reports?"

"Not completely. No, that isn't what I wanted to speak with you about." He glanced at Jake before he continued. "This may seem presumptuous of me, but if so, then I'd rather be guilty of presumption than lack of action." He cleared his throat again.

Kate was curious. She'd known Grell all of her life, and she'd never known him to interfere in someone's life a single time.

"It's about that body in the casino." He looked directly at Kate. "Jake didn't tell you about it because he was trying to protect you." At her expression he reached into the truck and touched her shoulder. "Listen to me, Kate. Jake was afraid it might be the remains of your mother. He wanted to spare you that—having to discover it in such a brutal manner. As it turns out, we know it isn't. So be angry at him if you choose, but temper your anger with understanding of his concern for you." He patted her arm awkwardly. "Forgive me for intruding. I was very fond of your mother, and I knew that the man she became involved with was a scoundrel. I should have spoken up, but I didn't. I didn't want to presume, and I've regretted it all these years. This time I was determined to speak my mind."

Before either of them could respond, Mortimer Grell turned and walked away.

Kate stared after him, her lips slightly parted as if she was about to speak. She finally turned to Jake. "You thought it was Mother?"

Jake couldn't help seeing the sixteen-year-old girl in Kate's expression. This was the pain he'd hoped to spare her. "It crossed my mind. When Ouzo found the body, I suddenly realized that I never truly believed that Anne would have left you. I wanted to have the facts before I had to hurt you."

"I see." And Kate did. She saw what a fool she'd been. Always rushing and jumping to conclusions. Always so afraid of being hurt that she hurt herself before anyone else could.

"Come inside and let's talk," Jake said.

She checked her watch. There was plenty of time to drive to Denver and get back. She owed Jake at least a talk. She owed herself that much.

Before she could answer, Familiar leaped from the window and ran toward the fire station.

"I think he wants us to talk. Either that or he's anxious to see Ouzo," Jake said, a wry grin playing across his face. "We shouldn't fight a cat that smart."

She got out of the truck and walked around it, letting Jake lead the way to the back entrance and up the stairs. Familiar darted ahead and disappeared into the bedroom. There was the sound of the dog and cat mewing and barking softly.

"Should I break it up?" Jake asked.

Kate shook her head. "I think Familiar can hold his own. He'll let us know if he needs help."

"Coffee?" he asked.

"Sure." It would buy her some time.

Familiar came from down the hall, a satisfied expression on his face. He rubbed against Kate's leg once, then curled up in a chair at the table. Ouzo trotted in, stopping beside the table and giving Kate a wag of his tail as he dropped a rolled-up piece of paper at her feet.

Absently, she bent to retrieve it, recognizing the map of the Double J. Apparently Familiar and the dog had been arguing over ownership of it. She put it on the table out of the reach of both of them.

"Jake, I owe you an apology." She swallowed. "I owe you a lot more than that."

Jake finished putting the coffee on and took a seat. His brown eyes were filled with what she could only describe as sadness. He reached across the table and picked up her hand. He examined it as if he expected to find some answers there, hidden in the lines.

"Can you tell my future?" she asked. He was so sad that she felt compelled to say something.

His brown gaze lifted to meet hers. "As you've probably observed, I'm a lot better at seeing the past. I would have spared you this. It's an old wound reopened."

Kate gathered herself. "I never understood how Mother could have left me like that. I suppose I never will. It's a door I had to close to survive."

"I should have trusted you to be strong enough to handle it, Kate. It was a choice—to protect you or to trust you. Maybe I made the wrong decision."

Kate shook her head. They'd finally come to the crux of the matter, and it was not Jake who was at fault. "It is a matter of trust, you're right about that. But it's my problem." Kate held his gaze. "I'm not as in control as you may think. I don't plan my actions, Jake. In the past, I've reacted. That's what I'm trying to change. This morning though, I fell back into the same old pattern. I lost my trust in you. I ran."

"Kate, I'm in love with you. I have been for years. For a long time I was too stubborn to admit it. Now I'm a smarter man, and I know you're the only woman for me. Long ago I made a mistake with you, one that can't be undone. But that doesn't have to be our fate. If we trust each other, we can learn how to avoid hurting each other."

His touch on her hand was so gentle. Kate wanted to wrap her fingers around his and hold on. There was such strength, such tenderness in his hand. She couldn't deny her need for him, and that was exactly what frightened her so. "We can't undo the past," she said. "No one can. I can't change who I am."

"But we don't have to live in the past."

"I thought you were the one who wanted to drag it all out and examine it." She gave him a rueful smile. "You almost had me convinced."

Jake took a breath and increased the pressure on her hand. "What I wanted was to get to a place where we both could quit running from it. I thought the way to do that would be to open it up. Maybe I had the wrong approach."

Kate considered his words.

Jake brought her fingers to his lips and kissed them lightly. "Tell me what you feel for me. This is the present, and this is a step toward the future."

Kate felt the panic begin. What she wanted was to snatch her hand away and run. This was going nowhere fast except to heartache. Jake wanted to wallow in feelings. What he didn't understand was that it was a conflict of emotion that made her so upset. Her body tensed, prepared for flight.

"Don't do it, Kate," he said softly, wrapping his hand around hers. "I can take the truth, whatever it is, just don't run away and leave me without even that."

Familiar sat up and looked over the table at her. He abruptly hopped up and went to Kate. "Meow," he said, rubbing against her shoulder.

"Even the cat is conspiring against me," Kate said, trying again for a light note and failing miserably. In fifteen years she hadn't admitted to a single person that she cared. Not deeply. There had been friends and flings and people she genuinely cared about. But no one had gotten close to her, not close enough to threaten. Not since her mother abandoned her and she'd run away from Jake.

"Do you care for me at all?" Jake pressed.

"Perhaps it's my destiny to be alone." She couldn't bear to look at him as she spoke. "I'm not any good at caring. I get scared and I run. And that's what I'm feeling now. Plain old scared. That makes me hate myself." She finally lifted her eyes and saw all the passion and compassion in his, as well as a lingering sadness. "I don't like feeling like a coward. It makes me angry at you when you force me to feel this way. The fear overrides everything else I feel." He wanted the bitter truth, well he had it. She was a yellow coward. But instead of disappointment or disgust, she saw something else in his face. Complete acceptance, and concern.

"You wouldn't want to run if you didn't care," Jake answered with a tone of satisfaction in his voice.

"What good does that do me?" she asked, her voice getting louder. "I care, Jake. I care more than I ever wanted to. Being with you last night brought back all the ways that I care. I've loved you since I was sixteen." She pulled her hand away and stood up. "What does it mean, though, if right along with all that caring comes a wagon-load of fear so terrible that I can't bear up under it?"

She stepped back from the table but before she could get away, Familiar launched himself at her. She had no choice but to catch the cat in her arms. Jake remained seated, his body as tense as if it were a coiled spring.

"I haven't even had a pet," she said, hugging the cat to her chest. "I was afraid it would run away or die, and I couldn't bear that. You're wasting your time with me. It's never going to change."

Jake stood slowly. "If that's the way you want it, Kate. I've done everything I can think of. Every move I make, I second-guess. I'm willing to work at this, the two of us together. But I can't make you want it bad enough to try."

"I have to go," she said, her voice almost a gasp.

"You can't run forever, Kate." Jake stood perfectly still.

She held the cat. "I can't do this, Jake. I have to go." She started backing up, her steps quick. "I'll go to Denver. I'll check out the leads on the timing devices."

"If you keep running now, Kate, you won't ever stop."

Familiar in her arms, Kate fled. This was what she'd

dreaded more than anything. Jake had finally had his way, he'd forced her to confront the truth about herself. In a small corner of her heart, she'd always hoped that when the right person came along she'd be able to care, to give her heart. Now that was a closed door. Jake was the one, the man she'd loved since she was an innocent. And if she couldn't give her heart to him, then she would be alone for the rest of her life.

What Jake had done, in an effort to reach her, was to strip away even the illusions she had left. Now there was only the ugly truth. She wasn't capable of loving. Not in the way necessary to form a bond. She would always be alone.

She ran out to the street. Familiar made no protest as she put him in the truck. Stomping the gas, Kate sped into the flow of traffic and headed straight for Denver.

Saints preserve us, I hate to admit it, but the blasted feline was right. Jake and Kate are in serious peril. A blow to the heart is a deadly wound, and poor Jake is suffering something fierce. Let me fetch the bottle of Jameson and see if I can't cheer him a bit. A little tipple of the bottle would dull the pain long enough for him to do what he needs to do. Perhaps a poem to cheer him.

There once was a fireman named Jake,
Who suffered hot fires for love's sake.
Fair Kate he would wed,
But she ran from his bed,
Afraid that his love was a fake.

Ah, enough poetry. I have my work to do. Perhaps I'll pen another verse tomorrow. Something a bit more cheerful.

JAKE SAT AT THE TABLE contemplating the cup of coffee that had grown cold. Ouzo had brought up a bottle of Irish whiskey, acting as if he understood what had just transpired. There were times when the dog was uncanny in his ability to sympathize.

The trouble was that a drink wouldn't help matters a bit, and Jake had no one to blame but himself. He'd pushed and pushed until he'd finally pushed Kate right out the door. Why couldn't he have just taken some time, worked with her.

He also had an additional problem, one that was also rooted in the past. The body in the casino wasn't Anne McArdle. So what had actually happened to her? Anne hadn't left with Johnny Goodloe. Kate hadn't been abandoned. At least that's what he wanted to believe.

It was going to be devastating news to Kate. She'd spent so many years believing her mother was alive somewhere, living with the man she loved.

If Jake had been able to win Kate, to make her believe she could trust and rely on him, then maybe he could encourage her to find out what had really happened to her mother. He could help her deal with it. As tragic as the facts were, they might even take some of the sting of abandonment away from Kate.

His whole intention had been to put himself in a position so that Kate had someone to lean on. But she'd never trust him now. She was gone, a creature so full of fear that her green eyes had been wild with it.

He felt Ouzo's cold nose brush against his palm and the lick of a wet tongue on his fingers.

"Hey, fella," he said softly, stroking the dog's fur. Ouzo was a rascal and a troublemaker, but there were times when he knew exactly what his master needed.

Suddenly he felt the dog's sharp teeth pinch down on

the base of his thumb. With a grunt of pain, he jumped to his feet. In the light from the kitchen window, he could already see the blood blister forming.

"Ouzo," he said with irritation.

"Arf!" Ouzo wagged his tail. "Arf!"

"I'm not in the mood to play." How had he ever thought Ouzo was sympathetic to his emotions? The dog merely wanted him to go for a walk.

Ouzo put his front paws on the table and nudged the sugar bowl with his nose. When Jake did nothing, he hit the spoon, flipping a pile of sugar on top of the map Kate had put near the center of the table.

"That's enough," Jake said. "Get your leash."

As Ouzo abandoned the table and dashed off to find the red nylon leash that matched his collar, Jake slowly walked to the counter and turned off the coffeepot. There was something he needed to check, and Alexis Redfield would be the best source.

"Come on, Ouzo," he called. "We've got to make some tracks and get some facts."

Ouzo appeared with his leash in his mouth. As soon as Jake opened the gate, the dog dashed out. The leash clattered down the steps after him.

"Ouzo!" Jake made a lunge, almost falling headfirst down the stairs, but the dog was gone. Only a few black hairs floated on the air to show he'd ever been there.

"That faking, low-down, good-for-nothing dog," Jake said. He picked up the leash. "If you get in trouble, Ouzo, you're on your own," he said to the empty air. Swinging the leash in his hand he hurried to the door. There was no sign of the dog outside. "That's right, you're on your own," he repeated.

Before Jake could even get out the door there was a loud cry. The sound came from the side of the building, and Jake started running. He couldn't tell it if was a man or woman, but whoever it was had to be in desperate trouble.

As he rounded the corner, he skidded to a stop. Reverend Theodore Lyte was pressed against the building. Ouzo, his tail in the air and ears cocked forward, lunged forward and scuttled back.

"This beast must be exterminated," Lyte said as soon as he saw Jake. "He's a menace and a danger."

"Ouzo," Jake called, relieved to see the dog respond to his voice. "Heel." Ouzo dropped into place perfectly.

"I come here to try and do you a favor and that creature almost takes my leg off." Lyte pushed himself away from the building. He dusted the elbows of his jacket as he pulled himself together. "I have a good mind to leave without telling you what I've learned," he said, still busy adjusting his clothes.

Jake couldn't help feeling a twinge of curiosity. Theodore Lyte wasn't in the habit of doing him favors. Still, the minister got around a good bit. He might possibly be a great source of information. "What did you want to tell me?" Jake prodded.

"Several of the local business owners are going to present a petition tonight at the citizens' meeting." Lyte cleared his throat. "They want the city to meet the demands of the DDC to bring in their casinos and theme park. As you know, I'm opposed to any more gambling dens in this town. In this one instance, I think you and I could work together."

Jake didn't relish the idea of working with Lyte for any amount of time, but what the minister said was true. "What do you want me to do?"

"Think of a way to hold off any official action."

"How do you suggest that I do that?" Jake was amused that Lyte thought he had such power.

"I don't know," Lyte said, obviously frustrated. "Isn't there some technicality you can come up with? Some archaic fire law? Once this petition is passed, we might as well give the key to the town to the DDC. They'll be in here and before long they'll own everything in sight. They've already been talking with Alexis."

"They still want to buy the Golden Nugget?" Jake felt his heart take another sinking spell. Anything related to Kate gave him a pain.

"They want that," Lyte stepped closer, "but they want the Double J more. You aren't considering selling that property, are you?"

"Nope," Jake answered immediately.

"If you are, I'm hoping you'd consider letting the church have it. We'll match whatever price the DDC offers."

"It's not for sale," Jake repeated. "Not to the DDC and not to you. That land's been in my family for three generations. When I was a boy I played all over Lookout Mountain." He gave Lyte a long look. "I still can't believe my daddy deeded that portion of the property to the church."

"As I understand it, your father was a very righteous man. One who knew the value of serving his church and his community." Lyte backed up several inches. "At any rate, if you decide to sell, keep me in mind."

"Don't hold your breath," Jake said. Every conversation he had with Lyte turned into a high-pressure job to sell his property.

"Will you try to stop the petition?"

"There's technically nothing I can do," Jake said,

"except maybe emphasize the fact that we have an arsonist on the loose. I don't think Roy would like that very much."

Lyte's eyes brightened. "Roy stands to benefit a lot from this. You know they're also looking at buying a chunk of his property."

Jake caught the drift of Lyte's inference. "Are you insinuating—"

"I'm not insinuating anything," Lyte said quickly. "It's just that Roy has insured every building that burned, including your ranch. Has that escaped you?"

"Those fires hurt Roy."

"In one way. But he also has access to a lot of information about the properties."

"I know. But if Roy has property to sell to the DDC, why would he start a panic by setting fires?"

"Perhaps you should ask Alexis or Evelyn Winn," Lyte's grin was widening with each second. "I believe he's offered to buy them out."

"Roy?" Jake was astounded. "Where did he get enough money to buy two businesses out?"

"Well, they won't go for a premium price. At least not the Golden Nugget. What better time to pick up an old historic building—"

"That needs half a million in renovation before it can even be used again."

"What's half a million to the DDC?" Lyte asked softly. "It's just a thought. I have no proof. I believe their approach is two-pronged: to offer to buy Alexis out and to also use Roy as a front to make another offer. With two low offers, Alexis will think it's the best she's going to get." He took several steps toward the street. "Think about it, Jake."

"I'll give it my undivided attention," Jake said,

watching Lyte back away, one eye still on Ouzo. Beside him, Jake could feel the dog bristling against his leg. Ouzo had taken a strong dislike to Lyte, and Jake couldn't blame the dog. The man was a snitch and a gossip. He certainly didn't mind hurling accusations, even when they were styled as "possibilities."

"Come on, Ouzo," Jake said. "Let's pay a call on Ms. Redfield."

When they got to the hotel in the center of Silver City, Ouzo slipped by the doorman and made it to an open elevator while Jake created a minor distraction.

"Okay, behave," Jake warned once they were both in the elevator.

Upstairs, Ouzo darted down the hallway and went straight for a lunch tray that had been placed on the floor. Before Jake could stop him he'd wolfed down half a chicken salad croissant, the remains of a roast beef po'-boy and a slurp or two of iced tea.

"Ouzo!" Jake caught his collar and pulled him along as he made for room 611, Alexis's latest living quarters. Jake braced himself for an orgy of pastels all madly run together, but no one answered his knock. He tried again, wondering at the muffled sound he heard from inside the room. Someone was in there. He considered forcing the door open but Ouzo had no such compunction. He charged against the door, pushing it back from a lock that had not quite caught.

Jake quickly stepped into blinding sunlight and found Alexis in a chair, with her mouth gagged and her hands tied behind her back. Her face was strained and white, and she made muffled cries around the gag.

"My goodness," Jake said softly as he took in the ransacked room. "What happened here?" Before the words were out, he saw the thin wire that ran from the rungs of Alexis's chair around a corner.

"Nnaake!" Alexis demanded. Her expression was murderous. Her eyes narrowed, and Jake walked over and gently removed the gag.

"Don't just stand around gawking, untie me," she commanded.

"Easy," Jake said, grasping her shoulders to keep her from twisting in the chair. "Be very still, Alexis."

"I've been very still for the past hour, you idiot. I've been still because I'm tied in this chair and—"

"I think if you move too much, you'll trigger an explosion," he said easily. "Now be very still."

"An explosion...?" Alexis stared at him. "You're kidding, right?"

"I wish I were." Jake traced the wire around the corner to the modern kitchen. It wasn't a complex device. It was simple, attached to the gas oven in the kitchen. If it ignited, a fireball would blow this hotel room right out of the building.

"Jake?" Alexis called, panic in her voice.

"Be still," he ordered. "I've got to defuse this thing." He talked as he worked. In a moment the explosive device was disarmed. He walked back and began to untie Alexis. "Who did this?" he asked.

"When I find out, he's going to pay. No one touches Alexis Redfield without her express permission."

"You didn't see who it was?"

Alexis shook her hands out and began to rub her wrists, which bore the marks of the tight ropes. "Roy had just left, and I was on the phone talking to Evelyn. Someone sneaked in behind me and knocked me out. When I came to, I was tied in that chair." She rotated her head. "My goodness, I have a headache."

"How long did this happen after Roy left?"

Alexis sat very still and thought. "Maybe five minutes. Why?"

"Do you remember anything? A footstep, a smell, the sound of the door? Anything?"

Alexis's eyes brightened. "There was one thing."

Chapter Fourteen

Kate pulled the truck to the side of the road and looked over the land she remembered so well. In the distance she could see a few stone pillars, but there was nothing else left of the Double J ranch. There was no reason for her to be there—except for the persistence of the cat. She had to pass the Double J to get to Lookout Church.

She had her emotions under control. She wasn't cornered. She didn't have to run. She was thirty-three, not eighteen. She had to keep the past and present from blending together. If she could do that, she wouldn't panic.

Against her better judgment, she turned down the road that led to the ranch and slowly drove to what remained of the gates. As she applied the brakes, Familiar was nearly bumped from the seat.

"Sorry," she said, "but you were the one with such a big interest in coming here. Remember? Let me take a few minutes here, then we'll head up to the church."

Familiar put his paws on the dash. He stared out the windshield as if he smelled something on the wind—something he didn't like.

She'd spent many a happy evening at the ranch with Jake and his father. Jacob Johnson had been a serious man with a warm smile. Kate got out of the car and walked beside the pillars that had supported the Double J sign. The stone pillars had once been wrapped in the wild roses that Jake's mother so lovingly tended.

The searing heat of the fire had killed the roses and even burned the sign.

Kate scuffed her boot in the dust, drawing out the two Js enclosed in a circle. Jake had had a ring made for her based on the Double J brand. It was to have been an engagement ring. The night he'd given it to her, he'd told her that he saw their future at the Double J.

Kate's hand rested against the pillar and she looked toward the blackened timbers of the ranch house. The past was so clear, so vivid that sometimes the future seemed pallid by contrast.

The night Jake had proposed, they'd been swimming at the little creek on the back of the Double J property. The day had been hot. High-school graduation was behind them, and Kate had remarked that she felt no more adult with her diploma in hand. Truth be told, she felt exactly the opposite.

So many of the girls she went to school with felt suddenly grown, ready for new lives, for college or marriage or entering the work force. Kate, who'd already been on her own for two years, felt only that the little security of routine that she'd found was about to vanish.

She had the money for college. Kitty had been a great believer in education, and a fund was waiting for Kate at the Silver City bank. She'd been accepted at the University of Denver, which was a short enough drive that she could commute. But she'd also applied at the University of Charleston, a fact she'd neglected to tell Jake.

She'd sent her application there because that's where Johnny Goodloe had been from. It had crossed her mind—more than once—that if she could get to Charleston, surely she could find her mother.

She'd even called a private investigator in the old Southern city, but he'd discouraged her from spending the thousands it would probably cost to try to locate Anne.

"Honey, if your mother doesn't want to be found, she won't be happy if you track her down," the man had said. She could clearly remember the soft Southern drawl and the hint of pity in his voice.

She hated it—to be a child whose mother had abandoned her. It was something that would sometimes catch her under her ribs with a sharp pain that almost made her cry out.

Jake was the closest person in her life, and she'd never once discussed the pain with him. Somehow, she was afraid he'd think less of her if he knew of the times she cried in the night for her mother.

She thought of Jake sitting at his kitchen table, a mug of coffee in front of him. He didn't believe that her mother had abandoned her. Perhaps if, long ago, she'd told him of her own fears, of her pain, he might have helped her. As the thought came to her, she knew it was true. Jake would have gone to the ends of the earth for her. She hadn't given Jake a chance. The minute Jake had slipped the ring on her finger, she'd decided that staying in Silver City was the last thing she wanted.

Now, looking at the ruins of the Double J, she finally understood that Jake had lost everything, too. His mother had died. Jacob had followed. Then the fire had destroyed the ranch.

With the cat at her side, she walked through the ashes. That had been the big family room. The stone fireplace remained, sadder than if it had fallen. Kate knew the loss of the ranch had hit Jake hard.

"What a pair Jake and I are," she said to Familiar. "If I can't find enough things to pine over, I can always come over and borrow some of Jake's."

"Meow." Familiar scuttled through the blackened timbers and stones, disappearing under a timber that had already settled deeply into the earth. "Meow."

"Be careful," Kate called as she started after the cat. "Familiar, hold up."

"Meow!" She could hear him beneath the timber, as if he'd dropped into a hole. "Meow!"

"Familiar." Kate got down on her knees and began carefully lifting the debris. After a moment the cat popped up, a small rock in his mouth.

"What in the world?" She took the stone and brushed at it. The glitter of gold appeared through the dirt. Kate had grown up in a town filled with stories of gold and silver strikes, and though some were hugely profitable, many were busts. Old mine shafts pockmarked the surrounding mountains. In fact, there were several near Sentinel Mountain. Jacob had never allowed her and Jake to explore them—the timbers were unstable and dangerous. And there was no real reason to go in them. There was no gold, and the old caves had filled with bats.

She rubbed the stone on her blue jeans. It looked to be the real thing—a rock with a vein of gold in it. But it could as easily be fool's gold.

"Where'd you dig this?" she asked the cat.

Familiar obligingly disappeared.

Kate pocketed the rock and pulled the remaining boards aside. "Well, well," she said, wondering how Jake's dog had failed to find the stash. She lifted up the Prince Albert cigar box with extreme care.

It was Jake's old treasure box. He'd kept his secret stuff in it since he was a kid. She'd never seen it, but she'd heard him talk about it often enough. And here it was. He was going to be so excited that she'd found it. She lifted the lid and a slow smile touched her mouth.

Inside were several miniature soldiers, undoubtedly favorite toys from childhood. There were marbles, one of them a vivid green cat's eye, and a pocketknife. Several smaller stones winked gold in the sunlight, but it was the ring that caught Kate's eye. She would recognize it anywhere, the two J's centered with two diamonds in a circle of smaller diamonds.

Her engagement ring. He'd kept it all this time. Her hand trembled as she slid it on her finger.

Amazing, after all that time, it still fit.

Marry me, Kate.

Jake's voice seemed to come from her heart and her mind. She felt again the rush of happiness, the feeling of complete and total joy. She and Jake belonged together. She belonged.

Both hands shaking, she removed the ring and put it back in the cigar box. She closed the lid and tucked it up on her hip. Even as she walked toward the truck she felt unsteady. Maybe she hadn't run away from Jake because he wouldn't leave Silver City, she'd run because she was terrified of loving him so much.

"Come on, Familiar," she called. "I've got to go back and talk to Jake. He's been right all along."

The cat popped out of the debris, but froze as the sound of a car engine came to them across the clear mountain air.

Kate felt her heart speed up. Was it Jake?

Her hopes flagged as she recognized the white Blazer that Roy Adams drove for his insurance business. He was no doubt hunting her down to demand that she solve the arsons. She needed to talk to him anyway. She wanted to know why he'd given Alexis more insurance when an arsonist was on the loose. Especially after his refusal to reinsure the Double J.

"Kitty, kitty," she called, hoping Familiar would pop up and run to the truck. She wanted to be ready to leave in a hurry.

"Familiar?" Kate went back to the rubble. There was no sign of him. "Come on, cat." She clutched the cigar box to her chest and started toward the truck. She was standing there when Roy pulled up. His face was grim and for a moment he simply sat with his hands on the wheels as if he were having a harsh internal dialogue.

Then he opened the door and got out.

"Is something wrong?" Kate asked. As she looked at the mayor, she forgot about Familiar. She'd never seen Roy so tense. He looked as if he might explode.

"What are you doing here?" he asked.

"Looking for clues," Kate answered, her concern for Roy growing. He was acting as if he might have had a small stroke. Almost disoriented. "Are you sure you're okay? I've got some water in the truck." She started toward her own vehicle.

"No, I'm fine." Roy hurried toward her.

Kate turned to face him and her gaze caught the edge of yellow on the passenger floorboard of his vehicle. Her mind registered it before her thoughts connected, but when she did, her hand went instinctively to her gun.

It was the fire slicker, the protective gear that was missing from the fire station. She had a mental vision of the man who'd struck her. He'd seemed taller than Roy. But in the heat and smoke...

She looked into the mayor's face and saw for the first time that he was carrying a gun.

"I don't want to do this, Kate," he said, sweat rolling down his face. "I honestly don't. I don't have a choice. I hope you understand."

Before she could say another word, he stepped over and swung the butt of the gun against her head. Kate dropped into the ashes of Jake's home without making even a whimper.

I hate hiding here in the rubble like a coward, but I have to remain free. Funny, but I never suspected Roy. Never. My thinking was going in another direction completely. This is troubling. I let Kate down badly by not warning her of the danger.

Perhaps she would have been better off with the dog protecting her. Ouzo may have been right. This is a bitter pill for a private investigator. But Roy is lifting Kate up and putting her in the Blazer. I can head back to town for Jake, or I can hitch a ride with Roy and see where he takes Kate. The second option is the best. I can't simply let Roy walk off with her. There's no telling what he might do. He's got her in the back, and now he's going to get the box she dropped. Here's my chance to slip into the Blazer with her. Pistol-Packin' Mama may be out cold, but the fight isn't over yet.

JAKE HANDED ALEXIS the ice pack, but his patience was growing thin. "Tell me again, what was Roy doing here?"

"He made an offer on the Golden Nugget." Alexis shrugged one shoulder but wouldn't meet Jake's direct gaze.

He knew she was hiding something, but what? Why would she protect the man who might have rigged her to a device that could have toasted her? Jake could feel the arsonist's obsession escalating out of control. First Kate had been knocked out and nearly killed, now Alexis.

Frustrated, Jake firmly grasped Alexis's shoulders. "Tell me what Roy offered you," he said. "Now."

"Or what?"

"Or I'll have Kate lock you up as a material witness."

"You can't do that!"

"Perhaps not legally, but Kate's on her way to Denver. She won't be back for hours, so if I put you in jail myself, say in protective custody, no one will be too upset with me. After all, I'm the fire chief, not the sheriff. I don't have to know all the ins and outs of the law."

"Jake," Alexis's eyes brimmed with tears. "I can't tell you. If I do, they'll hurt me."

"Hurt you?" Jake was incredulous. "Good God, Alexis. They tried to burn you to a crisp."

"But I can't be certain it was Roy. I never saw him. I never…"

"I'm not accusing him. You said he offered to buy the Golden Nugget. I'm asking what he offered, and I'm wondering why he'd want that old building." Jake was also wondering if Roy knew more about the old bones buried there than he'd let on.

"Okay, he offered me twenty thousand for what was left."

Jake was astounded. The dirt was worth at least a hundred grand. It was a prime downtown location for a casino. Even one that had to be built from scratch.

"And you said?"

Alexis made a face. "I said okay."

"I know you're a better businesswoman than that."

"Roy said he wouldn't hold up my insurance claim

if I said yes. He also said if I didn't sell, then I'd never get a penny of the insurance. He said he could find a million ways to keep the claim from going through.''

"And Evelyn? Do you know if he used the same tactic on her?"

"That's why I was calling her. I never got through though, before I got knocked in the head.'' Alexis frowned. "I was right in the middle of a sentence. You'd think Evelyn might have gotten worried that I just dropped the phone.''

"You'd think," Jake said. He grasped Alexis's arm. "Come on.''

"Where are you taking me?"

Jake only said, "Let's go.''

"YOU SIMPLY CANNOT do this!'' Alexis stormed.

"For your own safety," Jake said. "Really, Alexis, someone tried to kill you. You're perfectly safe here in the jail, until we can round up Roy and ask him some questions.''

"Don't be a nitwit. Why would Roy want to kill me after I agreed to the sale of the Golden Nugget?''

"You signed the sale agreement?"

"I told you I did.'' Alexis was beyond exasperation.

"And you told that much to Evelyn before you were struck?"

"That's as far as I got."

"Did it ever occur to you that once you signed the sale agreement, Roy had everything he needed from you? If you were to die, there's a chance he would never have to pay off the insurance at all.''

That fact silenced Alexis. "He meant to kill me so he wouldn't have to pay?"

"Maybe. That's why, until we get Roy in custody, you're safer here.''

"I'd much rather go with you. I'd be safe with you."

Jake shook his head. "I'm going after Roy. Deputy Rollings will take care of you." He motioned the deputy over. "Give her anything she wants within reason, but don't open the cell door," he said as he shook it to make sure it had latched.

He started to leave but turned back to Alexis. "One more thing."

"What?" she asked sourly.

"Roy let himself out of your apartment, didn't he?"

She thought a moment. "Yes. I was eager to call Evelyn, so he went out by himself."

"That's probably how he got back in—if it was him. He never closed the door. You should be careful about those things, Alexis."

"In the future, I'll do that. But at the present I see you've taken care of locking doors behind me."

"Deputy, maybe if you went over to the ice cream shop and brought her a double-dip orange sherbet and pistachio she'd feel better." He handed the deputy a five. "Just don't let her out." Jake would be damned if one more person was going to get hurt.

"Yes, sir," Rollings said.

To Jake's amazement, Ouzo had stayed right by his side, but as he started to leave Alexis in the cell, the dog started barking.

"Please shut that annoying dog up," Alexis said, covering her ears.

"Ouzo?" Jake was concerned. Ouzo was not a vocal dog in the worst of conditions. He much preferred sneaky, silent slithering to vocal protest.

"Arf! Arf! Arf!" The pitch made the walls ring.

"Ouzo!" Jake had never seen the dog so distraught.

"Arf!" Ouzo lunged at the door, but Jake was quick enough to catch his leash.

"Arf!"

Though the dog weighed only forty pounds, he was dragging Jake out of the cell area and toward the door. Ouzo detoured to the desk where Jake had dropped his keys. Picking them up in his mouth, the dog headed for the door again.

"I have to find Roy," Jake said, pulling on the leash. "Ouzo!"

But Ouzo went down the short flight of stairs and pulled Jake out into the street with breakneck speed. Paying no attention to traffic, he headed for Jake's truck.

"Ouzo!" Jake braced against the curb, but it was as if the dog was possessed by superhuman strength. He simply kept going, and Jake either had to follow or let go of the leash. He chose to follow.

When they got to the truck, Ouzo jumped in, dropping the keys on the seat.

"Which way?" Jake asked sarcastically.

"Arf!"

"Does that mean left?" Jake asked sourly.

"Arf!"

Jake took a left. At the next intersection, Ouzo barked twice.

"Right?" Jake felt more than stupid, but he'd never seen the dog so determined to have his way, and he'd seen Ouzo plenty determined.

"Arf! Arf!"

He made the right and two miles later another left. Jake immediately recognized that they were headed for Lookout Church. And the Double J. What would Ouzo want out there?

"Okay," Jake said, pressing the pedal to the floor. If he was going to be a fool over a dog, he might as well go whole hog and do it in style.

THE FIRST THING Kate felt was the pain. Her head throbbed and streaked lightning bolts of pain to her eyes and down her spine. Her second thought was that she was blind. She opened her eyes and saw nothing but blackness.

The panic that struck her was new—very different from the emotional demons that had driven her away from Jake. This was more visceral, more immediate. She was blind and injured and she had no idea where she might be. And no one else had a clue where she was either. When the deputies began to miss her, they'd start their search on the road to Denver. Damn! She'd made a royal mess of everything.

The silence seemed to echo, and for a moment she thought she was hallucinating when she heard the rumble of Familiar's purr. "Cat?" she whispered.

"Meow!" There was a note of relief in Familiar's tone.

He came to her, his rough tongue licking her cheek. The presence of the cat steadied her and helped hold back the panic. Lately, she'd been so busy protecting her heart that she'd half forgotten someone might damage her body. Had Roy Adams delivered a blow so severe that her eyesight was impaired? She blinked, still seeing nothing.

"We've got to get out of here." She spoke aloud and thought her voice echoed slightly. In the complete blackness, she began to work however ineffectually at the bonds that tied her hands and feet. Roy had not killed her. He'd left her tied. Did that mean he intended to return for her at some later date?

As she struggled, she thought back over everything that had happened. Roy had been so peculiar. He'd acted as if he were being jerked by strings, a marionette. After he'd knocked her out, he must have tied her and taken her— Surely she wasn't still at the Double J?

If she was, then Jake might find her. That thought brought a tiny bit of hope. Jake would look for her. He wouldn't give up. He'd promised that. He'd told her that he'd never allow her to run away again.

She clung to those words, hoping Jake had meant them. Surely their last conversation wouldn't keep him from looking for her.

With a groan, she realized it would take a day, at least, before her deputies determined she'd never made it to Denver. Kate swallowed and felt the beginning of thirst already. If she was at the Double J, laid out to bake in the sun, she wouldn't last forty-eight hours.

But she wasn't hot. She considered that. Perhaps it was night.

But it wasn't cold enough to be night. Where was she? Slowly, she started to move and explore.

"It's a cave!" She wanted to jump for joy. She wasn't blind! She'd been left in a cave. "Familiar!" She called the cat over. "You've got to help me." She sat up and shifted around so that the cat could get to her bonds. "I know it's going to be hard, but you're going to have to help untie me. We've got to get out of here. I have a really bad feeling that someone plans on coming back to finish me off."

"Meow." Familiar moved behind her and she could feel his claws and teeth at work on the rough rope that bound her.

Chapter Fifteen

Jake didn't believe it when Ouzo directed him to the Double J. This was hardly the time for a nostalgic visit to the past. But something about the dog's frantic persistence made Jake turn into the drive and pull up in front of the pillars that had once marked the proud entrance to his home.

Before he could react, Ouzo jumped out of the window and was busy snuffling the ground.

Jake didn't bother to call the animal. He'd had enough experience with Ouzo to know that once the dog had his mind set on something, he wasn't going to give up. The question in Jake's mind, though, was why Ouzo was suddenly so interested in the Double J. They'd been over the fire scene a hundred times.

What new thing had happened to get Ouzo, who was normally as lazy as a snake in January, shifting back and forth with his nose to the ground?

Jake was half expecting it when Ouzo stopped and howled. Jake hurried to the dog's side and knelt to examine the tracks. The ground was hard, but the dog had found two new sets of tire tracks. Both were large vehicles—trucks or sport utility four-wheel drives with tires equipped for handling the range—but that was about all Jake could tell.

And Ouzo was off again!

Jake trotted to keep up with him as the dog rushed back and forth.

They saw it at the same instant. Jake gasped and Ouzo barked as they both darted to the glimmer of white fire in the dirt. Jake picked up the ring and held it, not truly believing what they'd found.

"This burned in the fire," he said. He clutched the ring for a second before he turned to examine the scene more intensely.

When the Double J had gone up in flames, he'd been at the fire station. By the time he got there, it was too late to save anything—not even the box of childhood memories he'd tucked beneath the floorboard of his room in his own secret hiding place.

Among those things was this ring he'd had made for Kate. When she'd refused his offer of marriage and run away, he'd put the ring in the box of childhood memories, sealing it away with the things that represented his youth. He'd hoped that by putting away the past he could somehow get over it.

When the fire was extinguished, he'd combed the wreckage of his home for anything that might have remained, finally accepting that everything had been destroyed.

But somehow the box had survived—and someone had been there to find it.

Jake started as Ouzo howled again.

"Ouzo?" Jake knelt beside him, but the dog was inconsolable.

"What is it, boy?" he asked in desperation.

Now, Ouzo ran toward the truck, barking for Jake to

come. This time Jake didn't hesitate. Ouzo had some sixth sense of things that he didn't understand, but he was no longer a skeptic. Where the dog led, he would follow.

Once in the truck, Ouzo gave two barks, indicating a right turn. Jake idled in the driveway, looking up toward Sentinel Mountain. He remembered the map that Ouzo and Familiar had tried—twice—to get him and Kate to look at. It had contained the location of the ranch and the church.

Jake picked up the radio and called in to the fire station. "Have I received any calls from the sheriff?" he asked. Kate had gone to Denver, but she might have called in.

"No, sir," the fireman answered. "You have three calls from the sheriff's office. Deputy Rollings sounded a little desperate," the fireman said. "No other calls."

"Get back to Rollings and tell him not to let Ms. Redfield out of that cell no matter what she threatens. Tell him to destroy the key if he has to. I'll assume the full responsibility for whatever she does. I'm trying to make sure she stays safe."

"Yes, sir," the fireman said.

"If Sheriff McArdle does call in, patch her through to me instantly."

"You're breaking up a little," the fireman said.

"My reception should improve soon. I'm headed for higher ground," Jake looked at the mountain. "Over and out." He replaced the radio and spun gravel as he headed to the top.

The closer he got to the summit, the more Ouzo danced in the front seat. It was almost as if the dog sensed that time was of vital importance. Jake, too, felt the prickle of unspecified apprehension and hoped that he was only picking up on the dog's jitters.

The sun was beginning to set, and as Jake reached the plateau where Lookout Church had once stood, he was momentarily blinded by the brilliant colors of the sky. He drove forward. The ruins of the church were made more dramatic by the sunset, and as Jake slowed the truck, Ouzo began to bark.

The church wasn't the site the dog wanted. But where? The road dead-ended against a wall of boulders past the church property and up a steep incline. There was nothing there. A host of wild animals had found refuge on the mountain, but there was nothing else.

"Arf!" Ouzo clawed at the windshield.

There were old mines here, long abandoned, and Jacob Johnson, Jake's father, had told many a scary tale of the bears and goblins that inhabited them.

But ghosts and goblins were the only thing that had ever been found in them. The prospectors who'd worked the claim hadn't hit pay dirt.

The mines, if they still existed, were beyond the church property, and inaccessible by all except the most determined hiker.

Ouzo suddenly howled as if he'd been hit by a train.

"Here?" Jake stopped the truck. Ouzo leaped out the open window and disappeared in the shadows of some large rocks. He reappeared high on the trail, headed for the mines. Even as the dog began to climb the steep incline, small rocks clattered below him.

"Ouzo!" Jake called him back, remembering that the mine shafts were not that far away—at least to a dog.

Ouzo hesitated for a moment, looking back as if to ask if Jake were coming.

"Get back here," Jake called, worry in his tone. Ouzo

was smart, but that didn't mean he understood the dangers of an old mine shaft. Nothing more than his bark could set off a collapse.

But Ouzo churned up the side of the mountain, determined. "Damn!" Jake said under his breath. Well, in the past, Ouzo had led him to some unique discoveries. He checked his watch. He'd give it half an hour. If they hadn't found something by then, Jake would have to go back to town and track down Roy Adams.

Jake started up the mountain, he realized that the path was in better condition than he had hoped. The going was tough, but not the impossible hike he remembered from childhood. Had someone improved the path? As the thought came to him, Jake felt as if a cold breeze had touched his neck. He increased his pace.

The path leveled and he found himself on a plateau. In front of him was what appeared to be a solid slab of rock. The mine entrances were nearby. With the light fading by the second, Jake didn't have time to waste.

"Ouzo!" He called softly. There was an eerie silence about the place.

"Arf!" He heard Ouzo's sharp bark, then a muffled cry.

"Ouzo!" He plunged into the rocks, scrambling over the large boulders until he came to the mine shaft openings. There were three mines, and he had no idea which one the dog had run inside.

"He-l-p!" The call that came sounded watery, like small waves lapping against a shore. "He-l-p!"

"Kate!" Jake couldn't believe his ears. What was Kate doing in a mine shaft?

"Ja-a-a-ke? Is that yo-o-u?"

"Hang on," he called. But where was the cry coming

from? "Don't yell," he said. "Be quiet." The noise might bring half a mountain down on her head.

"Arf!" Ouzo appeared at the entrance to the center mine. "Arf!"

Jake snatched at him, but the dog disappeared into the mine. Jake felt his heart thudding. The old timbers that supported the mine looked as if they might collapse any second. He had to get Kate out, but he might have only one chance. He had to plan her rescue the safest way possible.

He headed back to the truck. He moved fast, feeling as if he were hurtling down the side of the mountain, but he had no time to waste. In the back of his truck he found rope and a flashlight. He also picked up an ax.

He made the climb up in record speed. Just as he prepared to enter the shaft he felt the slight tremor that was a warning. "Kate!" He ran toward the mine, heedless of the danger that he faced. "Kate!"

"Jake!" she cried, real panic in her voice. He knew that she, too, had felt the earth's tremor.

"I'm coming!" But even as he said the words the roof of the mine seemed to dissolve on top of him. Timber and stone came down in a brutal crash.

KATE SCRAMBLED FORWARD on her hands and knees. She'd distinctly heard Jake's voice—and Ouzo's unmistakable bark. That was before the cave-in. A fine dusting of grit had settled all over her, but other than that she was unharmed. She couldn't be certain, but she suspected she was somewhere near Jake's property. And Jake had come to rescue her.

"Jake," she called softly, aware of the danger of further cave-ins. If only she could hear his voice. Just some sign that he was okay. That he hadn't been badly injured or killed in the attempt to save her.

The trouble was, in the darkness, she couldn't be certain if she was crawling toward or away from Jake. She had no sense of direction. She had only Familiar to guide her, and the cat was steadily leading her on.

When her palms began to encounter loose stone and rubble, she was certain Familiar had taken her toward the mouth of the cave. Her hand felt bigger rocks, then finally a small mountain of them that seemed to reach taller than her head.

She had to get to Jake, to make certain he wasn't buried under a pile of rock, which might slowly be crushing the life out of him. She moved a stone and it started a small avalanche of others that bounced and tumbled, striking her head and feet.

"Damn!" she backed away. "What are we going to do?"

In answer, Familiar nudged at the pocket of her pants as if he sought something there. He left and returned, nudging again. She felt her pocket. The cat had put a couple of stones there. She patted his back, wondering how they were going to escape.

"Jake," she called again. "Please, if you can hear me, say something."

In the silence of the cave there was the whisper of soft wings. The bats were also trying to get out. Familiar moved slowly up the wall of rocks. She reached for the cat and caught only the tip of his tail. He was climbing to the top.

Kate hated the blackness of the cave, the inability to see. Jake could be two feet in front of her and she wouldn't be able to see him. Yet he was there. She sensed it. And he needed her. She had never been so certain of anything in her life.

In the hush of the cave there came a soft whine.

"Ouzo?" she whispered.

"Arrrr—arr."

Familiar sent a few loose stones scuttling toward Kate before he answered the dog with a plaintive meow.

From the other side came the sound of the dog clawing at the rocks.

Kate's fear blossomed, a fear worse than any she'd ever known. Jake had been caught in the rock slide. Ouzo wouldn't be bothering to dig her out—he was working to save his master. She hurried forward, moving up the wall until she could feel Familiar. Kneeling beside the cat, she began to dig. The smaller rocks tumbled beside her and she held her breath, fearing another cave-in. But Familiar continued to work and she set to it again with renewed intensity. Suddenly, a draft of fresh air came through the opening the cat had cleared. Good. They would get out. They had to.

Even as Kate and Familiar cleared a hole large enough for Familiar to slip through, Kate felt the rumble of the earth. The old mines had held steady for years, but if the beams supporting one shaft were weakening, it could affect all of the others. She had to move fast. Her time had run out.

There was the sound of intensified digging on the other side of the wall.

"Kate! Are you there?"

"Jake?" She couldn't believe her ears. "Are you okay?"

"Mostly. I got hit by a few rocks. I was out for a while, but Ouzo licked me awake."

Jake hauled at the rocks and Kate dug and scrabbled

at them from her side. In what seemed to take a lifetime, the hole in front of Kate grew larger. She pushed her arms and head through. The first thing she saw was dim light—and a begrimed Jake. He grasped her wrists and pulled her through the hole. Even as her body slid forward, Kate felt the pressure of the mountain coming down on her legs.

With a mighty tug, Jake pulled her free. The momentum carried them another ten feet toward the mouth of the cave.

Kate could see silver-gray twilight ahead. Silhouetted at the mouth of the cave were Familiar and Ouzo. The dog barked frantically, urging them to hurry.

Kate needed no such coaching. She grasped Jake's hand and together they ran as hard as they could. At the last minute they both dove for the opening. Behind them timbers cracked and rocks tumbled down.

Jake rolled on top of Kate, covering her as the mouth of the cave exploded with dust and debris. "Easy," he said, pressing her into the earth. "Easy."

In less than a moment, it was over. Dust was still settling as Jake helped Kate to her feet. She looked behind her. The old mine was filled with stones and dirt.

"If you'd been a moment later, I'd be dead," she said.

"If Ouzo hadn't awakened me, I would be too."

"And Familiar led me to the cave-in and helped me dig out."

Jake pointed to the cat and dog. "I think we owe them a lot."

"More than we'll ever be able to repay." Still shaky, Kate started toward Familiar. When Jake slipped his arm around her waist, she didn't pull away. Instead, she leaned against him, glad for the support, willing to let him help her.

"I can't begin to thank you," Kate said. "If you hadn't come after me…" She left it unfinished. They both knew what would have happened. And Kate was more than aware that Jake had risked his life to save her.

His arm around her was strong, and for the first time in many years, Kate let herself feel that she was safe and protected. She knew she wasn't the kind of woman who would indulge in such a sensation for very long, but at this moment, she yielded to it and felt the wonder of Jake's love for her.

His arm tightened. "You okay?" he asked as they paused on the steep trail headed down to Jake's truck.

Kate stood up straighter. "Yeah," she said, "I'm fine."

"What happened, Kate? Who put you in the mine?" Jake asked himself another question. "Who knew about them? There's something very wrong here."

"It was Roy. He attacked me at the ranch. He knocked me out and when I came to, I was in the cave." She brushed at the grime on her face. "I guess I'm pretty hardheaded, but I did learn something back in that cave."

"What?"

"I've been running so hard to protect my heart that it never occurred to me that I could be hurt as badly by someone I didn't love. It's a different kind of hurt, that's for certain. But Roy could have killed me. What I'm trying to say is that running away isn't a guarantee of safety. I've been the biggest kind of fool."

Jake didn't try to answer her. He simply held her tightly and kissed her. "You know, I never would have thought Roy capable of such a vicious act. Corruption, possibly. Falling victim to greed, possibly. But not violence or attempted murder. I think he may have tried to kill Alexis, too.'' He told her what had occurred at the old hotel.

The last light was almost gone from the sky, and a half-moon hung on the horizon. "We should get down this trail with what little light we have left," Jake said. He whistled to Ouzo and called Familiar. "Once we get down, I'm taking that dog and cat for a special dinner. Something expensive and totally decadent. Whatever they want.''

Kate nodded. "We'll do that, and when we're finished you can help me arrest Roy Adams for attempted murder.''

At last, they're talking sustenance. It's not enough that I've been bounced all around in a pickup, shunted into a cave, nearly crushed by falling rocks—I've been terribly malnourished this entire trip.

One thing I can say for the West, folks out here don't spend nearly enough time thinking about the menu.

One of the problems is that canine. I discovered, beneath Jake's bed, an open jar of peanut butter which Ouzo holds in his paws and licks.

Hey, I'm not one to turn down an occasional spoon of nut butter, but as a way of life! Let's be kind and say it's not for me. Up until today, Ouzo has been more nuisance than help. At last he's shown some tiny pinpoint of potential.

This case is coming to a head. Roy Adams never saw me, and I did manage to leave a clue for that witless canine. I must admit he was smart enough to pick up on it. And he did lead Jake to the cave where we were entombed. That little scene brought up some memories of that old master, E. A. Poe. He had a thing for walling his characters up in tombs and wine cellars and other dark, dank places. He really would have liked that old mine shaft.

But what troubles me is Roy Adams. I watched him haul Kate into the mine. She was unconscious, but he was careful with her. Not exactly your ruthless killer. It just set me to wondering. Perhaps Roy wasn't aware of how dangerous those old mine shafts were. Perhaps he thought it would be a good place to dump Kate and keep her out of the way for a little while.

No matter. I have full faith in Kate and Jake. Now that they're finally working as a team, they'll snap this puzzle together in no time.

Then I can head back to Washington, where hostesses know the meaning of a full buffet table including crab and shrimp and rare roast beef. Ah, all of that glittering silver, the beautifully cut crystal and the banks of candles and flowers. I miss the pomp and ceremony of my hometown. And in the middle of it all, I see my beautiful Clotilde, her black-and-orange-and-white coat blending perfectly with every style and occasion.

I suppose I'm a bit cat-sick. And a trifle homesick, too. But I think we're about to snare the mysterious arsonist. This hasn't been easy for me. I'm not fond of sharing the limelight with some slobbering dog. Speaking of which, he's practically dancing a jig around Jake. I swear, I think he'd almost blow a tin whistle for a little more attention. No, I won't even say that—it might give the hairy black beast some new ideas about how to fawn and grovel.

Chapter Sixteen

Kate slipped the last butter-sautéed prawn to Familiar and sighed. "I can't believe after everything that's happened today Ouzo and Familiar could eat all that food." After leaving the mines, they'd stopped on the outskirts of town and ordered takeout for the cat and dog.

Jake drove with one hand, casting glances at Kate as if to make sure she was really okay. "Why would Roy want to abandon you in a mine?" He fed the last piece of steak to Ouzo, who ate it and then slowly slid into a reclining position with his head on Jake's lap.

"Roy had no choice but to get rid of me—I saw the fireman's gear in his truck." Kate recounted, in more detail, what had happened at the Double J. "But why would Roy try to kill Alexis? Why burn down buildings he insures?"

"It almost sounds as if he's lost his mind."

"Maybe he hoped to drop the real estate prices so low that the DDC, or whoever he was working for, could come in and buy out the town."

"That's the thing I resent the most," Jake said, his frown deepening. "Roy will take the fall for this, but someone else is behind it all. The truly guilty will never do a day in jail."

"That won't happen if I can do anything about it," Kate promised him.

The lights of Silver City were coming up fast, and Jake's fatigue showed in the furrow on his forehead. "We've got our work cut out for us tonight."

"I know." The cat was stretched full-length on her lap. She stroked him and felt his purr rev even higher. "I've grown accustomed to this cat. Maybe, when all of this is over, I'll adopt a kitten."

Ouzo groaned in his sleep, and Jake laughed. "Good, that'll give this old boy something to chase."

Kate's eyebrows arched. "As the law in this town, I'm ordering his attendance in obedience school."

"He doesn't even get a reprieve for helping to save your life?"

Kate was so glad to see a twinkle in Jake's eyes that she almost relented. "We'll talk about it later. Maybe you could go to obedience school instead."

Jake's laughter stopped short as he pulled into the parking lot behind the sheriff's office. He rolled his eyes and lightly banged his head on the steering wheel in mock desperation. "Oh, no," he said. "I told you about Alexis and the bomb, but I forgot to tell you that she's in the jail."

"Alexis?"

"I didn't know what else to do with her. I put her under protective custody."

"You're not a deputy," Kate pointed out.

"I really didn't think she'd stay put—and stay safe," Jake said, nudging Ouzo awake. "Now I may need protection. From Alexis."

Kate couldn't help her smile. "You might. Just remind her that you saved her life."

"That's right. If I hadn't stepped in, she would be singing in a heavenly choir. That's what I'll tell her."

"Somehow, I can't imagine Alexis in any posture that might even vaguely be construed as angelic. I don't think they'd let her have plaid wings."

Jake shook his head. "I don't know if Alexis will ever have to worry about a *heavenly* dress code."

Kate laughed out loud, and in that moment she reached out to Jake. Her fingers curled around his arm and she squeezed lightly. She did it without thinking, but as soon as she felt his skin beneath her fingers she knew that it was more than a casual touch. Even the slightest brush with Jake had her wanting more. His gaze was on her, as intimate as a kiss, and she looked up into his brown eyes.

"You're a beautiful woman when you laugh, Kate."

Instead of the panic she expected, she felt a rush of warmth. "I wouldn't be alive to laugh if it wasn't for you. I can never thank you for saving my life."

"Oh, I'll think of a way." Jake's brown eyes sparkled with mischief. "Count on it."

Kate's expression turned thoughtful. "You know, I don't mind a bit being in your debt. You won't ever ask more of me than I can give. I believe that." Her hand reached out to touch his face. "Better than that, I trust it."

Jake caught her hand and lightly kissed the palm. "You can trust me, Kate, but it's more important that you trust yourself. I've always known what a special person you are. You just have to learn to see it for yourself."

"Meow." Familiar nuzzled against her leg.

"See, even the cat knows I'm telling the truth," Jake added.

Kate knew he was right. Part of her running away was to try to escape the pain, part was fear, and a large part was because she was afraid she wouldn't measure up—that she didn't deserve better. The woman she saw in Jake's eyes, though, was someone who was strong and capable of loving. That was the woman she knew she could be. "I have to believe in myself, if only to keep you from looking like a damn fool," she said, working hard to hide the emotion she felt so strongly. "I owe you that, at least."

Jake sighed, "Ah, Kate, why is it that you always melt for me just before we have to go out and kick some butt?"

"It's a tactic I learned from your dog," Kate said. She leaned across the seat and kissed Jake lightly on the lips. "It's how Ouzo keeps you so well trained."

"My life is going to be hell. I can see you and the dog teamed up against me." He clutched his heart.

"You should be so lucky," Kate said, laughing. "Now we have to think of a way to take Roy into custody. And we should send one of the deputies, first thing in the morning, to show his photo to the manufacturing company in Denver."

Jake nodded. "When we find Roy, let me go in and try talking to him."

"Why?" Kate frowned. "He's tried twice to kill me. And Alexis once."

"I've known Roy a lot of years. He stood up for me when I was first hired as fire chief, and he's the only one who's remained behind me during the fires. In all of my dealings with him before this, he was an honest man. Call it a hunch, but I'd rather try to talk him into surrendering than go in, guns at the ready."

"Okay," Kate agreed reluctantly. "Plan A is for you

to talk him into giving up. Plan B is that I and my deputies do whatever it takes to stop these fires.''

"I understand.'' Jake brushed his hand over her hair.

Kate captured his fingers and moved them to her lips. "Don't do anything foolish, Jake. Promise me that. I've finally come to the place in my life where I can tell you that I love you. Where I can admit it to myself that I've put my heart on the line. Don't hurt me by getting shot.''

"You have a peculiar way of telling me to be careful,'' Jake grinned, "and I feel the same about you.''

"Let's do it,'' Kate said. With the dog and cat behind them, they walked into the sheriff's office where half a dozen deputies were gathered and waiting.

ALEXIS GAVE JAKE a cold glare as she sauntered out of the jail cell. She stopped in front of Kate. "I hope your bond is good because I'm going to sue you for everything this county has.''

"Please, Alexis,'' Kate said. "I want to assign a deputy to you. Someone tried to kill you. They may try again.'' She had serious reservations about letting Alexis go, but Jake's methods of protecting the woman weren't something Kate could legally employ—not if Alexis didn't want help. Alexis had not been able to identify her attacker and she vehemently denied knowing anything about the body buried beneath the Golden Nugget. In fact, she'd paled when she first heard about it.

There was no physical evidence to tie Alexis to the body, so far, and the casino owner had steadily maintained that she was bushwhacked from behind and couldn't begin to identify the attacker. Kate had no choice but to set her free. She couldn't even force Alexis to accept protection from a deputy.

Alexis pointed a coral-tipped finger at Jake and Kate.

"I'll be perfectly safe on my own. I wouldn't dream of doing anything that will diminish my satisfaction in hounding the two of you out of office."

Kate gave her a long look. "It would seem to me that you'd be a little more interested in finding who tried to kill you and a little less interested in trying to get even with Jake for keeping you safe."

"It would seem you'd be more interested in identifying the body beneath my former casino than in harassing me." Alexis stalked down the corridor and left.

"I think we made her very angry," Jake said, with a sigh.

"*I* didn't arrest her," Kate pointed out. "And *I* didn't toy with her affections."

"I resent the word toy. I had dinner with her once."

"Sheriff, I checked on that list of suspects," one of the deputies said, hurrying toward Jake and Kate. He rubbed his jaw. "I came up with something interesting."

"What's that?" Kate sat on the corner of her desk and gave him her full attention.

"It's Ms. Winn. Evelyn Winn."

"What about her?"

"Well, she's dead."

Kate stood up. "That's impossible."

"That's what I thought. But it's true. Evelyn Winn of Denver, Colorado, was killed in a car accident two years ago."

"Get on the phone and get more details about that death. If Evelyn Winn is dead, who the hell is the woman running Evelyn's Boutique? Find out. And fax our Evelyn's photo over to the Denver P.D. See if they can give us an identification."

Before Kate could issue another order, the telephone

rang. A deputy answered it and held the receiver out to Jake. "It's for you."

Kate watched his expression change from interested to guarded to sad. When he hung up, she knew the news he had was not good.

"What is it?" she asked.

"That was Mortimer Grell. He got the full lab reports back on that skeleton at the Golden Nugget."

"And?"

"There's nothing conclusive. Not yet. The dental records don't match anyone who has been reported missing. It's still a mystery. The only thing certain is that the body was buried ten months to a year ago, and that it is a middle-aged male, Caucasian. That's all he has so far, but he's still working."

A few minutes later, a deputy rushed in. "I've got more information on Winn," the deputy said. His eyes were bright with excitement. "The Denver police department identified the photo immediately. Her name is Karen Black, but she has a string of aliases a mile long." His grin widened. "And she's wanted in Las Vegas on an arson charge. In the past she's worked with a partner. There's evidence she may be an arsonist-for-hire."

"That makes perfect sense. Vegas is where she got involved with the DDC," Jake said. "And I still believe that some outside force is behind these fires."

"Let's pick her up first. Maybe we can elicit some helpful facts from her," Kate said, waving the deputies into action. "We want to surround the Winn house and bring her in. Use extreme caution. She's a dangerous woman," Kate warned.

EVELYN WINN'S carefully decorated home was completely dark when Kate, Jake and the deputies pulled up.

The only sign that she was home was the car in the garage.

"Thank goodness we left Ouzo in the office," Jake said. Familiar rode beside him, but they'd decided that the dog was too headstrong to risk bringing.

Kate eased her truck into the shadows of a fir. "We don't have a lot of time to wait. I'm thinking we should surround the house, rush in through all entrances. I don't want to risk a chance that she'll escape."

"Remember, if Roy's in there, I get a chance to talk to him."

"I remember," Kate answered, regretting her earlier promise. She kept her attention on the job at hand, but she chanced a look at Jake. In the dimly lighted cab, his face was a mask of concentration. The idea that he might put himself in danger made her heart constrict with pain. In a single day he'd risked his own life to save hers. And he'd waited her out—until she could admit to herself how much she loved him.

"You okay?" he asked.

"I'm more than okay. I'm ready," she said.

Familiar sat up and put a paw on Kate's mouth. "Meow." His tail flicked as he stared out the windshield.

Kate saw the strange car slowing as it approached the Winn house. At last it stopped several houses back from Evelyn's. A tall, slender figure got out of the car and walked with fast clicks toward Evelyn's door.

"It's Alexis!" Jake and Kate said together. Kate punched her radio to alert the other deputies. "Hold your position. It's Redfield. Let's see what happens."

Unaware that at least a dozen pair of eyes followed her every move, Alexis went to the front door. When no one answered the bell, she banged with the knocker.

When that didn't work, she banged with her fist and kicked.

"Open this door, Evelyn. Open it this instant. Your car is in the garage and I know you're there. Open it now! I demand that you open—" She hurled her body against the door. "This—" And again. "Door!" Alexis fell back, panting.

With the same quick, high-heeled step, she headed back to her car. She started it up and drove away.

"Unit Three, follow Redfield. Everyone else, take a position. We're moving in."

Jake was the first one in the door, followed by Kate and Familiar. Even as Kate flipped on the lights, she knew the house was empty. There was the sense that it had been abandoned, though all of the furniture remained in place.

"Search it thoroughly," Kate told two deputies. She turned to Jake. She had put off the inevitable as long as possible, for Jake's sake. "We have to find Roy," she said softly.

"It's time," Jake agreed.

Across the clear night the clamor of bells rang out. Kate felt Jake tense beside her, an instinctive reaction to the summons. Her radio crackled. "It's a fire. Eighteen hundred Rock Court Avenue."

Kate was right behind Jake as he ran to the truck, Familiar on their heels. "That's Theodore Lyte's residence," Kate said, remembering the night that Ouzo had stolen the shoe.

"Let's go!" Jake slid behind the wheel while Kate and the cat jumped in the passenger side. Before Kate could close the door they were rolling.

They arrived at the scene seconds after the fire truck. Kate stood back, waiting for the moment when she might be needed. Flames were licking out the upstairs windows, and it was obvious to Kate that the fire had started somewhere on the second floor.

"Where's Lyte?" she asked one of the firemen.

"No one came out of the house. A neighbor called in the fire."

Even as the man spoke, Kate saw a silhouette in the top story. She pointed and yelled. "Jake! Jake! Lyte's in the house!"

"Get the ladders," Jake ordered as he took charge of the fire.

Kate watched, her heart pounding with dread. Jake was absolutely fearless as he donned the protective fire gear and started up the ladder. In a matter of moments he was guiding Lyte out the window.

"Grrrrrr!"

Startled, Kate looked down to find Familiar arched and spitting toward the back of the house. She leaned down to pick him up, but the cat darted away.

"Familiar!" He was running straight toward the back of the house, as if he intended to throw himself into the flames.

"Familiar!" Kate made sure Jake was coming down the ladder safely and then took off after the cat. As she rounded the corner, she caught sight of someone running through the yard. The fleeing figure darted from behind a tree just as the flames roared higher, illuminating the yard. It was a small, petite woman with dark hair.

"Halt!" Kate called. "This is the sheriff and I order you to halt now!" Her hand dropped to her weapon, but she couldn't bring herself to draw it. Instead, she took off in pursuit.

The woman wove in and out, among the trees, but she was no match for Kate. She had reached the property line when Kate launched herself in a flying tackle. She caught Evelyn Winn at the knees and dropped her hard. Evelyn hit with a thud that expelled the air from her lungs and left her gasping.

Barely winded, Kate rolled Evelyn on her stomach and cuffed her before she could draw a solid breath.

"You have the right to remain silent," Kate said, giving her the full Miranda recitation. "On your feet." Before Evelyn could protest, Kate had her up and moving. "Where's Adams?" Kate asked as she pushed Evelyn toward the car.

Still drawing ragged breaths, Evelyn stopped and looked back at the fire. The roof gave, collapsing down on the second floor. "He's dead, I suppose."

"He was in there?" Kate was horrified. "You left him in a burning building?"

"I don't have to tell you a thing." Evelyn tried to use her shoulder to rub her eye.

Kate nudged Evelyn toward the car. She had to tell Jake that Roy Adams was in the burning building, though there was nothing anyone could do to save him now.

Opening the squad car door, Kate put her in the back seat. "Duck. Lift your legs." She slammed the door and motioned a deputy over. "Take her to the office, lock her up, she's had her rights, and she gets one call."

"Yes, ma'am," the deputy said as he hurried around the car.

Jake was at the front of one of the fire trucks. The blaze was slowly coming under control, and Jake watched his men as they worked the hoses. Kate went to him and gently put a hand on his shoulder. "I just arrested Evelyn Winn. Jake, I hate to have to tell you, but she said Roy Adams was in that building."

"He was." Jake grinned, then pointed to the side of the truck where a man sat coughing. For a moment, Kate didn't know who she was looking at, but then she recognized Roy. A deputy stood over him, guarding him. "He's okay?"

"I'm certain he's felt better. He knows that he's going to jail. He's not going to try and run."

Beneath the sounds of the fire and the shouts of the firemen came a constant, grating bark. Kate's eyes widened. "If I'm not mistaken, that's your dog."

"Impossible! I locked him up." The conviction faded from Jake's face. "It's coming from—he's not after the cats this time."

"Finish it up, boys!" Jake called as he and Kate took off on foot.

"GET BACK! Get back!"

Jake and Kate, panting from the two-block run, heard the angry cries before they caught sight of a tall, dark-clad figure cornered in Susan Tanner's yard. It was too dark to identify the man as Theodore Lyte, but Kate recognized his voice. It took her a moment to see the can of gasoline in his hand.

"Jake," she said, pointing.

"Ouzo!" Jake started forward, but Kate caught his arm. Even as they watched, Lyte flung some of the gasoline onto the dog. Undaunted, Ouzo closed the distance, teeth bared and hackles raised.

"My God! No!" Kate couldn't believe it, but Lyte had drawn a cigarette lighter from his pocket.

"This is the last time you'll torment me." Lyte struck the flint of the old-fashioned Zippo, and a yellow flame jumped up.

"Don't do it!" Kate drew her gun and pointed it right at Lyte's heart. "Put out the flame!" Kate ordered.

"The penalty for killing a dog isn't much. I won't get any more time than I will for arson." Theodore Lyte's face was a mask of fury. "I've had it with this beast."

"You harm that dog, and I promise you that I'll make you wish you were dead." Jake had grown completely calm—deceptively calm. He stepped forward, softly calling Ouzo to him. "Easy, boy," he said. "Come on over here."

"Jake, be careful." Kate didn't have to tell him that if he was within ten feet of the dog and Lyte tossed the flame, Jake and Ouzo would be toast.

"You haven't killed anyone. Not yet," Kate reasoned with Lyte. "Jail time is a lot better than execution."

"Yeah, that's easy for you to say."

Jake crept steadily toward the dog.

Kate's finger itched on the trigger, but she was afraid if she shot Lyte, even to wound him, that he'd drop the lighter and ignite Ouzo.

"We managed to get Roy Adams out of your house," Kate said. She had to keep Lyte's attention focused on her. She had no idea what Jake had planned, but she imagined that it involved getting Ouzo out of harm's way. "Give it up, Lyte. There's no place else to run. Even if you got away from here, we'd find you."

"You never found Johnny Goodloe," Lyte bragged. "He got clean away with the money."

The statement was like a slap. "What do you know about Goodloe?" Kate demanded.

"How do you think I learned about Silver City?" Lyte answered, laughing. "He's the one who told me about the old mine shafts..." He broke it off.

"So that's why you wanted the Double J property.

You thought there was gold in the mines. There was never anything there except foolish dreams and the wild imaginings of the two old original prospectors.'' Jake was close enough to grasp Ouzo, who was still growling and ready to lunge at Lyte. He put his hand on the dog's fur and grabbed hold.

"That's where you're wrong. But you'll never live to enjoy it!" Lyte thrust the lighter forward.

A gusher of water erupted from the side of the house striking Lyte in the face and extinguishing the flame.

"Get away from that dog!" Susan Tanner came out from behind the hedges with her water hose blasting.

Jake saw his opportunity and leaped at Lyte, taking him down with quick efficiency. Kate rushed over and snapped the cuffs on Lyte and Jake hauled him to his feet.

"Put that scoundrel behind bars!" Susan ordered. "How dare he threaten Ouzo!" She bent down to the dog and patted his head. "When I bought this water hose, I intended to use it on the dog," she told Jake. "But I never dreamed I'd need it to help capture a maniac." She reached in her pocket and drew out a treat for Ouzo. "Now if you'll take care of that vermin," she squirted Lyte in the face again, "I'll give this fella a good old bath."

"It's a deal," Jake said.

JAKE PUSHED Theodore Lyte into the sheriff's office and stopped at the sight of Mortimer Grell standing pensively at the window. Grell turned to face Jake and Kate, then gave his attention to Lyte.

"Who are you?" Grell asked in his soft, cultured voice.

"I'm Theodore Lyte, and I've been falsely arrested." Lyte looked desperately around the room.

"No, really. Who are you?" Grell asked softly. He went to Kate's desk and picked up a report. Turning to Kate, he said softly. "Theodore Lyte is dead. It was his body beneath the casino." He turned back to Lyte. "This man is an imposter."

Kate directed Lyte to a chair. "You might as well tell us the truth," she said. "The entire truth." What she wanted was information on Johnny Goodloe. Obviously, this man, whoever he was, knew Johnny Goodloe.

"I want a lawyer."

"I think I'll bring Karen Black from the holding cells," Jake said. "I believe she's in more of a mood to strike a bargain with us."

At the mention of Karen's name, the man impersonating Theodore Lyte sagged. "So, you're on to Karen." It seemed for a moment that he would talk, but he straightened and glared. "Johnny always said never admit to anything. I'll die before I say another word."

"Then I suppose you'll die," Mortimer Grell said softly. "For the murder of Theodore Lyte. He was shot in the chest three times. It seems he was scheduled to take over Lookout Church. Instead, he was killed and this man assumed his identity. The question is why?"

"You'll never figure that out," Lyte snarled.

Kate nodded to a deputy. "Put him in isolation and bring Miss Black out. I think she'll sing a different tune."

In a moment the deputy returned with the petite woman. Karen Black looked around the room and saw the truth of the situation on everyone's face.

"I don't have anything to say."

"Talk now and I might put in a good word for you

at the trial," Kate said. She held the woman's gaze with her own. "This is your only chance. It's now or never."

"I didn't kill the minister," she said. "That was Harry. He had the whole thing set up before we got together in Vegas. I didn't know he'd already killed someone."

"Harry?" Jake asked.

"Harry Peebles." She nodded toward the jail. "That's his name. He's no minister and I'm not an interior decorator."

"What, exactly, were you up to?" Jake asked.

She looked around as if she expected deliverance. When she finally accepted no one was going to help her, she sighed. "It was like this. Harry wanted to buy that ranch, the Double J. He'd heard from a buddy of his that the mines held gold. So he came down here and did a little work. He said there was plenty of gold in there, but that guy who owned the property," she nodded at Jake, "wouldn't sell it. Some kind of sentimental attachment. Then he heard the church was due for a new minister, and that's when he hatched the plan. He thought for certain Jake would eventually sell to the church."

"He was very wrong about that," Jake said.

"So he found out. That's when he decided to start setting the fires. He burned the Double J first, hoping you'd decide to sell then. When you didn't, he thought he could force you out of your job. Once you weren't fire chief anymore, you'd have to sell."

Kate went to Jake and grasped his hand. "So very simple, and yet so devious. I'm sorry, Jake."

"What's Roy's role in this?" Jake asked. The mayor was also locked up in a cell.

"Nothing, really. He'd overinsured his business, and

Harry found out about it. I think he was making Roy help him.'' She shrugged. ''I don't know. The whole thing started coming apart. When Harry tried to burn down my business, I knew he'd gone out of control. I knew we were finished. I just didn't know how to get out. He wouldn't let me go. He said the same thing would happen to me that happened to Kate's mother.''

Jake stepped in front of Kate, as if to protect her from the words.

Kate walked over to Karen Black. She leaned down. ''And what exactly was that?'' she asked, her heart pounding.

''Harry said that Johnny killed her.'' Karen realized that she was on treacherous ground. ''I don't know the details. It was a long time ago. But Harry said that Johnny took the money and killed her, but that Johnny was smart enough to leave some cash for the kid. That way, everyone assumed the woman ran off.''

Kate took a deep breath as she straightened up. ''Where is my mother's body?''

Karen's eyes darted around the room. ''I don't know. I swear I don't. He never said. You'll have to make him tell you. Harry knows. Johnny told him.''

Jake suddenly caught her shoulder. ''This one time, Kate, trust someone else to take care of this.''

She hesitated, then nodded. ''Okay,'' she said.

KATE PLACED THE FLOWERS beside the new marker and stepped back. She read the words again—Anne McArdle, Beloved Mother Of Kate. Mortimer Grell had taken it upon himself to order the stone and have it installed high on Sentinel Mountain where Johnny Goodloe had buried Anne nearly two decades before.

Jake looked around. They weren't far from the mines.

It had been several days since Harry Peebles had been unmasked, and most of the threads of the case had fallen into place. This last, the formal visit to Anne's grave, was the hardest.

"I miss her still," Kate said.

Jake put his arm around her. "You always will, Kate. When you love, you love with every bit of your being. But she didn't abandon you. She was murdered. It's different, but still very painful."

"You had more faith in my mother than I did," Kate said slowly. "I should have hunted for her. I should have tried to find her. I was so ready to accept that she'd left me."

"You were blinded by pain, Kate. You were just a kid." He pulled her against his chest and held her gently. "You did the best you could at the time. And the hard truth is that nothing you could have done would have changed a thing. Anne would still be dead."

Kate thought back through the years. She'd been so young, so terribly wounded. Now Jake had given her a new view of herself. She was a grown woman now, one who could, and would, handle this new information with strength and pride and with love for her mother. She eased out of the shelter of Jake's arms. "If Johnny Goodloe is alive, he's going to pay for this. I have the training and the skill, and I'm going after him." She put her hand against Jake's heart and felt the solid beat. "And I have you to help me."

Chapter Seventeen

Alexis held the pen in her right hand and signed the legal document with a flourish. "That pile of rubble is yours. May it bring you happiness."

"You're too kind," Kate answered, picking up the paper. They were in the sheriff's office, and Alexis had just signed over the deed to what was left of the Golden Nugget.

"This closes the door on the arsons of Gilpin County," Jake said, his hand lightly rubbing Kate's back. "Who would have thought that Theodore Lyte would have burned down half the town trying to get me fired as fire chief so I'd have to sell the Double J to him." He shook his head. "Well, the last few days have been hard, but it's done. We can look to the future now."

Kate had traced Johnny Goodloe to Birmingham, Alabama where he'd opened a sporting goods store and was living the good life. But not for long. Alabama authorities picked him up without a hassle, and he was in the process of being extradited to Colorado for the murder of Anne McArdle.

"With my mother's murderer behind bars, maybe I can accept the past," Kate said, a wistful tone in her voice. "I'm going to take what's left of the old opera house and open that community theater." Once Alexis had cooled down, she was more than willing to make an equitable agreement concerning the Golden Nugget. Kate looked around the room at the deputies and firemen, the townspeople who had come to mean so much to her, and she knew that coming back to Gilpin County had been the smartest move of her life.

Roy Adams stood up. He was out on bond, but Kate had spoken to the judge in his behalf. "You all know I'm not proud of what I did to Kate, but I honestly was trying to protect her. I knew Lyte, or Harry Peebles, rather, was going to try again to kill her—he'd already tried it once in the Golden Nugget. And you know that he'd manipulated me into a position where I thought I was going to sell my land for a fortune to the DDC. I didn't go to Kate with what I knew because I was greedy. But when I thought he was going to hurt her, I did what I thought would keep her safe for a few hours. I never even considered that the old mines were dangerous."

Jake put one hand on Roy's shoulder and another on Kate's. "It was Lyte who attacked Kate in the Golden Nugget, and he also nearly killed Alexis." He grinned in response to the blonde's scowl. "Have a glass of champagne, Alexis, and celebrate with us. You're out from under the Golden Nugget and you escaped without singeing a single hair on your head."

Alexis pulled the veil of her sophisticated green straw hat over her eyes.

"What about the mines?" Roy asked. "Lyte was positive there was gold there."

Jake shook his head. "The cave-in was extensive. To reopen the mines we'd have to start from scratch." He waited until everyone was watching him. His gaze was only on Kate. "And that's what I've decided to do. Maybe there is something in there. I've always felt the Double J was special. So did my dad. We just never considered that it might be precious metals."

"Meow!"

From the desk Familiar demanded the attention of the room. When everyone was watching he nuzzled around on the desk, then hopped over to Jake. He dropped the nugget on the floor at Jake's feet.

"What in the—" Jake started.

"It's one of the rocks Familiar put in my pocket when I was in the mine." Kate picked it up and handed it to Mortimer Grell. "What do you think?"

Grell examined the rock, brushing it until the gold in it gleamed. "I'm a coroner, not a geologist, but this looks like gold," he said.

Everyone in the room, except Alexis, applauded. She stood up. "This is nothing but a cheerleader session. I'm going to get my things and head for the airport. I've had enough of this goody-goody crowd."

"Bye!" Susan Tanner said. "Have a nice life. Don't let the doorknob hit you in the— Can I have a little more champagne?" She held up her glass.

Alexis exited the room amid general laughter from those who had gathered. It was a celebration of sorts. Karen Black had turned state's evidence against Theodore Lyte, her romantic partner in crime. Her evidence was enough to put the pretend minister behind bars for the rest of his natural life. And Karen, too, would serve time for her part in the arsons.

Susan held up her freshly refilled glass. "To Ouzo!"

The dog sat up long enough to lick her kneecap.

"To Ouzo!" Everyone chorused.

"I can't believe that wicked man was going to hurt Ouzo," Susan said from the overstuffed chair where she sat, Familiar in her lap and Ouzo at her feet. "Wicked, wicked man. And all along he was involved with Anne's disappearance." She smiled at Kate. "I knew your mother wouldn't have simply walked out on you. Many was the time I wanted to tell you that, but I had no proof. None except what I felt in my heart. Anne loved you more than life itself. And as a surprise, I've got something for you." Susan reached behind her pillow and brought out a large book. "It's photos of Kitty and Anne and you. From the good old days."

Kate blinked back the tears. Now wasn't the time for grief. This was a party for celebrating. "Thank you, Susan." She took the book with extreme care and put it on her desk. "I thought I'd lost everything from my past."

"Everything except me," Jake said, stepping beside her so that he could put an arm around her.

"I have a toast." Kate held her glass aloft. "To Familiar. No matter what was happening, he kept his head and kept me out of trouble."

"To Familiar!" Everyone saluted and drank.

"And there's one more toast," Jake said. He turned to one of the firemen. "Now's the moment." The fireman stepped out of the room and came back carrying a large flat parcel wrapped in brown paper.

"This is for you, Kate."

She smiled her thanks as she stripped the paper off the gift. With a gasp, she recognized the portrait of her grandmother. Dangling from the top of the frame on a twisted gold chain was the ring Jake had made for her from the Double J brand. "How did—?"

"I didn't." Jake pointed at the fireman. "He did. I

was so busy making sure you weren't injured that I never gave the portrait a glance. But young fireman Tate realized that it might be of value and he took it out with him. Ouzo found the ring in the dirt at the Double J.''

Kate detached the ring, removed it from the chain and carefully slipped it on her finger. The late evening light coming in from the big front window caught the diamonds and sent multihued sparkles around the room. "It's beautiful, Jake."

"A small token of my esteem," Jake said, bowing gallantly. "I'm glad to see you put it on."

She looked up at the hint of mischief in his voice. When he didn't say anything else, she turned back to the portrait. An expression of longing crossed her face. "You know, legally, this belongs to Alexis."

"Wrong," Jake said, grinning. "You own the remains of the Golden Nugget. That includes everything left. Now may I make my toast?"

She lifted her glass.

Jake stepped up to her and lifted her chin with one gentle finger. "To Sheriff Kate McArdle, my future bride, if she'll have me. And she can't say no because the ring is on her finger."

Kate's answer was lost amidst the cheers and applause. Only Jake heard the yes that was spoken very clearly and without the least hesitation.

AH, TRUE LOVE WINS. It does the old cat ticker good to realize that sometimes even a human can get it right. As for me, I'm ready to go back to Washington. This case has been taxing, and working in this close proximity to a dog has nearly driven me mad. Not to mention that the cuisine out here in the West leaves a lot to be desired. Or maybe it's just that Kate and Jake have been so busy with each other that they'd failed to take notice of my gourmet needs.

Then again, perhaps it's the dog. He is such a common, hairy beast that he'd eat potatoes and pretend they were good. That's the problem with dog owners. They lose all refinement, all sensitivity, all delicacy of the palate. They become culinary bores. I want a good Washington soirée where the butter flows and the cream drips off every morsel.

Ah, look at that. It's Jake and Kate and they're wheeling in a tea cart filled with, my word, with butter-basted chicken livers, crab au gratin, a prime rib, for that Neanderthal dog, no doubt, and little silver goblets of cream.

Well, maybe I'll stay another day and make sure this tender young romance stays off the rocks. After all, a human may work from sun to sun, but Familiar's work is never done.

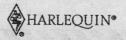

Take 4 bestselling love stories FREE

Plus get a FREE surprise gift!

Special Limited-time Offer

Mail to Harlequin Reader Service®

3010 Walden Avenue
P.O. Box 1867
Buffalo, N.Y. 14240-1867

YES! Please send me 4 free Harlequin Intrigue® novels and my free surprise gift. Then send me 4 brand-new novels every month. Bill me at the low price of $2.94 each plus 25¢ delivery and applicable sales tax, if any.* That's the complete price and a savings of over 10% off the cover prices—quite a bargain! I understand that accepting the books and gift places me under no obligation ever to buy any books. I can always return a shipment and cancel at any time. Even if I never buy another book from Harlequin, the 4 free books and the surprise gift are mine to keep forever.

181 BPA A3UQ

Name	(PLEASE PRINT)	
Address	Apt. No.	
City	State	Zip

This offer is limited to one order per household and not valid to present Harlequin Intrigue® subscribers. *Terms and prices are subject to change without notice. Sales tax applicable in N.Y.

UINT-696   ©1990 Harlequin Enterprises Limited

HARLEQUIN®

I N T R I G U E®

When little Adam Kingsley was taken from his nursery in the Kingsley mansion, the Memphis family used all their power and prestige to punish the kidnapper. They believed the crime was solved and the villain condemned...though the boy was never returned. But now, new evidence comes to light that may reveal the truth about...

The Kingsley Baby

Amanda Stevens is at her best for this powerful trilogy of a sensational crime and the three couples whose love lights the way to the truth. Don't miss:

#453 THE HERO'S SON (February)

#458 THE BROTHER'S WIFE (March)

#462 THE LONG-LOST HEIR (April)

What *really* happened that night in the Kingsley nursery?

HINKING